TABLE FOR TWO

STARLING BAY, BOOK 7

SIENNA CARR

AUTHOR'S NOTE

Table for Two is a STANDALONE romance in the ***Starling Bay*** series. While you do not need to have read any of the earlier books in this series, it might enhance your reading experience if you do because many of the characters in this book appear in the other Starling Bay books.

Starling Bay Series:

Whirlwind Kisses
Winter's Kiss
Maid for Him
Love Letters
Escape to Starling Bay (Books 1-3)
From Faking to Forever
Winter's Vow
Guarded Hearts
Table for Two
A Bouquet of Charm
Christmas Hope

Newsletter sign up: http://www.siennacarr.com/newsletter

CHAPTER 1

he smell of freshly cooked bacon assailed her as she rushed into the kitchen to place another batch of orders with her chef.

Roxy wiped a hand across her sweaty brow. It had been a long day, starting way before most of the people in Starling Bay got up. The lunchtime crowd had only just slowed, and she still had a good few hours ahead of her. She needed to get a bite to eat, to get some energy, before she started preparing for the evening rush. And in between that, she still had bills and her daily accounts to go through. This was fast becoming a part of the day she didn't like, so she was happy to put it off until later.

She barely had a moment to herself, and while she no longer spent as long in the kitchen, or waited on tables as much, there was still the paperwork, the planning, the budgeting, the constant whirl, whirl, whirl of the worry wheel in her head as to whether she would make enough this month to pay the rent, the wages, the supplies, and have money for taxes and bills, and then have something to set aside so that one day, *one day*, she could maybe have enough to extend the premises of the diner, expand the business, have more money and fewer headaches. And maybe buy a nice place of her own.

No sooner had she sat down to have her lunch, when her brother, Jax, and his girlfriend suddenly joined her. "Hey." They both greeted her at the same time and looked pleased with themselves. Jax always looked happy these days, and this fact made Roxy happy. He'd left his job as a security guard at the mall and was now working alongside Hailey—the Hollywood movie star—and keeping her safe.

"I was about to have my lunch." She was so bone-tired, so hungry, so in need of time to herself that, as much as she loved her brother, Jax, and had come to be good friends with Hailey, she wasn't in the mood or the right headspace to entertain anyone. She had initially been wary of Hailey and had even resented her a little for her seemingly easy life as a Hollywood movie star. But recent events Hailey had experienced had shown her that fame had its own price.

"You're finally getting to sit down, huh?" Jax swiped a piece of cucumber from her plate.

"We should maybe let you eat in peace, then?" Hailey suggested.

Duh.

Things were looking up for Jax. He'd been to LA with Hailey and had loved that lifestyle. He was making plans and had been talking about getting proper security training with a goal to build up a team to run operations in LA and here. He had tried that before, here in Starling Bay, on a much smaller scale, doing things like warning off abusive ex-boyfriends, but it hadn't really taken off. He'd given up and worked odd security jobs on the side while working at the mall.

But his life had taken a turn for the better now, and Roxy was happy for him. Her little bro was in love and had new dreams.

It was okay for some.

For others, life trudged along. "When are you guys leaving?"

"Tomorrow," Hailey answered, her blue eyes twinkling with mischief. "So …"

"So, we were wondering, why don't you let Hailey put in a word for you?" Jax leaned back in his chair.

Roxy couldn't taste the cherry tomato she had just popped into her mouth. These two were still entertaining that crazy business idea Hailey had mentioned; the one in which Roxy had no interest whatsoever. "The celebrity chef? Me going on TV? Oh, puh-leese. Can't you let that go?" She dipped a piece of her sourdough bread into her soup and wished she had chosen the path of a nun. At least that way, she would be afforded the peace and quiet which seemed so elusive to her now.

Hailey had mentioned her friend the famous chef a few times. Apparently, the guy was world-famous, but he couldn't be that famous because she'd never heard of him before. He also traveled the world, cooking for many famous people, had lots of restaurants in the country, had many cookbooks to his name, was seriously wealthy, and in recent years had become well known for his TV shows. Here, he sailed into failing businesses and turned things around.

Roxy had two problems with this. Her business wasn't failing. It was still making a profit, albeit not as big a profit as she would have liked, given the amount of blood, sweat and tears that she had put into it, and secondly, she wasn't about to let anyone tell her how to run her business. "Still no."

"Told you she wasn't going to come around." Her brother knew her well. There was no way in hell she was going to have a celebrity chef tell her what to do, or how to run her diner.

No way.

Jax had given up trying to convince her long ago, but Hailey seemed more determined. "Why are you being so stubborn, Roxy? What if this worked? What if this helped you?"

"Going on national TV and being humiliated?"

Hailey laughed, shaking her head slightly. "Mason isn't like that, I mean, yes, he has to put on a persona for his show, and he can be a bit in-your-face but—"

"In your face?" Roxy blinked at Jax. Did Hailey really not understand her? The idea of taking orders from someone was so alien to her that she wouldn't even consider it. And having someone who sounded like he would be loud and arrogant, well, that just wasn't going to happen.

There was about as much chance of her standing up in front of an auditorium, dispensing business advice, as there was of her doing what Hailey was proposing.

It would never happen.

"We're meeting Mason for dinner tomorrow evening. He's a really nice guy and his show is seen by millions. I really think you should at least consider it."

Roxy tore off another piece of bread. She and Hailey were worlds apart, and in the beginning, before she'd gotten to know the actress, she'd been unfriendly towards her, not realizing that Jax had started to have feelings for her.

Ever since they had been together, she'd seen how good they were for one another, and she had felt bad for her earlier prejudice towards Hailey. Because of that, she had tried to make it up to her. Now, they were good friends, but while she appreciated that Hailey was eager to help her with her business, she didn't want any help. She could turn things around herself.

"I have considered it. I've been considering it each time you mention it and I always come up with the same answer. 'No.'"

"How can you dismiss something without trying?" Hailey's refusal to give up was ruining her appetite. "Mason is always looking for new material—"

"I'm not *material*." That came out a little harsher than she had intended, but Hailey smiled. Maybe she was beginning to understand her better.

"You're not material, no, but Mason has a new TV show, Roxy, and this is *such* a great opportunity for you. Why not take that huge leap of faith? You don't know what you don't know."

"I know I don't want your friend coming here and telling me how to run my business." That would be like hell on earth. There was also that other minor factor of going on TV. She didn't know what was worse, going on TV and letting the world know that she was struggling or allowing a famous celebrity chef, and a man at that, to tell her what she ought to be doing.

"I have some things I want to try." She had customers. She wasn't as ridiculously expensive as Fellini's, the upscale Italian restaurant nearby, but she had been here for years, ever since she had taken over the diner from her parents.

There were things she knew she had to do, but there never seemed to be enough time. She wanted to revamp her menus and make better use of celebratory days. Have promotions and discounts and better advertise the diner on Valentine's Day and Mothers' and Fathers' Days. She had also toyed with the idea of having select hours for elderly people to come and have lunch on certain days at a reduced rate, and she wanted to introduce loyalty cards so her customers received points when they bought something. She had plans to improve the décor, to update the signage, to update the kitchen.

She had plans; of course she had plans.

It was time and energy that she didn't seem to have enough of.

"Then why haven't you tried them, Rox?" Jax attempted to swipe another piece of cucumber from her salad bowl but she swatted his hand. It was bad enough that they weren't letting her eat in peace, but taking the food off her plate was testing the boundaries of her patience.

Jax's life was working out amazingly well, but she didn't want to have her nose rubbed in it while she was struggling to find out ways of making her own life better.

"You know why, little bro. Maybe if you helped out more …"

"I said I'd help you. You only had to ask."

"Well, you're busy now, and you have your work to focus on." He used to help her, more than a few years ago, in between his various odd shifts of security work, but she had taken on a few more staff members, and Jax had obviously thought things were fine. With more staff came more responsibility, wages to pay, employees to train and manage and inspire.

"What if you doubled your income?" Jax sat forward and drummed his fingers on the table.

He knew how to get her to sit up and take notice. "Doubled?"

"Or tripled." Hailey pressed her lips together. They were lovely, pouty, full lips and even though she didn't dress like a superstar here in Starling Bay, or flaunt her celebrity status, Hailey being naturally beautiful meant that she was always noticed wherever she went. Roxy bet that she would be noticed even if she wore nothing but a plastic trash bag. She often felt a little inferior next to her, like a weed growing next to a sunflower.

"Tripled?" The idea speared her like a harpoon. If she doubled her earnings, that would be amazing, to triple them would be out-of-this-world crazy. It was something she couldn't comprehend.

She ran a hand through her hair as she considered the quantum leaps in income that Jax and Hailey dangled in front of her like tempting cupcakes. *Any* increase in her income would be a godsend.

"Why don't you look Mason up online?" Hailey suggested. "And look at some clips from his past shows? You'll see that he turned things around for a lot of people. I don't know if he tripled their income, but he left many with successful businesses and he transformed their lives." Hailey put her hand on Roxy's. "I see you working all the hours every day, and I just wish you could enjoy life a bit more. Have fun, do fun things. I just want to help you, Roxy."

Hailey's words made her warm and fuzzy all over. For two women who could not be more different, Hailey had become a wonderful friend and for that Roxy was grateful. Maybe it was time for her not to be so judgmental. She had been so wrong about Hailey, maybe she would also be wrong about the chef and his show?

For the sake of turning her business around, she could put up with someone telling her what to do. She only had to put up with the pain for an episode. One episode. How long would it take to film one episode? Not that long, she assumed.

She could tolerate the chef and his in-your-face ways for one episode.

CHAPTER 2

"*Y*ou're looking great, girl!" Mason got up and hugged Hailey, happy to see his dear friend again. She looked good. *Incredible.* She always did, but there was something different about her today. He cocked his head. "What's going on with you? Unless you've been nominated for an Oscar, I'm guessing this is due to the new man in your life."

"What is?"

"This glow?" He waved his fingers in front of her face. "You look terrific. Where is he?"

"You'll meet him soon enough."

They'd spoken many times in the past few months, but this was the first time they'd met face to face. He'd been in Paris, taking care of a private matter. The divorce had come through, and he had sold the home that he and Monique had owned.

They sat down. He'd been waiting for her, and she had run late. Something the prompt actress never did. Something had changed and he was curious to know what. "So, tell me all about it, your little vacation in … what's it called again?"

"My hometown? Starling Bay. It really does feel like home."

He sat up, because this was not the Hailey he knew. "Home? I thought LA was home."

She went on to tell him in great detail about Starling Bay, the place she had grown up in and how she had now fallen in love with it. So enamored was she that she was looking to buy a house there. "You're putting down roots?" With the ink on his divorce papers still not dry, a knot twisted inside him at what the idea of putting down roots felt like. For a few months, maybe even a year, back when they had first married, he also had believed he was putting down roots.

"I fell in love with the place."

He raised an eyebrow. "A place does not steal your heart, people do."

"Jackson has, but really, you should come for a visit, Mason. You might end up liking it."

"A small town?" He doubted it. He'd visited many places, had traveled around the world in luxury, stayed at the best hotels, cooked for dignitaries, diplomats, royalty and celebrities. He'd seen enough of the world in his thirty-three years that a visit to a small town wasn't going to make much of a difference to his life, even if it had done Hailey the world of good.

Everything was falling apart in his world.

A server came over and they ordered drinks. A smoothie for her, a fruit juice for him.

"It's been a while, hasn't it? It's so good to see you, Mason. How are you doing?" He flinched inwardly at the loaded question. They had talked on the phone a lot, and she had been supportive, had been a great friend while he'd gone through the tumult of realizing that he was the only person fighting to keep his marriage. "I'm glad to be back."

"Are you?"

"Yeah." He didn't want to talk about it. Not yet. "How about you tell me in detail what *you've* been up to, and how you met this man, again?" He knew the basics, but there was nothing like meeting face to face and getting the entire story.

He listened intently as she told him about the documentary one of the networks had filmed of her in her hometown, and of the second premiere of her latest film, and of how, through a strange sequence of events, she had met and fallen in love with the security guard who had been tasked with protecting her.

He slapped his hand across his neck; he suddenly remembered. "The stalker. Oh my god." He leaned forward and took her hand. "That sounded horrific. How are you?"

"I'm okay."

"You look unscathed, that's how good you look, but I was in shock when you told me what happened." They had spoken on the phone about it. He'd called her as soon as the story broke, about the intruder who had found his way into her hotel suite. Looking at her now, serene and stunning, he couldn't imagine her having been in that situation. Thank goodness she had been okay.

She recounted the story again, in more detail now, only stopping to thank the server when their drinks were delivered. "And Jackson came to the rescue."

"I like this man already." He didn't want to even think about what might have happened had the security guard not come to her rescue. He looked around. "Where is he?"

"He'll meet us soon enough. He's working out in the gym."

Mason held back a wry grin. Of course he was. "I can't imagine him doing anything else. How is this long-distance relationship going to work, Hailey?"

"It's not such a long distance—"

"Traveling across the country?"

"It could be worse. We could be in different continents," she countered. "I'm going to split my time between there and LA."

"Whatever for? Your career isn't over."

She giggled. "I don't film every month, and I'm going to get more discerning about the roles I take on. I can afford to split my time between the two places."

Love had made her thinking wonky. She was thinking of splitting her time between LA and Smallsville? But why, especially when she was at the peak of her career? "Aren't you being overly hasty?"

"I've done a lot of thinking recently. I've been able to prioritize what it is that I want out of life now, and it turns out that fame and wealth aren't at the top of the list anymore."

"You're brave. Bold, I would say. Insane, would be another word for it."

Her blue eyes twinkled under the sunshine.

"I love him. He's wonderful, you'll see for yourself when you meet him."

"It's serious, huh?"

Hailey nodded.

Her happiness meant a lot to him, and if she was happy—which looking at her now, he could see she was—then so was he. She'd had her share of failed romances, and the man who had saved her had to be pretty awesome if he had also managed to take a hold of her heart.

It was always a special, precious thing to find love. He wished he had been able to hold onto it for longer than he had. "I'm ecstatic for you." He took both of her hands in his. "I really am. It couldn't have happened to a nicer person."

"I'm sorry things didn't work out for you and Monique."

"That's the way it goes sometimes. I'm good. I'm surviving."

"Surviving." Hailey made a sad face. "I don't want you to just survive, Mason. I want you to be happy—"

"It's too soon for anything else. I will be happy when the new show works out. That will be a big help." He was hedging his bets on the show. With everything falling apart, not just his marriage, he was clutching to this one last hope; his last attempt to hold onto the crown that he had claimed years ago as a world-famous chef and restaurateur.

"The show will be a distraction." Hailey took a sip of her drink. "Distractions are good. Tell me all about it."

So, he did. He went on to tell her that they were getting ready to film the first episode in a few weeks' time and that he was looking forward to seeing how the new format would work out.

"New format?"

"It won't be one episode for each restaurant owner, but there will be more of a reality TV vibe so we're going to have eight episodes per restaurant owner."

"Eight?" Hailey almost choked in surprise.

"It's completely different than past shows." It had to work.

"Eight episodes on one person? Are you sure that will work?"

He wasn't, but it had to work, there was no way around it. His restaurants weren't doing as well as he would have liked.

He shrugged. He had no idea, but he had a lot riding on it. "People like getting to know the owners, they become invested in their life and business. In my opinion, it's a great idea to follow any one owner over a longer time frame to show the transformation of that person and their business in detail. In the older shows, we condensed everything down into one episode, detailing the restaurant owner's journey from the start, through all the blood, sweat and tears in the middle, to the happy ever after at the end. It's my gut feeling that people don't want to gloss over this. They want to follow the owner's journey as it's happening, and they want to go more in depth than the surface level gloss of what we used to show before."

"So …" Hailey set down her glass, her eyes twinkling with unbridled excitement. "I have just the person for you, but I'm not sure how she'll feel about this new longer format."

"Who is it?"

"Jackson's sister."

"Does she live in Smallsville?"

"Yes, she does, and what of it?"

He didn't want to go there. He had filmed shows in plenty of small towns, but he preferred cities more. The bigger restaurants, diverse clientele, the craziness and frenetic busyness added to the sizzle he wanted to depict. It made for better TV to have an overworked and struggling business owner rushing around in a busy kitchen, tending to a restaurant full of hungry people.

He didn't see that happening in a laidback small town.

"I'm not sure. I don't think a small town is going to capture the essence of what we want …"

"Listen to yourself. Jackson's sister would be great, and Starling Bay might be a small town but it's not dead. This is me; I've lived in LA for years and I love it so much I'm buying a home there."

"You're really trying to sell it to me, aren't you?"

"You might be pleasantly surprised. Don't knock something until you've tried it."

"I'm worried that it might be too small. Too boring. Too much of nothing going on."

"Mason! That's a preconceived idea if ever I heard one."

"It's what I believe." But Hailey seemed insistent, and she would have his best interests at heart, and for this reason alone, he was prepared to listen. "Tell me more."

"Her name is Roxy."

"Roxy? She sounds kind of foxy." He raised an eyebrow to enhance his cheesy line.

Hailey rolled her eyes. "That is lame, coming from you."

"I'm serious. Why is she a good fit for my show?"

She told him how Roxy was working hard but wasn't seeing the success she had hoped for. "I want to help her, and maybe going on your show could be just the thing for her." Hailey sipped her drink through the straw.

He already had the first contestant lined up to star in the first season. Buffalo Bill from Brooklyn, so called because his restaurant, Buffalo Bill's, had caught Mason's eye. The man was loud, brash, not prone to listening, and Mason could see at once why his restaurant was failing. The décor was outdated, which wasn't a big deal, but his food wasn't enticing, and his brusque manners, while they enticed some customers, frightened many others away.

"The problem is, we've drawn up our short list of people we want on the show, and we've just signed contracts with the first guy. Filming starts in a few weeks."

"So, I'm too late?"

"You must really like this woman, if you're working so hard to get her on the show."

"You should see her. She works such long hours. She's always working, and I feel bad that she's not seeing the results she wants."

"I'm looking for interesting characters. People with personality who will pull in the viewers."

"Roxy is interesting. She's stubborn and headstrong, and she'll give as good as she gets."

He was intrigued, just a little. "How's that?"

"Why don't you come and meet her."

"I'm a busy man! Get her to come and meet me."

"She won't come. She won't leave the diner," Hailey told him. "If filming starts in a few weeks' time, why don't you come back with us? You said things have been hard lately. You're dealing with personal stuff, and then you're diving headfirst into a new show."

"Always gotta be working. It's the best remedy for distraction." He'd been in Paris for too long. Selling the mansion, getting the divorce finalized, settling who took what couldn't be done in the blink of an eye.

"Come," she urged him. "We can hang out there, you can recharge. You might be surprised."

He could not believe the transformation in his friend. If Hailey was considering splitting her residence, he was intrigued to visit. And if her friend was half as interesting as Hailey had made out, she might very well be a good candidate for the later shows. There was no harm in finding out.

"Okay, then. I'll come back with you and stay for a few days. Meet your friend."

"Great." Hailey raised her glass to his again. "There he is." Her face literally glowed and she beamed for joy staring at something behind him. He turned to see what it was that had this effect on her. A tall guy, with a black t-shirt and jeans, and tattoos, walked towards them. He looked as if he had just walked off a film set. "You met *him* in Smallsville?"

"Starling Bay, Mason. Stop being so condescending."

He rose as Hailey introduced the two men. "So, you're the chef dude, huh?"

"I am. Mason Brandt, good to meet you."

"Likewise. I'm Jax."

They shook hands.

"I'm the only one who calls him Jackson." Hailey grinned as Jax put his arm around her and hugged her close to his chest. They sat down.

"Let's get you a drink." Mason summoned a server. "Hailey was telling me I should consider having your sister on the show."

Jax let out a loud exhale. "Good luck with that."

CHAPTER 3

She had finished for the day and was about to leave when her phone rang. With a sinking heart, she saw it was a video call with Hailey. She and Jax were enjoying the good life in LA where they had been for the past few days.

Roxy really wasn't in the mood to take a call, let alone one in which they could see her. Up until now, she had received only text messages—updates about Hailey's talks with the TV chef—and a few photos of them having fun.

Her phone continued to ring and she ignored it, hoping that Hailey would hang up. When she didn't, and because Roxy was too polite to send it to voicemail, she answered it.

"Hey." She was looking her worst, after a day at the diner, and Hailey would be all glammed up and looking glamorous as usual.

"Hey! Are you busy right now?" Hailey's voice was loud, and Roxy could hear music in the background.

Roxy rolled her eyes. When was she not busy? "I was about to go home."

"Oh, good. You've finished for the day. Do you have a few moments?"

"I do now." She pulled up a chair and sank into it.

"We're with Mason, you know my chef friend, the one with the TV show. He wants to meet you."

"Meet me?" Roxy bolted upright, and ran a hand over her hair, trying to smooth it down. "Meet me where?"

"Calm down. He suggested it might be a good idea to do a video call with you so that he can get a feel for the type of person you are."

"He needs to get a feel for the type of person I am?" Roxy chortled. "I need to get a feel for the type of person he is." The deal cut both ways. "It's noisy," she pointed out. "Where are you?"

"At a bar. Someone's playing the piano."

"How nice." What a lovely life for some. She couldn't remember the last time she had gone out for dinner or spent an evening with friends. She didn't really have a group of close friends. If she had any evenings out it was attending the SBWEB meetings. The Starling Bay Women's Entrepreneurial and Business evenings were attended by women she aspired to be like, though even on those nights she barely had much to say.

"He only just suggested it. Sorry to put this on you without any prior warning. Jackson and I are busy for the next couple of days and this is the last time we're meeting Mason. Are you free to talk to him now?"

Roxy blinked in hesitation. The opportunity was as enticing as running naked through a crowded mall. She didn't like video calls, and she was very aware that she didn't look her best.

Hailey had met with him a few days ago and discussed the possibility of Roxy being on the show. The fact that he was now interested in speaking with her indicated that things were moving on. She wiped her hand across her brow. It was the end of her long shift at work, and she wanted nothing more than to go home, shower and collapse in front of the TV. A bit of notice would have been good. "Do we have to do it now? As in right this minute?"

Talk about springing something on her when she was least prepared.

Hailey winced. "Yes. He's not going to get on a plane until he's got some idea of what you're like and whether you'd be a good fit for his show."

"I wish you'd let me know sooner."

"He didn't tell me until now. Let him see you in your natural environment. It's now or never, Roxy. He already has someone lined up for a show but I convinced him that you would be great. Let me get him to come over."

"No!" But Hailey's face disappeared, and as the camera phone zigzagged, it was too dark for her to make out anything clearly.

Then Hailey appeared again, a real close-up as her voice dropped to a whisper. "Try to impress him. You've got something on your cheek."

"Where?" Roxy rubbed her cheek, then saw Hailey turn her head and speak to someone. It sounded like Jax.

Hailey came back on the screen again. "The other side. Good luck. This is Mason. She's all yours, Mason. This is Roxy."

In the next second, a stranger suddenly appeared on the screen. Roxy sat up even straighter and wished she had at least taken her hair out of the ponytail. But it was too late. Her face was sweaty, the way it always was at the end of the day, and her hair was probably greasy enough to be noticeable. She wanted to vanish in a puff of smoke.

She's all yours? Roxy resented that, and just as she was about to protest, a young man appeared on the screen. She blinked a few times. She hadn't expected him to be so young looking. She'd been meaning to look him up online, but she hadn't had time yet. The shock of his youthful face surprised her because from the way Hailey had described him, from all he had achieved, and all the things he had done, she had expected him to be old.

"Hi." She forced a smile, mentally adjusting herself to his age, and his looks. She didn't feel anywhere near 'presentable' and felt ill prepared to impress him.

"Rox, is it?" he asked.

"Roxy." Only certain people called her Rox. This man certainly didn't qualify for that.

"Ah, Roxy." He stopped and took a sip from his glass. "Is that short for something?"

"Is what short for something?"

"Roxy."

"It's short for Roxanne but most people call me Roxy." She wasn't sure exactly where he was going with this conversation.

He nodded, as if he were assessing her. Already she felt on edge. Uncomfortable, not only because there had been no preparation for this, but because this man was … peculiar. She didn't know what to make of him.

He touched his cheek. "Uh, Roxy … you have something on your cheek."

Hailey had told her. Too bad she'd rubbed the wrong cheek. She rubbed her cheek briskly. "Gone?"

"Gone."

She felt foolish, as if she had physically tripped and fallen flat on her face in this interview.

"Tell me about yourself." He smiled, but it was no ordinary smile. He looked smug. She could imagine what he was thinking, probably that she was struggling and desperate and she needed his help to save her.

"What do you want to know?"

"I want to know everything about you."

That sounded creepy. "I don't want to tell you everything about me."

"I don't need to know your dress size, or your favorite color, or what your favorite designer label is. I want to know about your *business*."

That told her. Also, she didn't shop for designer labels. Already, he was making assumptions about her that were so wrong. But she needed his help. "Okay." She let out a slow, shaky breath. This was worse than going to the bank manager to ask for a business loan. Being as brief as she could, she told him how she had taken over the diner from her parents and that she'd been working hard for years but was getting frustrated with the way things were going.

"You've taken over the family business."

The way he said it made it sound as if she'd made a mistake, which, to be truthful, is what she'd started to feel lately. "Is that a bad thing?"

"No, but in my experience, when people take over the family business, it's often not because they have a passion for it, but because it seems like an easy option."

"It's not an easy option," she shot back. He was making it sound as if she'd done something wrong, even though he hadn't come out and said those words, it was the way he was making her feel.

"I know that. It's not. You'd be better off going and getting a job. Why don't you?"

Get a job? Why was he asking her such questions? It took her all the way back to high school when her careers teacher told her that it wasn't going to be easy, finding her feet in a world with her grades. Even now she could see Mr. Greyson staring at her and telling her it was a good thing her parents had a diner she could help out at. She never forgot his laugh, and his conviction that she would never amount to anything. The man was waiting for an answer, his hard eyes unflinching as he dared her to give him a reason. "Because I want to be my own boss, and because I can make this work. The success of my diner is proportional to the amount of hard work I put in."

"Is that what you think?"

"What?" The man was beginning to confound her. These were not the types of questions she'd expected.

And when she didn't reply, "Is it?"

"What are you asking me? Are you trying to bait an answer out of me? I wanted to run the diner because my parents were looking to get out of the business, and I thought I could run it. I'd helped them out for years. I knew it."

"And how's that going for you?"

She stopped, clamped her jaws together as she wondered at this man's superpower to piss people off. "It's going well. It's going wonderfully well. I don't even think I need to be on your show to turn my business around."

"Then why are we having this conversation?"

"Because Hailey wouldn't let up."

"You're blaming Hailey?" He lifted his glass again, the corners of his lips turning upwards before he took another sip.

"I'm not blaming anyone. I'm trying to answer your questions, your riddles, as best as I can, but I think you've maybe had too much to drink and you're not making sense."

He chortled. "You think I'm drunk?"

She forced herself not to answer.

"And what is it that you're hoping to get out of this relationship, if by some miracle I decide to let you on the show?"

This *relationship?* She didn't like the way he phrased that. She also didn't like his tone, and what he was saying. She didn't need this. A few minutes of phone conversation had her wanting to throw something at him. She couldn't see how she would cope doing one show with him. But just as she was about to fire off a hotheaded reply, the bone-tired weariness crawled across her neck and shoulders, reminding her that the last few months had been like banging her head against a wall. Working hard and not seeing a corresponding improvement in her bottom line.

Maybe this pigheaded and insufferable man might have the

keys to her success? She schooled herself to calm down. "I'm hoping that you will be able to give me advice on my business and help me figure out where I can do better, what I should stop doing, and how I can increase my profits."

"What do you think you need to stop doing, Roxy?"

If she knew that then she wouldn't need to go on his show. It was beginning to annoy her that he was asking her these questions when she was just so tired, and she was already annoyed that he'd sprung a phone interview on her when she was least prepared.

"I'm hoping that going on your show will help me to see more clearly, at least, this is what Hailey thinks. She says I could benefit from being on your show."

"She also says, as does your brother, that you don't like being told what to do."

"I don't."

"I see that about you."

"But I've reached a stage where I'll take all the help I can get."

"What would you consider to be your strength?" he asked, his eyes shimmering.

"My …. uh … my strengths?"

He hadn't asked her a single thing about her the menus, or the people she employed, or the hours she opened the diner.

"Being stubborn and sticking to my guns."

"Interesting." Then he laughed, as if she had amused him. "I've heard all I need to." Without even saying 'goodbye' or finishing off nicely, he handed the phone back to Hailey.

"How was it?" Hailey whispered.

Roxy forced a smile. "Great. Just great."

"Oh, good!" Hailey's high-pitched squeal told her she bought it.

Roxy hung up and stared into space, going over the conversation again.

"Was that the bank manager again?" Ella walked past carrying a tray full of dirty plates and cutlery, only this time she stopped and placed them on the table.

Roxy set her elbows on the table and scrubbed her face. "No. He doesn't call this late." She always dreaded the bank manager's phone calls, but she would have gladly spoken to him now instead of that man.

"Everything okay?"

"Yes. It was one of the suppliers. Nothing important." How easily the lie fell from her lips. She breathed out a sigh, forcing herself to make a move otherwise she could easily sit here all evening and fall asleep. It wouldn't do to tell Ella anything yet, or the rest of her small staff. Her chances of being on the show didn't sound too promising.

Ella picked up the tray. "Have a good evening."

"You too. See you tomorrow." Roxy got up slowly. She had to stop thinking that Hailey's famous chef friend was the answer to her prayers. It was probably just as well. He had a slight arrogance, and I'm-better-than-you air about him. Not to mention that annoying little smirk on his face.

While she needed help in her business, she wasn't sure that this man could help her as much as she wanted to believe he would. Being around him would probably cost her sanity.

CHAPTER 4

The woman was as abrasive as steel wool. He liked that. Of course, he could also see that she had a problem with taking orders; Hailey and Jackson had warned him as much.

But she had character. She had gallons of feistiness; and he could see all this after a quick first video call.

Most people he met were ready to roll over and do everything and anything he suggested. He could tell an interesting character within a few minutes of talking to them. Most people were deferential to him. They were in awe, hanging onto his every word just because of who he was. Many were more prepared to listen to him without questioning anything.

He didn't want that.

Of course, he had the occasional ones who gave back as good as he gave them. People like Buffalo Bill, who he'd be meeting soon enough. But on the whole, most normal people made for boring TV and he didn't want boring TV. He was already taking a risk with the new show format.

He welcomed people like Buffalo Bill, like Roxy. They had substance. Character.

"So?" Hailey stared at him with her huge saucer-like eyes. "What do you think?"

"She's … interesting."

"You can say that again." Jax lifted his beer bottle in agreement. "My sister has been called many things and 'interesting' is one of the better words."

Hailey crossed her fingers. "You'll have her on the show?"

He scratched his jaw. "She's going to be interesting, but I can't tell from one video call."

"Then come over and meet her in person." Hailey's excitement was hard to damp down. It was also infectious and, having spoken to the potential new candidate, he was starting to feel a quiver of excitement himself. That was usually a very positive sign that he was onto a good thing.

Visiting her in person was the right thing to do. He shrugged. "Meeting her face to face would help cement my final decision."

Hailey clapped her hands together, and even the oh-so-cool and laidback Jax ventured a smile. "Rox might get a chance?"

"She told me to call her Roxy."

This made Jax roar with laughter. "Come to Starling Bay. We'll take care of you, show you around."

"We will," Hailey said. "You might find yourself liking it more than you expected."

"I don't recall you being so mushy about the town you grew up in," he said.

Hailey tucked a lock of hair behind her ear and gave Jax another one of her dreamy looks. "Maybe not while I was growing up there, but when I went back, I was older and wiser and then I met this wonderful man …" She held hands with Jackson, and he kissed the back of hers. There was no disputing the fact; this was a new Hailey, and he could see from how she and Jax were around one another that they were completely in love. She gazed up at him in total adoration while he stared at her as if she were the only woman in the world.

Who was he to begrudge them their happiness? Maybe it was fitting that Hailey had found her chance in love and happiness not here in LA, the land of made-up magic, but back in her small town.

"Starling Bay, eh?" He lifted his glass and considered his options. The chances were that Roxy might not be as entertaining as she had been on the phone. People developed a certain type of brazenness that vanished when confronted with someone face to face but taking time out to visit this place that seemed to have captured Hailey's heart wasn't a bad idea. It wouldn't do him any harm to visit, and it would even be like a small break for him. "Okay. I'll come."

"Yes!" Hailey was so delighted she got up and hugged him. "Starling Bay is a gem. You'll love it."

~

This wasn't bad.

Forest Heights. An upscale luxury development away from the town. He had rented a condo here. Hayley had suggested he book into The Grand Hotel, but he preferred not to stay in such places unless he had to. He preferred to have his own kitchen where he could cook his own food.

The apartment was tastefully done, and he had a nice, sleek kitchen with all of the best appliances.

This was perfect, almost a home away from home. Forest Heights was picturesque. There was greenery around him. No palm trees, but plenty of trees and woodland nearby, and a lake which he could see from his apartment.

He loved nothing more than opening the doors to the veranda

and having his morning cup of coffee there while gazing at the beautiful scenery around him.

He hadn't realized just how much he had been in need of a break until he'd arrived here.

Hailey had come to visit him on the day he'd arrived, making sure that he had settled in. He had. The view of the lake was breathtaking.

Not wanting to waste time, he and Hailey had hatched a plan for her to bring Roxy over to his place for an introduction.

For that reason, he had thrown together a few canapés. He hoped to get to know her in a more informal setting. As he buttoned up his black shirt and smoothed down his sleeves, he surveyed his reflection in the mirror. He ran his hands through his copper-colored hair. He was aware that he was going beyond his normal routine for interviewing potential candidates for his show. He'd never invited them to his home for an interview much less prepared canapés for them.

This was different, because Roxy was a friend of his dear friend, and he was here not so much to meet her, but because an escape, a break from his life, was something he badly needed.

The doorbell rang, and he felt a tiny flutter of anxiety flash through him. It disappeared as soon as he acknowledged it. Maybe it wasn't nerves, after all he had no reason to be nervous. This was his show, and he was in charge. Maybe the nerves were due to the fact that Hailey so badly wanted Roxy to be on his show and he felt a sense of pressure.

If she wasn't suitable, he would let her know.

He didn't suffer fools, and he wouldn't tolerate boring people. The show was the most important thing. Its success was paramount and nothing else mattered, not Hailey's hopes, or Roxy's need for help.

He opened the door to find the three of them staring back at him expectantly. Hailey and Jax were holding hands, and Hailey looked hopeful. Seeing Roxy in the flesh was strange. Up close she was softer, shorter and slimmer than he had expected.

"Ta-da!" Hailey gestured with her hands as if putting the spotlight on Roxy, who grimaced and looked uncomfortable.

"Trust you to get someplace like this." Jax nodded his approval as they shook hands. He kissed Hailey on both cheeks, and was about to do the same to Roxy, when she held her hand out like a defense shield.

He shook her hand. "Enchanted." She snatched her hand back as fast as she could.

"You're staying here for a week?" she asked as he opened the door and they filed in. Roxy stepped inside and looked all around.

"We suggested that he stay at The Grand Hotel, but it's not grand enough for him," Hailey told her.

"That's not quite what I said." Mason didn't miss the look of surprise on Roxy's face.

"I hate to think what you're going to make of my diner."

"There's nothing wrong with your diner," Jax interjected quickly.

"We love your diner," Hailey announced. "And I can't see why Mason wouldn't." Roxy looked at him, perhaps hoping for verification. He couldn't give her something he didn't yet know. This was a business decision, and he didn't know if he would like the diner. He wasn't even sure if the two of them could work together. But he could sense that she was nervous, even if she was doing her utmost to hide it.

Hailey and Jackson milled around, obviously feeling comfortable in Mason's presence. She was not comfortable at all. Her first glimpse of this man had affirmed her worst fears. His strong jaw spelled confidence. He seemed sure of himself, and worse, that smug smile of his, the one which made the corners of his mouth turn upwards, made her wary.

"Relax and don't look so worried." Mason handed her a glass of champagne, which she took with uncertainty.

"Isn't it too early for this?"

There it was again, that smug smile, the slight tilt of his head as if he were trying to figure her out. "It's never too early for champagne. Whoever told you that?"

"My dad." Champagne was only for very special occasions, like birthdays and big family get-togethers. "This is a beautiful place," she murmured, more to herself than to anyone. Jackson and Hailey were staring out of the window, giggling about something and wrapped up in their own little world. She and Mason were the awkward ones left to stand in pained silence, while pretending to get along.

"I made some canapés. Come and try them." Mason nodded towards the kitchen area and she followed him. The kitchen area was enormous. Sleek and shiny surfaces, everything new and the best appliances. A pang of envy scorched her as she ran her envious gaze over everything. She didn't even have anything close to this in the diner, let alone in her home. Everything was outdated.

So what, she told herself, determined not to feel inferior, second best, second class, or broke. Determined not to let this man make her feel like this.

But boy, was it difficult.

She had been so busy admiring his kitchen decor and appliances that she didn't immediately see the kitchen island full of tiny trays filled with colorful and interesting-looking appetizers.

"Try some." Mason held out a tray for her.

"They look too good to eat." She didn't want to ruin the display.

"Thank you, but they must be eaten. I didn't make them to be admired."

"What are they?"

"I've got deviled eggs, caviar, pate, salmon and cream cheese here and in this—"

"I'm vegan."

His face dropped, filling her with a burst of satisfaction. That was something he hadn't considered.

"Vegan?"

She nodded.

"All is not lost." He started to walk towards his fridge when she called out. "I was joking. I'm not. I was just testing you." She couldn't read his expression because his back was turned to her. For a split second of silence, when he didn't reply, she felt a rush of heat go through her.

"Mason … I'll try these."

He turned around and walked back. "You have an unexpected sense of humor." He picked up a tray of canapés and shoved it under her face. "Try something."

She didn't want to try something which would crumble when she took a bite, nothing that was too big that required taking a bite, something that wouldn't leave crumbs, or was gooey in the middle and would dribble down her mouth.

"I went to great effort," he pressed, when she stared at the delicacies but wasn't moved to taking one.

"For me? You didn't need to go to any effort for me."

"Au contraire. We want to impress, do we not?"

"You don't have to impress me. I'm not looking to impress you."

"How lucky for us both that we're not going to be on a dating show." He picked up a canapé and expertly plopped it into his mouth. When he swallowed, and spoke, there was nothing stuck between his perfect teeth. Some people made some things look so effortless.

She tried not to stare at this shirt, or the way his copper-colored hair contrasted so well against it.

"Come on." He walked over to her side of the kitchen island so that they were standing side by side. "Try these, please. I'm begging now, and that's not something I often do." This time he picked up a different platter.

"What's that?" She had a feeling she knew, but she wasn't sure.

"Caviar. Ever tried it?"

"Once. I didn't like it."

"Try again." He motioned for her to take a cracker, but she declined.

"I see you two are getting to know one another."

"She doesn't trust me," Mason declared. "She refuses to try any of these canapés."

"Come on, Rox."

"He's a great cook," Hailey said, "You don't know what you're missing." She and Jax each took a plate and put a few starters on them.

"Have you told Roxy about the new show format?" Hailey bit into the caviar cracker, splitting it evenly. Nothing dribbled down her mouth. No crumbs fell down the front of her clothes. She seemed to have perfected the art of eating.

Roxy was hungry. The canapés did look divine, but she was too self-conscious to try. Hopefully if Mason slipped out of the room, she could.

"What new show format?" Roxy picked up a strawberry.

Mason wiped his mouth. "There's no point in discussing that until I've determined that we can work together."

"I'm not entirely sure I want to work with you either, yet." Roxy picked up another strawberry and put that on her plate.

"Maybe eight weeks in each other's company might be too much."

"Eight weeks?!" she screeched. This was news to her. She turned to Hailey. "You said it was just one show."

Mason stepped in and explained the new format and the logic behind it, but the more he told her, the less appealing this idea became.

The phone rang in the other room and Mason excused himself to answer it. No sooner had he left than Roxy piled a whole heap of canapés on her plate. Jax and Hailey looked at her as if she'd grown a third arm.

"I'm hungry." She picked up something that looked fishy but wasn't caviar.

"Why are you being sneaky about it?" Jax demanded.

She popped the canapé into her mouth, not bothering to answer because he wouldn't understand. She was certain this was a woman's problem. Men didn't care if they had crumbs around their mouth or spinach in their teeth.

"Have you and Mason clashed about something?" Hailey lowered her voice. "I'm sensing a chill."

But Roxy was in food heaven. Mason's canapés were out of this world delicious, and she was going to try as many as she could while he was out of the room.

CHAPTER 5

Why had she allowed Hailey to talk her into something like this? Why? She wasn't that desperate for help, was she?

Or was she?

She came into the diner early the next day after a night of hardly being able to sleep. She had managed to sneak some canapés while Mason's back had been turned, and there was no denying, the man could cook. But did she need his condescending smirk when he was talking to her? Did she need the extra stress of having him in her diner today, doing a routine inspection? Wanting to take a good long look at her diner?

She did not.

She did not need this level of stress in her life, not when her life was already stressed out to the max. She glanced around. Ella would be coming in soon enough, and then the others would all be here. She had to tell them. She hadn't even consulted them about the possibility of them being on a television show.

What if they didn't like the idea of being on TV?

Nothing she had so far seen of the man excited her too much.

She had spent last night, when sleep had been scarce, looking him up online, and going through reviews of his past TV shows.

Not everyone had done well after appearing on the show. A few business owners had shut down their businesses while a few had gone and prospered.

Surely this came down to the individual?

She made small talk with her staff, and only Ella commented on the fact that she had dark circles under her eyes. Observant and smart. Ella reminded her of herself in a lot of ways.

Mason had told her he would be coming in the morning, before her diner got busy. He said he wanted to have a good look around, to 'see what he had to work with' and 'the scale of the problem.'

There was no time like the present to tell everyone one what 'might' happen, depending on this final visit from the chef.

As soon as her workers had shown up, she turned the door sign from OPEN to CLOSED and clapped her hands together. "There's something I want to talk to you all about."

Ella raised an eyebrow. "Are things that bad? Are you going to let us go?"

Her employees looked at her with worried faces. She'd had no idea that they were worried about something like this. Things weren't that bad, they weren't that bad at all, but if things didn't improve, if things suddenly took a downward turn, it wasn't inconceivable that she might reach a point where she would have to reduce some of their hours, or lay some people off.

Maybe she could put herself through the stress of taking orders from Mason Brandt, after all.

"No. No." She shook her head, needing to drive the message home. "No one is getting laid off. We're doing okay. But I don't want to be doing okay, when we can do better."

A few of them folded their arms in defense. As if preparing themselves.

"I have good news." This was how she would sell it. "There is a chance—a very slim chance so don't get your hopes up too much, but there is a chance we might get a shot at being on TV."

A collective gasp echoed around the room. "What?" Ella was so visibly surprised she advanced two steps closer. "On TV? Who, *us?*"

"It hasn't been decided yet. I'm giving you all the heads-up. We have a visit from the man whose show it is." She glanced at her watch. "He'll be here in the next hour."

"Who?"

"Quit teasing us, Roxy." Lewis looked impatient.

"Have you heard of Mason Brandt?" When they looked at her with confused faces, she whipped out her cell phone and found him online, something she should have done before to put her own mind at ease. "This chef." She handed her phone over to them and they passed it around.

Murmurs of "Oh, him," were followed by, "Yeah, I know him."

"He's cute," said Ella, staring at the cell phone a moment longer, before Lewis held his hand out for it.

"He's vicious." Lewis handed the phone back to her.

"Vicious?" she asked.

"I've watched a couple of his shows. He can be really patronizing. Looks down at the poor owners as if they're stupid."

Roxy wiped her hand across her brow. She should have watched some of his shows. She should have done her research. If only she had time. She smoothed down her apron. She attempted a smile. "He's not perfect. As you know, Jax is dating Hailey Ross, and she knows him very well. She says he's not so bad."

"She would say that," retorted Lewis. "They all stick together, all of those Hollywood people."

"I've met him, and he's … not … that bad…"

This elicited a chorus of excitement, so she told them how the entire thing had come about and that she'd had a telephone interview followed by him actually flying over to Starling Bay, and staying at Forest Heights, and the meeting she'd had with him.

"I think it could work. I'm not saying it's going to happen. It probably won't but I wanted to let you know it could happen, and if it does, well, we need this. I need this, but I want to know if you're going to be comfortable being on TV."

"I'm not comfortable with him shouting at me." The defiant look in Lewis's eyes worried her.

"Or acting like we're idiots." Ella folded her arms even tighter.

"Oh, puh-leese. No one is going to make out we're idiots, because we're not. And I won't let him get away with looking down on us. If you're not comfortable, I need to know, and maybe we can have you work behind the scenes and stay out of the camera angles."

Her heart sank. Who was she kidding? She wasn't so sure herself. Yesterday's little get-together at his place had been … awkward. The only fun she'd had was when Mason had stepped away to answer the phone. When he had returned, they hadn't spoken much more about the show, but she had a feeling that he was watching her and trying to determine if they could work together.

She wasn't so sure they could.

It didn't really matter what they thought or not. The final decision was Mason's.

"He'll be here by eleven. Let's clean this place up and put on our best faces."

"We always leave the diner so clean you could eat off the floor," Ella threw back, as she disappeared behind the serving station.

"Do you think this is the right way to go about making things better here?" Lewis asked her.

And that was the problem. Things had reached that stage, and no one knew but her.

CHAPTER 6

"Not a bad location," he muttered to himself as he followed Hailey and Jackson into the diner.

Meeting Roxy last night had been interesting. It had showed him another side to her that the video conference had been unable to.

Talking to her that first time, she had been hard as nails. Meeting her in person had been another matter entirely. The nuance in the tone of her words, her expression, the thinly veiled act of her being strong and undeterred, all of these things were hidden away, but he could see them, because he had become a master at reading people and assessing what went on beneath their show face facades.

She wouldn't eat when he was around, but he was sure she'd enjoyed his canapés the moment his back was turned.

Hearing about the things she had tried to turn her business around told him that she wasn't coming to him willingly. He was a last resort. She was vulnerable, more vulnerable than she would ever admit to. The defiant upturn of her chin, the steely hardness in her eyes, told him she needed his help, but it was killing her to ask him for it.

He wanted to see her in her natural surroundings, at the diner. After today he would have to make a decision, and then he would have to let the show producer, Gerard, know that they might have to move Buffalo Bill to a later date.

He was thinking about putting Roxy first. Gerard wasn't going to like it one bit but, in his gut, Mason knew this could work.

People related more sympathetically to women. Roxy was small, yet a powerhouse of energy. Determined not to give up, hard-working, by all accounts from Hailey and Jax.

She was cute too, and viewers liked cute.

Buffalo Bill was spiky and sharp. All angles, no softness. Roxy was multi-faceted. She had spark. Sizzle.

And there was something else.

They reacted to one another.

She had clearly found him irritating; and he'd found her to be the same.

Why start with a whimper when the enigmatic Roxy offered so much more?

"What do you think?" Jax asked him. "Nice and cozy, huh?" Roxy's brother was eager to paint the diner in as best a light as possible. Mason stood near the door, his discerning glance around the inside allowing him to take in everything and commit it to his memory for safekeeping.

"Roxy!" someone shouted, and soon enough, Roxy appeared, her cheeks flushed, her hair up in a pineapple hairstyle, her chestnut brown locks heaped prettily yet casually atop her head. "You're early." She walked towards them, then hugged Hailey and Jax.

"Don't I get one?" he asked, when she didn't do the same for him.

She blushed, the tell making him tilt his head. She held out her hand and he took it, deliberately holding onto it for longer than was necessary. He didn't shake her hand but held onto it as if he didn't want to let go, because he had no doubt that it would make her uncomfortable, or embarrassed, or hopefully both, and for some reason, he liked getting a reaction out of her.

It wasn't that he was attracted to Roxy.

He wasn't.

"Can I have it back?" Her dark eyes glared at him.

"What's that?" Although he knew perfectly well what she was alluding to.

"My hand." She snatched it back just as he let go of it.

Hailey gave him a peculiar look, and Jax didn't look too pleased. He himself had no idea why he was behaving like this. It was thoroughly unprofessional, and yet he couldn't help it. "Sorry." He gave her a tight smile, resolving to be on better behavior. "Show me around and introduce me to your staff."

She introduced him to her staff, giving him too much information of the wrong type that he didn't need—how long each of them had been here, where they had worked before, what they excelled at.

She was a good boss, proud and protective, and he liked that. Her employees seemed like a decent bunch of people too.

As Roxy showed him around, he slid his finger across the surfaces, checking for cleanliness.

"And this is my kitchen." She swept her hand in front, highlighting the small work area at the back. "It's not as slick and shiny as the places you've worked in, I'm sure—"

"Are you embarrassed?" It was only the two of them now, the other people in the kitchen were busy getting on with their tasks.

"I'm not embarrassed. I'm just letting you know in case you were expecting something more glamorous." She had already contradicted herself in that sentence, but he didn't want to point that out. She was embarrassed. He ran another finger over the cupboards and worktops. It was clean, even if it was slightly outdated.

"It's small but …"

"It's the size it is," Roxy threw back. "I can't do anything about the size. It's a diner. It's not a sprawling big restaurant like the ones you're probably used to."

"I meant with regard to the film crew. We'll have people here. We should also set up at the back." He opened the door to the kitchen that led to a yard outside. This would be perfect for putting up a tent for makeup and prep and for the TV crew. "Is everyone on board?"

"They are."

"Are you?" he asked.

"Yes, why?"

"Are you happy about everything?" They were in a corner of the kitchen.

"I don't know what your decision is yet."

"No, you don't. I haven't made up my mind. Talk me through what you serve."

"Serve?"

"Your menu options. Do you provide lunch, brunch, dinner, what?"

"I provide it all."

"Shall we step outside," he suggested, not wanting to say anything in front of her employees.

"Anything you want to say to me, you can say in front of the others. I don't hide anything from my employees."

He was thinking more about her, and not wanting to embarrass her, but if she insisted … "Let's step outside." Once outside he told her, "You've got to stop being so defensive."

"I'm not being defensive."

"I'm observing things, and you're a little too … on edge."

"I am not."

He lifted his eyebrow, questioning her. "I'm here to get a feel for your working environment, Roxy. I'm not here to take a dig. I've worked in worse places."

Shock jolted through her eyes. Her mouth fell open.

He lifted his hands to placate her. "That's not what I meant."

"Then what did you mean?"

"You can't take offense at everything I say."

"I'm not taking offense, maybe you shouldn't be too abrupt and assume that I'm going to do everything you say. I won't, unless I understand the reason why."

He liked that. That was exactly what he was looking for in a suitable candidate. She turned to him. "I'm not sure I can give you any more of my time. I have a business to run."

"Filming here, if we decide to move forward, will interrupt some of your day-to-day routine." He had touched upon some of the filming logistics and timings yesterday.

"I know. You already spelled it out for me in great detail."

"I'm touching on it again to make sure you get it this time. I couldn't help but note your shock at the two months of filming involved." He had to stop himself from lifting his eyebrow as he wondered whether this woman was capable of talking without a gallon of sarcasm injected into her words.

"Two months is a long time to spend with someone like you."

This woman had guts. He couldn't help but admire her. He had to respond in a similar fashion. Leaning in towards her ear, knowing that she flinched whenever her personal space was invaded by him, he whispered, "You might learn something." He'd been tempted to say something else, something flirtatious, but stopped himself.

It was unprofessional to make such comments, especially to show contestants. What he didn't understand was why Roxy pressed his buttons. He had sworn off women, had ejected them from his radar ever since he and Monique had separated a year ago.

To be feeling something, even if it was good old-fashioned bickering, for a woman he barely knew, let alone cared about, niggled him.

She backed away as if he'd tasered her. "That's the objective, isn't it? That you, the almighty rich and successful chef, will pass down some grains of wisdom to a mere mortal such as myself."

He bit down on his teeth. She knew nothing about him or his failing businesses, but she definitely knew how to drive a stake right through him.

The sniggering laughs of his peers at the Parisian restaurant where he had received his training still rang in his ears. No matter what level of success he reached, he couldn't eradicate it. He was always conscious of who he was; the poor boy from Maine who had done well. "I can only try. Thanks for showing me around."

"I hope it was worthy of your time," she shot back.

"That remains to be seen."

"Have you finished?" Hailey asked when they walked back through to the diner.

"I've seen all I need to."

CHAPTER 7

$\mathcal{N}$o way. She couldn't work with that man. She couldn't.

"He's so nice!" Ella stared dreamily into space, making Roxy wonder what part of the entire time Mason had been here Ella had missed. She'd obviously been too wrapped up in awe to notice how obnoxious the man could be.

"Do you think he might offer us jobs at his restaurants?" Lewis asked.

Roxy threw him a contemptuous look. "Why, aren't you happy here?"

Lewis looked sheepish. "I was just asking."

"Because if you do, don't let me stop you." She stormed off into her office and closed the door. It was a tiny little room, past the entrance to the kitchen. Sometimes, diners mistook it for the washroom. She'd now put up a small sign saying, *Office*, and kept it locked.

Now, stepping inside, she bolted it, needing to have some quiet uninterrupted time to herself.

This was a mistake. She'd gotten so wrapped up in Mason Brandt being the answer to her prayers that she hadn't fully considered the enormity of the situation. A TV show, with him? Was it really the best way for her to get ahead?

He had grated on her nerves today, and she'd tried hard to keep herself from responding. She hadn't always succeeded. She didn't like the way he observed her kitchen and her appliances, and she was sure he had an opinion about the menus and the rosters, and the layout of the diner.

He came from a different world.

What had she been thinking allowing him to come here and tell her what to do? Her parents hadn't needed anyone when they had run the diner.

Of course, back when her parents had started this, it had been another time. Starling Bay had been a different place.

Now, new places were springing up all around town. She needed to change things up in order to retain her customers as well as gain new ones. A knock at the door stopped her thoughts. "I'm going through my bookkeeping," she shouted back. "What is it?"

"Nothing. I just wanted to talk to you about the chef," Ella called out.

"Not now, Ella. I need to concentrate."

"I liked Mason." Ella's voice floated from the other side of the door.

"I'm happy for you."

"Can we at least talk about it?" The door handle turned. "You bolted it?" Roxy sighed, Ella wanted to talk, she did not.

"I'll be out when I'm done, Ella. Don't you have things to do?"

She had dinner with her parents this evening, something else she wasn't looking forward to. She had a lot of unwanted things to deal with, and now Mason Brandt and his show. She didn't think she stood a chance, but he had riled her up, and that had soured her mood for the day.

~

"Mason who?" her father asked.

"Mason Brandt, the chef who does the TV shows." She had decided to tell them, in case news got around that the chef had visited her diner. Rumors spread fast in this town. She felt she owed it to her parents to hear the news from her.

"His name sounds familiar," her mother said.

Roxy found a clip of a one of his shows and passed it to her dad. Her mom leaned huddled in, pulling down her reading glasses from her head so that she could see the video clip. "Oh, yes! I remember him. I've watched his shows. He's not very nice." Her mother pushed her glasses up and gave Roxy a what-were-you-thinking stare.

"But why are you going on his show?" Her father's thick eyebrows raised angrily. "Are you running a diner or looking for fame?"

"He offers advice. He helps restaurant owners turn their businesses around."

"Turn them around from what?"

"Dad, calm down!" This was why she never came to her parents with her financial troubles. They should have been her first point of contact when she had started to struggle, but they judged her. Jax could do no harm, but when it came to her, her parents weren't so forgiving. "I'm sure it won't come to that. We're just having initial talks, but I don't think we're a good fit. It's a long shot that he'd have me on the show."

"But that man has come all this way to see you," her mother cried. "This sounds to me like it could happen."

"Are things that bad, Roxanne?" Her father handed her the cell phone back. She had reluctantly stopped by for dinner on her way home from work, but it was the last thing she wanted. After Mason had left, her day had seemed doomed. Customers complained about their salads, citing that the lettuce was limp. Ella had slathered it with too much dressing. Lewis had overcooked the huge pot of pasta. One of her suppliers was hiking up his prices, and the bank had refused her the new loan which she needed to overhaul the kitchen. The bank manager had told her he would review the situation after six months, but her business projections to date weren't good enough.

Failure was written over her heart as she walked into her parents' home. To add to her dismay, Jax and Hailey weren't there, although having decided to keep her parents in the loop regarding Mason and the show, it was probably easier without them both.

She felt a certain pressure to not voice her real opinion about Mason in front of Hailey, but she had doubts and things she wasn't sure about. She didn't blame Hailey for pushing her into this predicament but having seen Mason again today made her even more hesitant.

"Roxanne?" Her mother's tone didn't bode well. "Are things really that bad that you're going on national TV?"

Her father pushed away his empty dinner plate. "You don't come to me anymore, eh?"

As if she could come to him. Every time she had tried, she was always met with the same 'we told you this was hard,' 'you didn't listen to us Roxy, running a diner isn't for you.' She couldn't tell him the truth. "Dad, this is a great opportunity. There's a slim chance I'll get on it, and if I do, it could help me and it could be great publicity for the diner."

Her mother placed her hands on her cheeks in a woe-is-me pose. "Roxanne. You can't control your mouth. I've seen that man, this… this... Mason fellow. He's like you, he has no filter and he's rude."

"I'm not rude!"

"You're not very tactful," her mom retorted. "I'm worried, honey."

"Worried about what?"

"That he will show you up. He'll make you look like a fool. He does that to people."

Roxy chewed her food, but her mouth was dry. She needed to watch his older shows and read up about people who had been on them, find out how their experiences had been. She was going in blind and hadn't checked anything. She had simply taken Hailey at her word. Maybe this was her failing? Maybe she was at fault? Maybe she was not well equipped to be a businesswoman. Maybe her parents and her teachers had been right.

"My Roxy isn't going to let anyone make a fool out of her, eh, Roxy?" Her father winked at her.

"You know me, Dad. I give as good as I get."

"That's my girl."

"Are you going to get your hair done? What about a facial? Your skin's looking greasy." Her mother had other concerns.

"Mom!" She raised a hand to her face. She'd come over from the diner, so it was to be expected after spending a day in the kitchen. She didn't cook as much anymore, or wait on the tables, but on Sundays when she had limited coverage, she ended up doing more than usual.

"I think you should get some highlights put in, some flecks of gold to lift the dull brown of your hair."

"Thanks, Mom." She didn't feel like finishing of the rest of her dinner.

"Eat up. I don't want you wasting your food, Roxanne."

"Then you'll complain I'm going to look too big in front of the cameras."

"Big? You?" Her mother cried. "You could always eat like a horse and not put on an ounce." These were the words her mom spoke with pride, as if being able to stay thin was something to be proud of.

"I don't know about this, Roxy. Going on this chef's show isn't going to fix your problems as easily as you think." Her father gave her the same disapproving look he'd given her each time she'd shown him her report card at the end of every school semester.

"Why don't your mom and I start helping out one day a week, eh? And we can see where you're going wrong, since you refuse to talk to us."

Her parents working with her, even if it was just one day a week, was a big no. She would rather put up with Mason and his scathing retorts than that.

Her mom gave her an empathetic look. "If this isn't working out as you wanted, then maybe it's time to give up, honey."

They had already attributed her being a huge failure and all because she said she wanted help from a successful chef.

"Running a diner isn't for everyone," her father continued. A heavy, unsettling feeling weighed in the pit of her stomach. The leg of lamb with roast potatoes sat undigested in her belly. "We told you it would be hard work, but you didn't listen."

Her mother tapped her father on the arm playfully. "Don't be so hard on her, Pete. At least she's giving it a try."

"It's hard work. We told her that. And now she's suffering so much she has to go on TV and tell everyone she's failed."

"Dad." Roxy put down her napkin, the desire to leave making bile rise up her throat. "I haven't failed. I'm not failing. I'm just not where I want to be." This was the reason she never told her parents anything. She kept it all to herself. It was only recently that she'd let Jax know that things were hard, and she had regretted that decision because that was what had led to him telling Hailey. Hailey had gone to Mason, and now here she was, stuck in a situation she didn't want or need, and having her parents make her feel even worse. "I have to go."

"What? You've only eaten half of your dinner, Roxanne."

"I'm not hungry, Mom."

"That was a good piece of lamb, and you like this Greek recipe."

"It's delicious, but I'm not that hungry."

"We made so much, thinking your brother and Hailey would come but they're always so busy."

"They're always so busy," her father echoed.

"Jackson is talking about setting up a security firm in LA." Her mother's eyes shone with pride and she spoke as if Jax could accomplish anything.

She'd heard of his plans, and of Hailey wanting to buy a place in Glassmere. She didn't want to bring that up in case they hadn't told her parents. She didn't need another bullet point showing how well Jax was doing, and how she wasn't.

"He's talking about setting one up here, too," her father announced. "I always knew he was going to do well."

This was too much. "I'll take this with me to have tomorrow." She took her plate and started to walk into the kitchen.

"But I've made apple pie, Roxanne. You like my apple pie."

She'd made up her mind and needed to tell Hailey, who was at Jax's place, so she passed by on her way home.

"Well?" Hailey opened the door to her. "What's the verdict?"

Roxy walked in and handed over a big plastic container of food her mom had packed for them. "From my mom."

Hailey opened the lid and inhaled. "It smells divine."

"I hope you have a better appetite than I do."

Hailey set the container on the countertop. The door to the

backyard was open and she could see Jax working on his bike. They both stepped out. "What did you think of working with Mason?" Hailey asked.

"No. Definitely no."

"No?"

"Why not, Rox?" Jax wiped his hands on a rag which was dirty with black grease.

"But I thought the morning went well?" Hailey cried.

"I've made up my mind, Hailey, and I don't want you to talk me into this—"

"Talk you into this? Roxy, I'm not forcing you into anything, and I'm sorry if you feel that way."

"You've been really eager for me to do this, but I don't do things like this. I never go to people for help—"

"Isn't that half the problem?" Jax asked. "This is a great opportunity, Rox."

"Don't you start," she snapped. Everything and everyone around her were conspiring to make her life difficult.

"Yeah, when are you ever going to get the chance to be a part of something like this?" She realized it wasn't just Hailey who was pressurizing her. Jax was just as bad.

Hailey poured some iced tea in a glass and brought it out for her. "Thanks."

"No hard feelings?" Hailey asked. "I was only trying to help."

"What happened?" Jax wanted to know. "It looked like you guys were getting along." He motioned for them to sit down under the patio umbrella.

"Is that what you thought?" Roxy sipped her iced tea. Jax clearly hadn't been paying attention. She had been thinking about this all day, and the conversation with her parents had cemented her decision. Mason Brandt had nothing to offer her except humiliation and a lowering of her self-esteem, and no amount of being on a TV show, no amount of having this man look down on her, was going to make anything better.

"Mason isn't the easiest person to get along with," Hailey said. "I understand where you're coming from."

"He probably isn't interested in working with me, so, the problem is solved anyway." She sat back and closed her eyes, letting the warm sun kiss her face. This was a solitary moment of peace in a day that had been nothing but full of headaches.

"If you don't want to do it, Rox, then don't."

"We were only trying to help," added Hailey.

"I appreciate that," she replied, still soaking in the sun, "but I'll find a way to make things right, and I'll do it my way."

CHAPTER 8

"I've made my mind up, Gerard, and you can't talk me out of it. Make the switch."

"We already have the contracts signed. The filming is due to start in a few weeks. Why the change? Why now?"

Mason pressed his thumbs into the space just at the start of his eyebrows. He didn't know. He'd be damned if he could answer that question without sounding too mysterious or vague; he wasn't sure he could explain this in a way that made perfect sense, because to him, it didn't.

But Roxy Miller had a certain way about her, her acerbic tone and sarcasm wasn't lost on him and it would translate very well to the TV show. He was taking a big gamble with the new format and felt that she would be less of a risk than the middle-aged and grumpy Buffalo Bill.

The timing was bad.

But he went with his gut. After all, his gut had never failed him. Not when it came to a new recipe, or taste, or dish, or new way of serving it. And not when it came to the important decisions in his life, like this new show.

"I have a good feeling about this. Trust me."

He'd been talking to Gerard for almost an hour. His producer hadn't been happy and had complained at the other end. Mason was relieved that he wasn't there, face to face in a meeting with him. "Buffalo Bill isn't going to like it."

"He can go second."

"He won't get his turn for a couple of months. He's not going to be happy."

Mason sighed as he swirled his whiskey glass around. "Tell him we'll have ironed out the problems in the show by the time we come to film with him. Tell him what you need to, Gerard."

"This is very eleventh hour."

"I know." He lifted the glass to his lips and sipped. The view from the sofa, with his veranda doors open, was heavenly. He liked it here. He'd felt a peace he hadn't in a while. He wasn't a man who handled failure well. The year-long separation had been a helpful prelude to the finality of the divorce, but it had shocked him how much it had still hurt. Here, he had been able to finally push the hurt and failure behind him. He hadn't had time to think about it. Starling Bay and Roxy had been a welcome segue from his failed marriage and the business problems he was facing.

"I'm used to it." Gerard sighed out loudly. "She'd better be good."

"Wait till you come and meet her."

An awkward silence descended before Gerard thundered, "Come and meet her where?"

"In Starling Bay. It's a small place, on the East Coast, an hour's drive from New Haven."

Gerard groaned loudly. "This isn't helpful, Mason, moving the shooting location and changing things at such a late stage. Do you have any idea of the logistical problems this presents?"

Mason scratched at a fleck of flour on his jeans; he had been expecting this reaction. "It's not too late, and everything is flexible, Gerard. Better to be flexible than to be fixed. Please take care of all the paperwork. I'll email you all of her details so that you can draw up the new contracts. Send them to me quickly."

Mason got up and walked out onto his veranda. The lake glistened in the distance, and he considered going for a walk in those woods.

Forest Heights was no Beverly Hills, but that was no bad thing either.

"You're going to give me a heart attack, Mason."

"Don't be so dramatic." He hung up. With filming a few weeks away, there was much to be done in the way of getting Roxy's Diner and the employees prepared for all that was expected.

Of course, he'd need to look at her financials as well, to see how much she was making, and how much was going out, and what he could do to advise on the best practices.

Speaking of which, maybe he ought to call the woman and tell her that he'd taken her on. She was going to get a lucky once-in-a-lifetime chance to be on his show.

She would be grateful, no doubt. She should feel honored. Most were. A chance to be on his show could be life-changing.

He tipped his head back and took another long sip of his drink.

Perfect.

This was the perfect end to a perfect day. Pulling his cell phone out of his pocket, he speed-dialed Hailey to tell her to pass the news onto Roxy since he didn't have her direct number.

"Hailey? I have news." He paused for effect.

"News? What news?"

"I'm taking Roxy on. She'll be the first to be on the new show—"

"The first? As in … you'll start filming soon? Didn't you already have someone lined up?"

"Don't worry about him. I've taken care of everything. I've

spoken to my producer, and we're getting the contracts drawn up as we speak. Expect to have them here in a few days' time." He was puzzled by the lack of excitement from Hailey.

"We might have a problem."

The glass he had lifted to his mouth in readiness stilled. "What sort of problem?" He didn't like problems, and when he was confronted by them, he liked to resolve them quickly; hence why he was so good on his show.

"You need to come over, but hurry. I'm not sure how long I can hold her for."

"Hold who for?"

But Hailey had already hung up, and given the context of their conversation, he had an idea who she was talking about.

Well, this was a turn of events he hadn't been expecting. What the heck was going on? Rather reluctantly—for he had been enjoying his drink and quiet evening—he got a cab over to the address Hailey had given him, where her boyfriend lived. He wasn't used to being summoned, or having his plans changed unless he was the one who was doing the changing.

"This had better be good," he muttered, striding through the door as Hailey greeted him.

"She's in the backyard."

He followed Hailey out to a small yard where Jax was sitting, and where he could see the back of Roxy's head. When Jax stood up to greet him, Roxy turned and looked at him.

"That's why you didn't want me to leave?" Roxy picked up her jacket and made as if to leave.

"Mason has news for you, and you need to hear him out." Hailey blocked her exit.

"What's going on, Hailey?" Jax didn't seem to know either.

"What the devil is going on?" Mason growled. He had given up a perfectly good evening and he wasn't pleased.

"Roxy says she doesn't want to do the show," Hailey announced.

Mason groaned, then scrubbed his hand over his face. He examined Roxy's expression for clues as to what was wrong. This had to go through. He'd spent an hour telling Gerard why he was making this change. Roxy couldn't back out now.

Unfortunately, he'd jumped the gun and rushed on ahead, assuming, as with many of the other contestants, that Roxy would be thrilled to be on his show, that she would value his experience, that she would welcome the fifteen minutes of fame and short-lived publicity which could turn her business around and change her life.

He should have checked with her first, he would have, but Gerard had called him to discuss a logistical issue with the filming, and Mason had ended up telling him then.

"Why are you backing out now?"

"This show is not going to work for me." Roxy examined her nails, her mouth set in a stubborn line.

"What?" He moved toward the table so that he was standing in between Roxy and Jax. "What do you mean it's not for you?"

"You can't force her," Hailey murmured, as she poured him a glass of iced tea which he declined because he was so angry.

This was rich, coming from Hailey. "You're the one who told me to come all the way here." He wasn't going to let anyone off the hook. What a mess this had quickly descended into.

"I mean," Roxy stopped to swallow, the first indication that she was nervous. "Why is this such a big deal anyway?"

Mason slapped a hand to his forehead. "It's a big deal now because I've given the go-ahead to my people. I've told them that we're moving you to be the first candidate. I've moved the guy who thinks we're going to start shooting in a few weeks' time to the next slot."

Roxy's dazed expression told him she hadn't been expecting any of this. "You did what?"

"You heard. You're on the show. We start filming in a few weeks' time." She was speechless, a rarity for her. "What went wrong?" He gesticulated with his arms, not caring to hold back his temper.

"I ... I don't want to do this anymore. I didn't think I stood a chance."

"But that's not why you don't think you want to do this, because you felt it was a long shot. Don't dance around the truth, Roxy. Have the guts to be honest with me."

Silence fell. Hailey coughed lightly. "If she doesn't want to do it, she doesn't have to do it."

"Steady there, Mason," said Jax.

"Why didn't you check with me before you told your agent?" Roxy asked.

"My producer," he corrected. "Why? Because I assumed we had a deal. You said you needed my help. You said you were struggling. What changed?" He glared at her. He had come all this way for this woman and had allowed Hailey to twist his arm and convince him to interview her, and now she was walking away.

Did she have any idea what he could do for her restaurant? For her reputation? For her bottom line? Appearing on his show would help her get an initial burst of publicity that no amount of advertising could get her.

What he was giving her was priceless.

Was she really too stupid to see that?

"Why don't you think about it, Roxy?" Hailey tried to appeal to her. "Did you two argue?" This was directed at him.

"No, we didn't argue."

"I don't think we get along." This from Roxy.

"We're not supposed to be best friends. I'm not supposed to be gentle with you. You're trying to turn your business around. This isn't kindergarten where I compliment you for every mistake you make."

Rage simmered beneath his skin. She had no idea of the mountains he'd moved. Of the costs, the extra work involved in making this happen. He was going to have to get her on, no matter what, which meant he was going to have to appeal to her, beseech her, convince her, be nice to her; something which didn't come easily to him and which was as rare as a flawless diamond. He had been put in the position of having to win someone over, and he hated it.

Exasperated, he drew out an irritated breath. Maybe he should cut his losses, let Gerard know that he had messed up again. It wasn't too late. Maybe they hadn't let Buffalo Bill know yet?

"What made you change your mind, Rox?" Jax asked, but she was quiet, her head lowered, probably feeling put upon and outnumbered.

Mason sat down, taking a seat opposite Roxy, and picking up his glass of iced tea. He was tempted to ask if they had anything stronger, because he was sure as hell in need of something strong. "Tell me what it is, and I'll cut you loose," he said, curious to know why she had changed her mind at such a late hour. "It's not too late. I also could do without the headache, and this," he waved his hand between them both, "has been nothing short of a headache and we haven't even started filming yet."

"You bully the people on your shows. You make them look bad, and you laugh at their expense—"

"I do not laugh at their expense." He couldn't excuse himself with regard to that. It hadn't been bullying, exactly. The format of his earlier shows had dictated that he give people hard advice. He was known for being loud-mouthed, opinionated, selfish, and with a temper, but he also understood that many wouldn't listen or heed his advice unless he spelled out the disaster for them continuing on their current path. Some people didn't hear, and he didn't dress up his words. He doled out advice in no uncertain terms. But he had also been called out for doing what was right for him. For using the restaurant owners and their paper-thin fragility to advance his own ratings.

He was guilty of that, too, but he was trying to move on. Audiences might have tolerated that approach years ago but not so much now. He had been advised to soften up.

"Are you scared of me being hard on you?" He dropped his voice to a softer tone, difficult for someone like him to do. He wasn't used to having to treat people with kid gloves, and he resented that he had been put into this position now.

"I'm not scared of your bullying," Roxy shot back. "I can't see how the intrusion and cameras, and everyone getting in the way will help. I don't want it to scare off my customers."

"I have lots to explain to you, but if you no longer want to be a part of this, if you're too scared to take good advice, and you don't want to be taught, I understand. This isn't for everyone. You're fine to continue as you are, which, from what Hailey tells me, means that you work all the hours and don't have a life. But you continue with that, because you obviously know better. What do I know? Me, a world-famous chef. I've cooked for dignitaries and—"

"And there you go again, tooting your own horn."

He narrowed his eyes at her. She spoke to him in a way that most people hardly ever dared. He needed his show to be off to a great start, he needed great ratings from the outset and a firecracker like Roxy would definitely boost his ratings.

"I can't see how this is going to work," said Jax, propping his arms on the table and locking his hands.

"It's such a shame. I thought you two could help one another." This from Hailey.

He drained his glass, eager to be done with them and to return to Forest Heights. If he left now, it might not be too late to get a hold of Gerard and get back to having Buffalo Bill on the first show. "I understand. Some people can't handle the pressure. They can't put in the hard work. They don't want to push themselves further and do things that I recommend because it involves doing hard work."

"I'm not scared of hard work."

He stared into Roxy's dark eyes, saw the fear. "Then what are you afraid of?" Even though she didn't answer, he knew. Like him, she was afraid of failing.

"It's been a great evening." He got up. "But now I must get back and call my producer again. Stay," he told Hailey. "I'll see myself out. Have a good evening, all."

But when he reached the door, he heard footsteps behind him and knew, without turning around, that it was Roxy.

"Mason." Her voice was raspy. He turned around, curious to hear what she had to say.

"I'm not afraid of hard work."

"You're afraid of failing, I know."

"I'm afraid of being made to look like a fool."

His eyes widened and for the first time he had an inkling of the real her. "I won't make you look like a fool."

"You won't?"

"That's not my style."

This seemed to reassure her.

"Then, okay."

"Okay what?" He needed clear words, not vague promises.

"Okay, I'll go on your show."

CHAPTER 9

She loved being the first one in the diner each morning.

The quiet, the absence of clattering utensils and dishes, was heavenly. It was against this that she enjoyed her first cup of coffee in the morning alone, left to her thoughts, thinking of the day to come, and all that she had to do.

But again, she hadn't slept well at all. She had been stressed out, not that this was anything new. This, even despite Mason's assurances about the show, once she had agreed to be on it.

She had been satisfied with his assurance that he wouldn't make her look like a fool. She didn't want to fail, and she worked hard, so failure wasn't an option, but being made to look like an idiot? That was her greatest fear, because it would bring to fruition the messages she had learned about herself from school. From her parents. That she couldn't cut it.

She agreed to Mason because perhaps this was her last chance to prove everyone wrong.

The turn of events yesterday had made things more complex, because even though she was now doing the show, the dynamics between her and Mason had shifted even more.

She wished she could walk away. She had been about to, until

Mason had shown up at Jax's and didn't seem too pleased about her decision to quit.

As much as she appreciated all that Hailey was trying to do for her, she felt as if she'd been pushed into this; the whole entire journey, from Hailey first suggesting the idea to Mason suddenly arriving in Starling Bay, was something she wasn't ready for.

She'd been scared off not only by their chemistry—or lack thereof—but by her mom and employees telling her that Mason was nasty to people on the show.

But he had gone ahead and chosen her. Yet now that things were back on, she still wasn't sure that it was going to work. Not only that, but he was pushing out the person he had lined up for the first show and putting her first.

She sensed that Mason was a man who wasn't often turned down, and the fact that she had turned him down had hit hard. And too late.

He'd apparently told his people she was on board.

It was all premature, and not her fault.

Hailey had seemed caught in the middle, and Jax had tried to make her see she was turning down the opportunity of a lifetime. In the end, she and Mason found themselves going forward with a deal that neither of them felt one hundred percent sure about.

They'd both talked inside for a long time after that. Mason had explained to her how this would work, that someone from the production team would arrive to scope out the diner and see where and how they would film it. Soon after, the film crew would arrive and then filming would start a few days later. He assured her that she would get timetables of everything, so that she would know in advance.

She had been worried about the interruption to the restaurant, until Mason had explained that a lot of the filming would take place behind the scenes, in the kitchen, and after-hours. A lot of it would be conversations between her and Mason with him making suggestions.

She was happy with that, and when things were quieter in the diner after the lunchtime rush, she got her crew together to tell them. When she told them the dates of the first show, Ella whooped with joy and decided she would get her hair and nails done.

"I doubt that you'll have to go to such lengths," Roxy replied. Trust Ella to think about her looks over the lessons to be learned in the diner.

"We're going to be famous." Lewis clapped his hands together, seeming super pleased that this would be his claim to fame, and maybe the stepping stone to a better job.

As for herself, Roxy had no such ideas.

She still had suspicions that Mason's intentions for the show were to help people. She didn't believe him.

A few days later, Rourke, one of her old friends, came by around noon to get his lunch and couldn't help himself. "I've heard rumors, Rox," he said, paying for his lunch.

"Oh? And what rumors have you heard?"

"That Hailey and Jax are looking to buy a property in Glassmere."

"Are they now?" She waited, knowing that Rourke started with one thing, but he had a whole heap of other questions stacked up his sleeve. As one of Starling Bay's realtors, he would be privy to such matters, seeing that the place where he worked was the prime realty business when it came to buying the huge multi-million-dollar properties which were par for the course in Glassmere, an exclusive part of the town.

"Jax sure did hit the bigtime when he ended up taking care of Hailey Ross." He winked at her.

"I would say that Hailey hit the bigtime when she ended up with someone as lovely as my brother."

Rourke took the change, and grinned as Roxy handed him his lunch, but he made no move to leave. "When's the wedding?"

"Oh, puh-leese." She waved her hand in a dismissive gesture. "They've barely known each other long enough." But it was clear to her that Jax was smitten. She worried about him at first, wondering what it would be like for him to be with a world-famous actress. She couldn't abide wealthy, famous, celebrity people. She hadn't exactly been welcoming to Hailey when Jax had first met her. But over time, as she got to know the actress, she could see how right these two were for one another.

Maybe her suspicions about wealthy and famous people were something that tainted her relationship with Mason Brandt?

"But he's definitely moved up a rung in the income bracket."

"Hailey's buying the house, not Jax." Her brother didn't have that kind of money. He had plans though, and he didn't plan on being Hailey's security detail forever. "Did you come here to get the lowdown on Hailey and Jax? Because you're better off asking them than asking me." She was fiercely loyal and protective when it came to people close to her.

"I do remember." Rourke looked at her for one wistful moment, but she didn't buy that either.

"What?" she cried, knowing that this one-time high school ex-boyfriend of hers had no such feelings for her, and nor did she for him. They were amiable enough, friendly enough, to tolerate one another and be just good friends.

"Do I have to pry this out of you, Rox?"

"What?"

"I heard you're appearing on Mason Brandt's show."

"News does travel fast." She was surprised it had taken this long for Rourke to make a comment.

"Is it true? It's awesome if it is."

"It is true." Just about.

"You don't sound your usual enthused self about it."

She made a face. It was easy enough to put on a facade with others, and she and Rourke hadn't dated for more than a few weeks, but they had come to trust one another, and she found it easy to tell him things that she ordinarily wouldn't have told anyone else. "I'm not sure. I'm not sure we'll get along. He's not the easiest of people to get along with."

Rourke laughed. "Many people would say that about you. You're not exactly an angel yourself, Rox. Maybe you're both more similar and that's the real problem."

She wasn't sure it was that. Mason Brandt was all sorts of problematic. Rich, and famous, smug and self-assured, and in the coming weeks, he was going to look through her business and pick holes in it.

She didn't like that one bit. It was going to be hard to keep her mouth shut and let him tell her what she needed to do.

Rourke leaned over the counter, that sexy, slightly irritating grin of his dancing on his lips. "Want some advice?"

She folded her arms. There was no point saying 'no', because he was going to give it no matter what. "What?"

"Brandt is a world-class chef. How will you ever meet anyone of that caliber? Consider this a lucky break; go for it. Enjoy it or try. Don't look upon it as him being judgmental or critical. Let him guide you. Look at his success, look at his business. The guy has a TV show, for crying out loud. He knows what works, Rox. Listen to him."

She inhaled deeply. Rourke was right. Mason had fame and fortune—the things she didn't care for. She wanted to be successful, but here in Starling Bay, she wanted her diner to be one of the go-to places when tourists came to the town. She wanted to be known for great home-cooked food, and if Mason gave her the keys to that kingdom, she was a fool for not taking advantage of it.

Of course, she could always blame Hailey if things didn't work out.

"He's super successful at what he does, Rox. This is a great opportunity, and you should make the most of it."

"You're right."

He cupped his hand to his ear. "I'm right? You said that? I'm right? This isn't like you, to admit that someone else is right. You're ready to work with Mason, I'd say."

"Thanks for the pep talk."

"Anytime. You have a good day now. Let me know when the show airs."

She needed to dive into this opportunity. Learn what she could, take what lessons Mason had to offer, apply them to her business and with some luck, and a lot of patience, she might do better than she expected from it.

It wasn't a cast-iron guarantee that she would get these results, but it made her feel a teeny bit better about her next adventure.

CHAPTER 10

Fellini's was a lovely place to have lunch. He liked it so much, he had taken to coming here every day. The head chef and manager recognized him instantly. Nice to know that even in such a small town, he was still noticed.

Usually after lunch, he chose to walk around the town, often walking along the beach, in order to walk off the extra calories.

He wasn't young anymore, rather *youngish*, and at thirty-three, he had done more than most people would have accomplished in a lifetime, but because he enjoyed his food, he had to keep an eye on his waistline. In recent years, it was starting to grow. The paunchy softness of his waistline wasn't something he relished about growing older.

He was a man who liked to be in control of his future and his plans, but in recent years, life had given him a kick in the teeth and he felt the control slipping out of his hands. It was happening with Roxy Miller and her diner. He didn't like to appease anyone. He didn't like to beg, or plead, or cajole, or go easy on them, but Roxy had asked him in a roundabout way to do just that—to go easy on her—and because he needed her for the show, he had agreed to do just that.

Having this woman on his show was already turning out to be such a headache that he couldn't wait for it to be over with.

As he walked around the beach, he decided to go to the diner to see her. He'd received the contracts and, since he had pretty much commandeered this entire change in the filming schedule, he took it upon himself to make sure that things went as smoothly as possible. He needed to get Roxy's signature before she bailed out again.

He walked into the diner. In the late afternoon, it was half-empty. A waitress hovered around the counter, and looked up as he entered, greeting him with a smile that hinted at admiration as well as recognition.

"Hi, nice to see you again." She spoke with a familiarity that eluded him. He couldn't place her or remember her name. Obviously, he must have seen her the last time he was here.

"I'm Ella. We met the other day. Would you like to take a seat and have a look at the menu?"

"I'm not staying. I'm not eating. Is Roxy here? I have something for her."

"She's in the office. If you follow me, I'll show you the way." He was about to ask her to warn Roxy, because he was certain she wouldn't want him walking into her office while she was unprepared, but it was too late. Ella knocked on the door, then opened it, something he found a little forward.

Roxy was standing in the middle of the room, with her eyes closed, and slowly turning her head around. Ella coughed, and Roxy's eyelids flew wide open. Her face flushed to a beet red. She gave them a look that could have skewered them.

"I knocked," Ella tried to explain herself.

"I didn't hear you..." Roxy looked embarrassed. He frowned, wondering what she had been doing. Relieving tense shoulders and neck, from the looks of it.

"I came to give you your contract." He stepped forward and handed it to her.

"That will be all," she said to her waitress.

"Could you get me a chair, please?" he said to Ella as she opened the door to leave.

"You're staying?" Roxy stopped flicking through the contracts, her tone suggesting she wished he was gone.

"I can go through those if you need. Yes, I'm staying."

"Uh … do you need these back now?"

"Now would be good. Thanks, Ella." He sat down. "Before you change your mind again."

She moved over to her side of the desk, sat down and continued reading. Silence mushroomed in the space between them.

"I can explain the fine print," he said.

"I can read."

Twiddling his thumbs, he waited for her to finish. "Need more time?"

"I'm still reading."

"There's a lot of legalese there I can explain if you want."

"Do you think I'm illiterate?"

"No. I'm just offering to help you, Roxy." How could she take it to mean anything else?

She put the papers away. "I'll read through them carefully and get back to you."

"You'll have to sign it, on the dotted line."

"I know. I've signed paperwork before."

Roxy Miller wasn't talking to him as if he was a multi-millionaire celebrity, she was talking to him as if he were one of the staff at her diner.

Ballsy.

Gutsy.

Feisty.

"Do I make you nervous?" He could see that her hand was shaking.

"Ha! No. But would you prefer it if you did? Would you feel more manly if I quaked in my shoes?"

That told him.

He cleared his throat, feeling uneasy with the direction that their conversation had taken. This woman didn't take any baloney from anyone. "Now that I'm here, how about we get started and you talk me through your financials."

"My financials?"

He sat back, his hands on the table, used to this type of reaction from people who were creative and liked cooking and believed they could make a business out of it, but didn't care much for the administration side of things. Running a restaurant wasn't that easy. If it were, every mom, dad and grandma would be doing it.

"You want to see my financials *now*?"

"Are you hiding something?"

"No." The lines in the middle of her forehead begged to differ.

He hazarded a guess. "It's okay to take out loans, and be in debt, and try to make your dollars grow. It's all part and parcel of running a business, but the bigger picture has to be you making money, otherwise, why do it?"

"I took over the diner from my parents, like I told you."

"Did they demand that you do that? This is hard work, why not go out and get a job? It's way easier." He had met many business owners who had just sleepwalked into owning and running their current businesses. There had been no weighing of pros and cons, no looking at the good points or the bad points.

They had put no serious thought into it. At all.

"Because … I thought … I wanted to do this." Her voice was quiet.

"How about we look through your menus? Talk me through

what choices you give your diners. Menu choices and financials, this could take a while, so let's get started."

She looked as if he were torturing her. "Is this what it's going to be like? You wanting to see every little piece of paper I have? And observe everything I do?"

He leaned forward, lifting his thumbs and crossing and uncrossing them. "I'm good at what I do, but I'm not telepathic. Do you want my help or not, Roxy?"

CHAPTER 11

She didn't like this one bit. She didn't like having to tell Mason Brandt, a relative stranger—and someone she felt sure looked down on her behind her back—about her financial details, about the loans she'd taken out on the business in order to keep it running.

Her parents had taken out loans when they had started the business, but it seemed as if her business was bleeding money. It was gushing out faster than it was coming in and now for her to be in this man's company and share such details, it was humiliating.

Ten minutes into showing him the financial information, she had to get up and open the window. Breathing was becoming difficult. Her small office always got stuffy and hot in the summer months and now, with Mason sitting across the desk from her, the situation felt intense. The room wasn't built to house two of them, but she was grateful that he sat across the desk from her, instead of by her side.

He helped himself to a pen from her desk caddy, then tapped it on the table as he read through her paperwork, asking questions, so many questions. Luckily, she was always on top of her paperwork, and knew her figures inside out which, something told her, Mason seemed to be surprised by.

"This isn't so bad." He put his pen down and clasped his hands together. It almost sounded like a compliment.

"Really?" He sounded impressed.

"It's not great. I've seen worse business plans and figures."

Trust him to bring her back to reality. A compliment followed by a put-down. "Would you like a glass of water or iced tea?" she asked, sliding her finger in the collar of her waitress's outfit. She fanned her face, the heat making her feel stifled. The small space and the proximity to Mason adding to her feeling of discomfort and claustrophobia.

Opening her small window hadn't helped much, and the stagnant air outside didn't help to cool the temperature. This was the only room in her diner which didn't have air conditioning, but she had never before felt it as badly as she did today.

"No. I'm fine. We need to get on with this. Tell me about your menus, about how you put them together."

She gaped at him, as if he'd spoken in Russian. "The … menus?"

"Yes, the menus. The things you give to your customers when they arrive."

There he went again, talking to her as if she were an idiot. She fished a menu out from one of her drawers and handed it to him.

He gave it a cursory glance, then closed it, and nodded as he read the back of it. "This is what I would call … basic. I was hoping for some inspired choices, something exciting, something beyond the basics of breakfast, and hot chocolate, and sandwiches and salad."

He threw it onto the desk, dismissing it with a flourish of his hand, as if he couldn't bring himself to say more. "What made you decide on these options?"

What sort of a question was that? "Where do you want me to start?" she volleyed back, because she was afraid of what he would think when she told him that her menus were a continuation of her parents' menus, with some minor changes over the years.

"Start at the beginning. This isn't a difficult question, Roxy."

"I kept it in line with what my parents had."

"That's nice and easy, isn't it? You take over a diner and you can't even be bothered to make any changes."

A heavy ball of lead landed in her stomach and sank lower, dragging her spirits and energy with it.

"I bet you expected money to rain down as well." His humorless laugh made her want to run for her life. "When did you take over?"

She coughed. This sounded bad, now that he was drilling deeper and deeper. She shifted uncomfortably in her chair, felt her blouse sticking to her back. "Five, um … six years ago."

"Six years!" His eyes widened, and her heart pitter-pattered as if she'd committed some terrible culinary sin. "You haven't updated the menu in six years?"

"I have updated it. I've updated it many times, but a lot of those dishes are staples from what my parents used to serve. They've been popular menu choices and, apart from making minor adjustments, I didn't see the need to change them so much."

He picked the menu up again and opened it. "What sort of stuffed shells? What sort of burritos?" he wrinkled his nose. "This looks pretty basic and plain to me. There is nothing here that makes me want to order anything."

How dare he. Just because he had pretentious tastes, because he liked to dress his food up and make it look good, rather than taste good, didn't mean that her basic dishes were no good.

Her customers would beg to differ. She folded her arms, the

defenses going up like sheets of steel. "I want to focus on good, simple, home-cooked food, without drowning everything in unnecessary flavor."

He tipped his head back and stared at the ceiling. For a moment she thought he'd lost his mind. Then he hooted with laughter, and she was certain that he had.

"Unnecessary flavor? What in heaven's name is that?"

She clamped her teeth together so tightly she was in danger of grounding down her molars. "I'm not a huge fan of throwing every jar of seasoning into a dish."

His face twisted in disbelief. "You're a cook, yes?"

A sarcastic answer danced on her lips, but she didn't want to make things worse, so she nodded.

"And you expect your customers to pay for the food you serve them?"

"Yes."

"So why give them boring, bland and flavorless food when—"

"It's not flavorless. It's good simple food."

"People don't eat out and want *simple*. They want something that is delicious, with a twist, something colorful and which looks good and sets their palates on fire."

"My food is delicious, and it does set their palates on fire." At least, she hoped it did. She thought it did. People still came here. A knock at the door stopped them. "Come in," she cried, grateful for this interruption.

The door opened. It was Ella.

"Someone has come in and wants to speak to you concerning catering for their parents' fiftieth wedding anniversary."

Escape. She breathed a sigh of relief. "Can we pick this up another time?" she asked him. "I need to meet with this customer."

"You do catering, too?"

"Yes." She wondered what sniping comment he would make about that. "Thanks, Ella. I'll be out in a minute."

"I can wait while you tend to your customer."

Her insides sank. She didn't want to take this up with him again. Mason had a knack for draining the energy out of her, for making her feel like a failure and as if she was doing everything wrong. She couldn't handle another minute with him, not today. "This is going to take some time."

"Like I said, I've got nothing else to do today. I can wait."

"I'm still running a business here, even if you're on vacation." She got up, forced a smile. "I can't give you more of my time today."

"It seems to me that you're pretty glad for the interruption." He stood up and placed his hands on his hips.

"You're mistaken. This has been … enlightening. We'll pick this back up again soon." She couldn't wait to get away from him.

He got up. "I wanted to talk to you about the filming of the show and the disruption."

She glanced at her watch, aware that a customer was waiting for her, and irritated by this man's refusal to leave quickly. "I'm busy now."

"Just to keep you informed, very quickly, you should know that there's going to be a whole heap of people coming here soon. A location manager, someone to scope out this place, someone to walk you through it all, how the daily filming will go. Don't worry, we film behind the scenes, and we'll only have a few scenes in which we'll film you talking to the customers. It will be good if we can include your catering event."

"I'm not sure." In fact, she was sure. There was *no way* that this could happen. Events where she catered were busy. Not only did she worry about getting everything cooked and delivered, and laid out on time, but she had to be mindful of the people hosting the event, and make sure that she and her staff didn't get in the way. There was so much to juggle. Having Mason and a TV crew following her and filming here was a big 'no.'

He turned towards the door. "Think about it. The more we have to show different facets of your business life, the more it will make for interesting viewing."

"Is that all you care about? The viewers and the show?" She was still wary that he had his best interests at heart, not hers.

"You seem to be dreading this, Roxy. Are you still having doubts?"

She had doubts every day, but she was determined to press on. Like Rourke had said, she was going to go for it. "I tell myself that this will help me."

"You make it sound like torture, something to be endured."

She plastered another smile on her face. "That's a great way to put it."

His expression turned serious. "This will be over before you know it, and you can go back to your life again."

"I can hardly wait."

"Oh, me too, me too."

She opened the door to leave.

"Personal life?"

She turned around. "Excuse me?"

"Husband, partner, boyfriend?"

She didn't understand the relevance of this. "What does that have to do with anything?"

"Partners often have a huge part to play in a business, so it might be wise to let yours know what you're up to—"

"I'm not having any cameras invading my personal space."

"That's not what I said. I asked about your partner, the significant other in your life. Business owners don't operate in a vacuum, Roxy."

"I do." She was very much alone, not even involving her parents in her business decisions for fear of them thinking she couldn't handle it. "There is no significant other. Not that it should be any of your business."

"It's not. I'm only asking for the show. Everything has to do with the show."

She showed him out. She knew. She understood Mason and the type of man he was. He was concerned only about himself.

CHAPTER 12

"Is it true, about you being on Mason Brandt's show?" Jenna asked as she and Shay removed their handbags and propped them on the empty chair.

She had known these two from her school days. She sometimes saw Shay at the business meetings she attended. Shay worked at a recruitment agency and was always decked out in sharp suits, her hair in a slick ponytail and wearing super smart reading glasses. She'd taken things up a notch in recent months; it seemed like she'd had a complete new makeover.

Jenna was dating Reed Knight. Theirs was the stuff of dreams, the lowly housecleaner who had fallen in love with her boss.

"It's true." Roxy got ready to take their orders. The diner was really busy today, more so than usual and she wasn't sure if the news was spreading around town like a hurricane.

"Awesome!" Shay cried. "Sit down." She pulled out an empty chair for Roxy to sit on, and when Roxy hesitated, she said, "You're the boss, you can."

Once again, Roxy's gaze went to Shay's ring. "That is a gorgeous ring."

"Thank you."

She hadn't known that Shay was seeing anyone, so when she suddenly announced, not long after Christmas, that she was married, it had taken her by surprise, and Jenna too, judging by the conversation at that time.

It turned out that Shay had gone and married a local factory owner, and they were now happily settled down.

"Sit down," Jenna said, so she did. "How did this happen? You being on that man's show?" Roxy told her as briefly as she could. "You're going to be famous," Jenna squealed.

"It's not fame I'm after." Roxy blinked as the light glinted off Jenna's hand. A ring? On Jenna's hand? Her mouth fell open in shock and awe. Jenna too wore a huge ring. Looked like an engagement ring. "You're engaged?"

"I am." Jenna displayed her hand, showing off the beautiful glistening hunk of diamond on her finger.

"It's disgustingly big, isn't it?" Shay said.

"You're one to talk," Roxy piped back. Both these women now had beautiful diamond rings on their fingers. One was married. She shrank back into her chair, the weight of failure weighing heavily on her shoulders.

"I expected nothing less from Reed," Shay said.

"When … when … did you … did Reed propose?" Roxy wanted to know.

"Two weeks ago. He surprised me. Said he'd cook dinner, and there, on the plate alongside my chocolate cheesecake, was a box with this inside." She flashed her hand around again and examined her ring with pride.

"Congratulations. It's beautiful." Roxy hadn't ever wished or dreamed about rings or having a diamond that size. Getting engaged wasn't something that filled her mind. She hadn't considered being in a relationship, but suddenly, everyone around here was getting paired up. Even Jax.

She felt alone, and lonely, and left out, like never before. She got up, seeing some more customers come into the diner. "I'd better take your orders. It looks like we're getting really busy."

"Good luck with the show," Jenna said. "That Mason Brandt is quite something."

She wasn't sure what Jenna meant by that, but she didn't want to get into a conversation about him, so she let it go.

"Are you coming to the SBWEB meeting?" Shay asked.

"Maybe."

"We can catch up them."

"I don't know why you don't consider attending Hyacinth's monthly town hall meetings." Jenna looked up from her menu at them when they fell silent. "She's not that bad when you get to know her."

She and Shay exchanged glances. The SBWEB meetings were better. Many of the women felt more at ease. They had been set up by a few local businesswomen who didn't like the formal tone of the town hall meetings.

Roxy was aware of the meetings at the town hall open to business owners. Rourke often attended them.

"The SBWEB ones are nicer," Shay replied.

Roxy had to agree, while she didn't attend as regularly as she should have, the times she had gone out, it made her feel good to be in a space where other women business owners could talk about their struggles as well as celebrate their wins.

She hadn't considered attending this month's one; she often forgot about them due to pressing matters at the diner, but now that Shay had mentioned it, she decided she would attend. There was something to be said about females helping one another, and she needed a boost of confidence if she was going to survive two months of filming with Mason.

She hadn't liked the meeting with him a few days ago. Not one bit. It was intrusive. He had encroached on her personal space, her privacy, and on top of that he had asked her a personal question—about a partner, and whether she had one. Even Hailey and Jax didn't press her for such details. Of course, they knew she didn't have time for romance.

For Mason Brandt to ask her was out of order.

Since then, she had even more doubts about working with him, but it was too late to back out now. The contract was signed. Mason had seen her profit and loss statements. It was a small comfort that he'd been impressed with her business plan and had said that her figures weren't too bad.

She feared his questions, and that he would probe and dig deep to unravel her, that he would see through her. If he dug too deep, he might discover that there were days when she regretted taking over the diner.

There were. During hard days, she had started to think of other things she could do, easier things that didn't break her soul. Years of working hard just didn't seem to be paying off.

If this—baring her soul and letting Mason trample all over her reputation at the expense of her pride—didn't work, she would have to seriously consider selling the diner and moving on.

Maybe she could move out of Starling Bay, go to a big city and try that life.

CHAPTER 13

ere it not for the SBWEB meetings, Roxy would hardly get to meet other like-minded businesswomen. They were the closest thing she had to friends.

While she was well known in and around Starling Bay, her relationships with most were superficial. Even when it came to people like Rourke, or Jenna and Shay, who often came to her diner, she didn't hang out with them outside of work. She didn't have a close best friend to discuss ideas with, so this was a good alternative.

This time they were meeting at The Olive Tree, and if nothing else was great about the night, the food certainly was.

She sat next to Francine, Shay's boss from the recruitment agency, though there was no sign of Shay. There were others such as the owner of Books & Buns, the coffee and bookshop place, and Mackenzie, the owner of the florist shop, whom she was friendly with because she sometimes came to the diner. There were also a handful of others she hadn't seen in a while.

At this event, they all shared in turn what they had been up to since the last meeting, and how their businesses were going. There was no chair, no agenda, nothing set in stone and this resulted in a friendly and relaxed evening, more like a getting-together-with-friends night, rather than a business talk.

"I suppose we should go around the table and see what everyone's been up to," said Francine. She was good, and often seemed to lead the meetings if no one else jumped at the chance. She guided the evening so that it provided some sort of business help, even if it was just a chance for the women to air their concerns and get things off their chests. Achievements and success were enthusiastically celebrated, while struggles and problems were discussed, for those brave enough to air them.

Roxy listened as they went around the table, and each person shared their trials and tribulations since the last meeting. She hadn't attended one of these for a while, and so it was good to hear what everyone was up to.

She scratched her nape, worrying about her turn. Should she tell them about Mason and the show, or not? They would have started filming on the show by the time of the next SBWEB meeting and she would look silly if she didn't say anything now.

"Your turn," said Francine.

She often froze when the spotlight was on her. She never froze in her comfort zone of the diner but here, where the women were smarter, more successful, where they were more than her, she felt paralyzed. Often, she would talk briefly, without giving too much away, and she never asked for help. Today, she had something else to share, something that they would find new and exciting, even if she felt slightly reticent about it.

"I have an announcement." She swallowed and traced her fingers around the base of her wine glass. "I'm not sure if the rumors might have reached you but ... I'm going to be on a TV show and it's going to be filmed at my diner."

A gasp of excitement rippled around the table.

"I knew it," Leigh exclaimed. "I'd heard rumors. Mason

Brandt is in town, and he came to the coffee shop. People said he was filming on your premises."

"Mason Brandt?" another woman cried; someone Roxy didn't recognize. She placed her hand on her heart as if she were about to swoon. "You lucky woman! That man is a dream."

Roxy coughed. "I assure you he's not."

"Is he the guy who goes around helping failing restaurant owners?" Francine asked.

"He's the one," Mackenzie, the florist, answered. "And he loves flowers. He's been into the shop many times and ordered armfuls of flowers."

"He has?" Roxy asked, surprised.

"I can't believe you've been sitting on this news the entire evening," said Francine.

"I was waiting for my turn." It was just as well she had shared now. Clearly the women were besotted by the man. Why, she didn't understand. He was tall, and slim, and looked somewhat good in a black shirt. But a dreamboat?

No way.

No freaking way.

"This is going to be great for your business!" someone cried out. "Well done."

"Thank you," she murmured, feeling uplifted by the excited response.

"Where's he staying?" someone asked.

"How did you meet?"

They all turned and stared at her.

"Roxy?" Francine raised her eyebrow. "Spill all."

She told them all that she knew but didn't divulge anything about where he was staying. She understood, from Hailey, that he probably had a desire for privacy and wouldn't want people showing up and standing outside Forest Heights. Why anyone would do that she had no idea, but from the way these women had reacted, they were clearly enthused by him.

Or maybe it was his wealth and fame which attracted them. In telling them, she was asked the usual questions about Jax, and his dating a Hollywood star. Wanting to preserve their privacy, she cleverly sidestepped those types of questions.

"The Millers are definitely having their fifteen minutes of fame," someone said. It was yet someone else she didn't know, a sign of how long she had missed out on these get-togethers.

"I'm hoping to have more than fifteen minutes," she quipped. "And Jax isn't with Hailey because she's famous, but you don't know my brother, which is why I'm guessing you would make such a nasty comment."

"I … I didn't mean it like that."

Roxy waved her hand dismissively, her newfound courage at the ready especially when it came to defending those she loved.

"When will they start filming the show?" Francine asked, smoothly moving the conversation on.

"Next week."

"As soon as that?"

"As soon as that." A few days ago someone from the TV crew had come to the diner to check things out and informed her. Mason hadn't been with them, thank goodness.

"And the first show? When do we get to see that?"

"I have no idea. Sorry. Everything has happened really quickly. I don't know all the ins and outs, and the dates or anything, but I'll let you know."

"Good luck," one by one everyone around the table told her.

"Moving on to the next person." Francine moved the meeting along and Roxy was grateful to not be in the limelight. Later, as the women talked among themselves over dessert, she and Francine got to talking.

"I'm so excited for you." Francine lifted a fork to her mouth, then hesitated. "You don't seem that excited. Is it still sinking in?"

Roxy twisted her lips, unsure of what to say. She liked Francine and found her the friendliest to get along with, but Roxy wasn't one to let her guard down or get too close to anyone. She always maintained a good distance between herself and others and what she shared.

"I'm not sure how I feel, to be honest."

Francine set down her fork. "What are you worried about? Being on TV?"

Roxy grimaced.

"Making yourself vulnerable? Having someone dictate what you should and shouldn't do?"

Francine seemed to have read her mind completely. "Yes." The lightness that someone understanding her so clearly, was liberating. "Yes, exactly that."

"You're brave."

"Try foolish." Roxy tucked a lock of her hair behind her ear and picked up her cup of filtered coffee. It was late to be drinking coffee, and it would probably lead to another restless night. With so much going on and happening so fast, she was feeling as though her grip on life and her business and her sanity was fast vanishing.

Francine shook her head. "Not foolish. Not foolish at all. Brave. It takes serious guts to ask for help, and then to go on national TV, and with someone like Mason."

"Have you seen his shows?"

"He has a tendency to overdramatize things. I've seen a few of the business owners in tears."

Roxy's eyes widened. "In tears?" She should have done more digging. His past shows were online for anyone to watch, and even though she had intended to have a good look through, she hadn't. She hadn't had time. Every evening when she came home, she wasn't in the mood to watch Mason, even if it would have been in her interest to do so, to prepare herself.

Francine opened her mouth, then paused before asking, "Did you not see any?"

"I've looked at a few clips and read a few reviews, but this was after he'd come to Starling Bay. It all seemed a little too late then to back out." She pressed her hand against her forehead as the reality of it sank in. "What have I done?"

"Don't be nervous. He's a changed man. The last few seasons were different. People are saying he's softening."

"You're only saying that to make me feel better." She had messed up. Even after she'd seen the clips and freaked out, she should have trusted her gut instinct. She had always done that before and it had served her well.

"You're going to be fine, Roxy. If anyone can put up with Mason Brandt, and put him in his place, it's you."

She murmured a thanks but knew that putting Mason in his place was something she couldn't afford to do. Nor did she want to try.

"Deal with it, Murphy. That's what I pay you for." His fear of failure made him snap at people and ride roughshod over them without a regard for their wellbeing.

Buffalo Bill, the chicken wing guy from Brooklyn, was threatening to sue him for breach of contract and all because he'd moved him to a later filming date.

This was the last thing he needed, on top of all the current melodrama going on in his life.

This new show was never supposed to be this difficult, and with the obstacles he had faced and dealt with lately, he was growing tired and fed up.

He slammed the bottle of whiskey onto the table and strode over to the veranda again with his whiskey glass in his hand.

Looking out, he felt a sense of calm. There was something about this apartment, no, this place, this woodland paradise, and the lake and the privacy, that soothed this soul.

Even in the midst of the mayhem going on in his life, he could feel the tension flow out of his tired muscles.

So much was riding on this show. So much rode on every single venture of his. He approached everything he did with a steely determination of winning. Of having success, whether that manifested itself through high ratings, rave reviews, or invitations to guest shows.

Celebrity chef Mason Brandt does it again.

Those were the types of headlines he wanted to see. Not headlines alluding to people who wanted to sue him. The funny thing about all of this? He hadn't even shot a single episode of the show yet. Not one darned episode, and yet he was dealing with problems coming at him from all angles.

Jack would have to take care of Buffalo Bill. He didn't have the headspace to even think about it. This was why he used the services of the finest lawyers that money could buy.

The longer he stayed on the veranda, the deeper he breathed, the more he looked around and admired the beauty of nature, the calmer he felt.

Things were going to be all right if he stayed here in this apartment, surrounded by all of this woodland beauty. He would be fine. He could suffer even Roxy Miller. Heaven help him when they started filming the show and he had to tell her what to do.

Yet, at the meeting the other day, he had been surprised. Her business plans were good. She had concrete goals. She had figures she wanted to hit. She had planned and figured it all out in great detail.

The problem wasn't in her planning. It was in her execution. She was bone-tired. Even he could see that. It was a common problem he saw in many struggling business owners. They were so focused on the end line, the income, the profits, that they didn't stop to think about why they had opened the restaurant or diner in the first place, or why they sacrificed their precious time—

weekends and evenings, when most people were socializing—in running the business. He had paid a price, too. Monique hadn't liked spending her evenings or days alone. Married life wasn't supposed to be like that. He had tried to explain to her but failed. He was one of the top chefs in the world because he worked so hard. It wasn't fair on her. Could he blame her for finding someone else to confide in? She denied an affair, but he could never be sure. The trust was forever broken.

In her desire to have a successful business, Roxy had reached a plateau, and had started to give up. She maybe didn't know that yet, but he could see it in the menus that hadn't been updated for so long, in meal choices that were bland and boring and didn't tickle the tastebuds.

And she hadn't changed her prices.

She priced way too low.

Could he help her? Most definitely. Was it going to be easy? Hell, no.

His cell phone rang, and he plucked it from his pocket and answered without looking to see who it was. The light reflecting off the lake in the far distance caught his attention, soothed him, calmed him.

But then Roxy's, "How long are these people going to be here for?" broke the peace and quiet. He had expected her to complain about the intrusion, he was surprised she hadn't done it sooner.

A couple of people from the TV crew had gone over to the diner to take a look at the location and interior, and to do a health and safety check, for filming purposes.

He had warned her about it, but there were no cameras rolling yet, so the fact that she was already complaining didn't bode well for later on.

"Why are you getting so worked up?" He took a sip of whiskey to calm his nerves, numb him.

"Because they've been here all day."

He frowned. It shouldn't have taken all day. "All day?"

"Well, since three."

Given that it was now almost six o'clock, he didn't consider that to be all day. "What are you complaining about?"

"They're in the way."

"They have to take a good look so that we can see how much space we have for filming. I already explained that your diner is going to be a film set for a couple of days a week, Roxy. Get used to it."

"But it's going to scare my customers away."

"Is it? Or will more customers flock there because of curiosity? You'd be amazed how many people long to be on TV."

Hearing her stifle a groan, he gritted his teeth again, something he seemed to do on a fairly regular basis. This show was going to fail. It didn't take a genius to see that. He had never before had so many problems. First Roxy threatening to quit, then Buffalo Bill threatening to sue him.

He couldn't back out now.

He wouldn't let her back out either, in case she started to get any funny ideas. "They'll only be there today. They're getting ready to film the show. Are you ready?"

"Ready?"

"Yes, ready, as in calm and happy, and excited to be given this once-in-a-lifetime experience."

She scoffed.

Something in his gut tightened at her audacity.

Who did she think she was? Her basic failure to appreciate and value who he was, her constant disregard for him and her inability to treat him with respect, angered him. He had never met anyone like her before, and he hoped he would never again.

"You need to toughen up, Roxy. I suggest that you make this work. I have to make this work. Otherwise, we will come out of this with less than what we went in with. Do you understand?"

There was silence at the other end. He'd used his extra harsh voice, the one he reserved for the people on his show when they messed up badly. It always worked. "Did you understand?"

"Yes."

"Good, then at least we're on the same page regarding something."

"Yes."

"The sooner we get this over and done with, the better," he said.

"The end can't come soon enough."

CHAPTER 15

She clamped her mouth shut. Mason's team of assistants and his TV crew were in full flow. Luckily, a tent had been erected in the back and most of them were hanging out there.

It was an intrusion even worse than she had feared, but she forced herself to accept it and say nothing. The onslaught of people, the interruption to her daily tasks, not to mention the makeup and lighting and staging, or trying to pretend that a cameraman didn't have his camera shoved in her face for a close-up when Mason was asking her pointed questions was a shock to her system.

One of the TV guys had explained the format of the show, and told her that she would get used to having people around and would soon forget that the camera was on her.

She braced herself for this new adventure, knowing that it was already making her so uncomfortable having the crew around. She dreaded the filming.

And then, a few days later, filming began. Everything sped up, and everything was new, like a shock to her system. People everywhere, lights, camera, action. But it turned out to be a gentle introduction with Mason asking her why she had taken over the diner, what her goals were, and what she hoped to achieve. She answered the questions, and it seemed like they were just having a normal conversation. The first day had gone relatively smoothly.

The second episode, a few days later, Mason dialed up arrogance. His questions were more pointed, more accusatory, more antagonistic. He looked through her menu, reading it off loudly and staring into the camera, making faces as he mocked her several times.

I can't find any pizzazz in your menus. There's plenty of zzzzzz though.

That's an insult to pancakes.

We're in the business of making taste buds explode, Roxy, not put them to sleep.

That sauce looks dead.

Since when and how was a sauce supposed to look alive? She hadn't had time to think, hadn't had time to be shocked, or want to throw something at him, because he said these things while she rushed around. The diner was busier than ever, on that aspect Mason had been right, customers weren't so easily scared away, even by a TV crew.

She told herself that it was only two episodes a week and it didn't take the entire day either. She could get through this.

Over time, she discovered that sometimes the camera crew would film during the day, sometimes they would film in the evening. It wasn't always in the kitchen or the dining area. Sometimes it was in her office, which wasn't easy given how small it was. It made things extra claustrophobic, extra tight, with her and Mason squashed up really close side by side on chairs, with the crew in front of the desk.

In these moments, Mason seemed to be able to smell her fear, her reluctance, her timidity.

She, who had always been fearless, especially in her territory, the diner, seemed to be growing tamer, and in danger of losing her power.

"We need to change up the menu," Mason said one day as they were bunched up side by side at her desk. He crossed his arms, then leaned forward on the desk, posturing for the camera no doubt. Observing him, she had come to know when he was hamming things up for effect, for the audience, though she was surprised he hadn't mentioned her menu sooner. He hadn't liked her menu choices from the start.

"What's wrong with it?" She braced herself for the inevitable standoff, knowing that there was nothing wrong with the choices. It was all basic, good, decent, home-cooked food. Pancakes and bacon, spaghetti bolognaise, a variety of sandwiches for lunch. Hash browns and sausage.

Mason laughed. He didn't so much as laugh as he bellowed. "What's wrong with it?" He looked at the camera, "Do you want to retain your customers or—"

"My customers keep coming back."

"What, the same ones?"

"New ones, too."

"What new ones, Roxy? I've been here a few weeks now and I see the same old people."

"They're called loyal customers," she shot back.

"Loyal as in they feel sorry for you." Another laugh, and another look at the camera at her expense.

"Why are you being like this?" she whispered.

"You told me you wanted to make more, have more customers and take in more profits. Isn't that what you said? Isn't that what you want?"

"Yes, but ..."

"Yes, but ... yes but ... Get your act together, Roxy. You have to change things up. You've can't do the same old, same old. Your customers will die of boredom." He flung the menu across the table, which, because the table was so small, landed on the floor. His comment about her customers dying of boredom stopped her cold. She didn't like him talking about her customers like that.

She got up, saw the menu lying on the floor, decided that she couldn't reach over to pick it up, and promptly sat back down again. "That show of force wasn't necessary. You don't have to behave like a caveman."

He roared with laughter. "I've been called worse. Look, I'm here to make you meet your goals, and years-old menu choices, and boring food isn't going to help you accomplish what you want. That's why I'm here. So, let's brainstorm some menu ideas."

She had been meaning to give her menus a good overhaul before, and while she had made small changes, she didn't want to risk making changes that were too drastic, especially when what she served worked.

Despite how much Mason liked to portray her as having only a few customers, a lot of her regulars had their favorite dishes and they told her this time and time again.

She knew what she was doing.

"Why not have chili and cornbread? Offer spaghetti with

meatballs. Why not do something a bit different and offer green spaghetti?"

"Kids wouldn't eat green spaghetti."

"How do you know? Have you ever tried? Are you too scared to try?"

She clamped her lips together.

"What about mac and cheese, and thick garlic bread with some special Italian style veggies on the side?"

He looked at her expectantly, but she was feeling increasingly hot. The heat of the lights on her face made it seem to her as if her makeup was melting. She dreaded the thought of it dribbling down her face.

"Why not go all out, Roxy?"

She hated the way he said that, as if she were a child he had to prompt and coax into doing things. "And do what?"

"And do what, Roxy? Are you a chef or a sleeping partner? Or a lazybones? Do you want to give your customers something to get excited about?" More laughs. He was taking a jab at her expense, making it sound as if she didn't care about her customers. Making it sound like she was lazy.

"I'm not lazy."

"Then prove it to me."

"I've been working all day, and you've been talking all day."

"That's because I've proven myself, Roxy. I don't have anything to prove. I have restaurants all over the world and I've cooked for—"

"Yes, we know. You keep telling us."

He stared at the camera. "I think she's getting annoyed," he whispered, conspiratorially into the camera. "If you're not lazy—"

"I'm not." That came out as a snarl. She was reacting to this buffoon, but she had to remind herself that everything she said, every expression on her face was magnified by the camera. He would come out of this smelling like roses. She would not. It was his show. He could manipulate and cut it and edit it to portray her as something she was not. He wouldn't hesitate to do so.

"Then show me you're not."

"What do you want me to do?"

"I want you to work on the menu. I want you to change five things on it, for now, for starters, and we'll see how it goes."

"Five things?"

"Five things." He held up five fingers, and counted through them, "One, two, three, four, five." Humiliating her with his tone.

"I can count, Mason. I'm not in kindergarten. You don't have to knock me down to make yourself look better."

He wasn't expecting that, his quick glance at the cameraman, without a smirk, told her, before he quickly recomposed himself. "Do you think you can do it?" he asked her.

"Yes, I can do it. This is what I do for a living."

Another laugh. "Is it? Is it really, Roxy? Because up until now, I thought you were doing this part-time."

She wanted to throw something at him, and it was a good thing that there was nothing at hand.

*D*id she really want to be the owner of a restaurant business, or would Roxy be better off doing a paid job, working set hours, getting a set wage?

This was the question Mason often asked himself. He thought he knew which one Roxy was, but as the weeks rolled by, he wasn't so sure.

He had met all sorts of people during this career, but it was the business owners on the show, the ones who came to him wanting his guidance and advice, and were desperate for him to put things right, that revealed themselves in the way they conducted their business.

Surprisingly, working with Roxy hadn't been as bad as he'd expected. Theirs had gone from a hate-to-be-around-you type of relationship, to something that was more like a push and pull of similar personalities vying for looking good on TV. Roxy was making an effort. She listened to him, let him have his way. He started to take liberty with that.

Sometimes he laughed too loudly, or too much, pooh-pahed her suggestions. She sometimes fought back. Threw back a comment or retort she knew would hurt. He liked that. He had never had anyone on his show, especially not a woman, who answered back the way she did.

Men did. There was often a battle of the wills. A lot of restaurant owners were older than him and he detected in them a hint of jealousy, a begrudging acceptance of his advice.

With women, it was different. They were often eager to please. Eager to take on every suggestion he gave them, eager to show him. Sometimes he detected a hint of flirtation, but he was always professional and turned a blind eye to it. Pretended he didn't notice.

With Roxy, there was no danger of that. The woman hated him with a severity he was not used to.

After week three, when the third episode had been edited, they could air it. This way they had a three-week lag between when an episode was filmed and aired, and he was most interested to see how his ratings would be.

At the end of the previous episode, he had given Roxy five new menu choices to come up with and he was eager to see what she would think up. He had decided to film this scene early in the morning, before any of the other employees came in.

The crew was all set up, the smell of fresh coffee wafted through the air. He liked this time of day himself and hungered for the peace and quiet before a busy day. He imagined Roxy did too.

"So, excite me." He huddled across the table, warming his hands around the big coffee cup. This time they weren't in her teensy little office but sitting at one of the large tables in the diner. "What have you come up with?"

"I'm going with the spaghetti and meatballs, then my mom's beef stew and homemade biscuits."

"I like that." He nodded, in complete agreement. "Beef stew and homemade biscuits. I'm getting hungry just thinking about it."

She smiled. It was a rare sight, and at seven o'clock in the morning.

"Uh... and I was thinking about maybe having stuffed shells with salad."

"Stuffed with salad?" That didn't appeal. "Since when have you tried shells stuffed with salad?"

"I'm not stuffing shells with salad, Mason. I'm serving stuffed shells and having salad on the side."

"Good, I wasn't sure, knowing you." He had attempted to make a joke, but she didn't laugh.

"I'm going to have breakfast burritos with eggs, bacon, sausage, hash browns, diced green peppers, diced onions, shredded cheese all wrapped in a soft taco tortilla."

His stomach rumbled. He ordinarily didn't have breakfast, aside from a cup of black coffee at home. Brunch was more his thing, but with Roxy talking the way she was, conjuring up these magnificent dishes was making him super hungry. "You're going to have to make me breakfast at this rate." But he was impressed. She had really thought things through. She'd come back with a feast of goodies that had him salivating and not many people could do that.

Maybe it was the air, and the strangeness of being here, in this small coastal town where time seemed to stop.

"I haven't finished," she looked down her list. "A seafood feast, baked shrimp, scallops with seasoning—"

"Seafood, scallops," he moaned. He loved seafood. "You're killing me."

"Really?" She flashed him a huge smile that made him feel as if the sun had shone inside him. "Lasagna with Greek salad and garlic bread," she continued.

"You already have thick garlic bread."

"Then lasagna with Greek salad."

"Feta cheese, kalamata olives, cucumber, vine tomatoes ..."

His mouth was watering.

"Red onion, extra virgin olive oil, dried oregano …"

"Yes." True to form, his stomach made a loud gurgling noise as if on cue.

"You are hungry," she remarked, before looking down her list of notes. "And shrimp Alfredo served after a bowl of clam chowder."

"I love seafood." It was his Achilles heel. "I'm already dreaming of your clam chowder."

"What do you think?" she asked.

"That's more than five things."

"I got carried away."

The woman had outdone herself. She'd done that within a day. Nothing that he'd had to drag her to do. She'd come up with simple, delicious, mouthwatering dishes, and he was hungry. "Roxy."

She took a sip from her coffee, her brown eyes staring at him over the rim.

"You've done wonderfully well."

"You approve?"

"Approve? I am starving, woman!"

"You really like the choices?"

"I love the simplicity of them, aside from the clam chowder."

"Clam chowder isn't that difficult to make."

"Make some today, let me see how you do it."

Her hand flew to the back of her neck, and she was about to do the thing she always did when she wasn't sure of something. "Are you nervous, Roxy?"

Defiant eyes burned back at him, she was about to glance to the right, as if to check whether the camera was rolling. It was. She didn't need to check, and then she froze. "You don't scare me, Mason. It might have worked in your earlier shows, but I'm not scared of you."

"That's a wrap." Someone called.

"Do we have enough?" she asked.

"We have some footage from the other day. This is good. This was good." He picked up his coffee cup again.

"I don't appreciate you asking me on national TV if you make me nervous. Do you get a thrill out of saying that?"

She'd hit him where it hurt. He'd been told to soften up, to be more mindful and respectful of the people on his shows, and here he was doing it again. "Sorry."

"You don't have to put me down to make yourself look good." She got up, looked down at him through her dark lashes.

"I'm sorry. I didn't mean to. You just seemed nervous."

Her brows pushed together. "I'm not used to having anyone second-guess me."

"I'm not second-guessing you."

"I've seen some of the clips from your old shows, Mason. You said you wouldn't ridicule me."

"I'm not ridiculing you."

"You don't seem to have any faith in me, or that I can cook."

Now she was being petty. Nitpicky. "I have faith. How else are you running this place if you can't cook?"

She changed the subject abruptly. "Are you hungry? You said you were hungry."

"All that talk of seafood and scallops made me hungry."

"I'll rustle you something up now."

He paused. She was at the start of the day and offering to make him something when she no doubt had plenty on her plate. "I'll make you one of my new breakfast burritos."

"That sounds good." He would normally wait until brunch before eating something that substantial, but Roxy's new menu choices had put a hole in his stomach. "Thanks."

"You don't have to thank me but let me know if you think I can cook or not once you've tried it."

CHAPTER 17

*H*ailey took a lick of her bright blue ice cream. Soon her tongue would turn the same color. Roxy looked on in bewilderment. "Bubble-gum flavor?"

"It's not as bad as it looks."

"You can't beat dark chocolate with hazelnut."

They walked silently, heard the excited cries of children playing nearby and the gulls screeching.

"Let's hear it then. How are you finding it, working with Mason?"

Roxy suppressed a smile. Working with Mason? There was nothing equal or partnership-like in this equation. One didn't work with Mason; one chose to let him trample all over them as recompense for being on his show.

She tried to choose her words carefully, knowing that Hailey and Mason were good friends. "It's been an experience."

Yesterday hadn't been so bad at all. He had been surprisingly pleasant. He'd even complimented her on her breakfast burrito. What had possessed her to make him something? Had it been because he had given her a rare compliment on her new menu choices? Or because he'd seemed normal, and they'd had a normal conversation during which he hadn't made a single sarcastic comment.

He had so mocked her before that nothing in her DNA would ever have made her get up and cook something for him, but she had. And he had been grateful for it.

"An experience?"

"I wouldn't call it working *with* him. He's more like an angry teacher, looking for ways to tear me down."

Hailey gasped. "He's not still doing that, is he? He told me he was going to be better. Kinder. This show means a lot to him."

"I'm aware of that. He postures a lot, makes himself look good. Me, not so good."

Hailey sighed. "I'm sorry he's still doing that. I'll have a word with him."

"Don't. He's better than he was in the beginning."

"He's a lovely guy. He needs this show to work," Hailey said.

"Even if it failed, he'd be all right." Unlike her. For Roxy this was a last resort. If Mason's show didn't work out for him, he would be fine. He had so many other things going for him.

"He does like to brag about his own achievements sometimes."

"You think so?"

They looked at one another and laughed. Roxy took a nibble of her ice cream cone again. The only people who liked to brag were those who needed to make themselves feel better.

Everything she'd seen about Mason told her that this self-assured and super successful man had the world at his feet.

Kind of like how Hailey did.

How different these two were than her and Jax.

"Just ignore him when he's like that," Hailey suggested.

"That's easy enough for you to say. You're not on national TV, and you don't have to worry about him chewing you up and spitting you out."

"Mason would never do that to you."

Roxy frowned at Hailey. "Are you kidding me?" She shook her head. "You're friends, and you're both superstars. He's going to treat you differently than how he treats me."

"Mason has worked his way up. He wasn't born into fame and fortune. He's worked hard."

"You wouldn't think it to look at him. The man who has restaurants in every major city," Roxy mimicked his voice, eliciting a knowing grin from Hailey.

"You're good."

"He loves the sound of his own voice."

"I'm sensing some sort of complaint here."

"Or truth," Roxy said. "I can complain about him now that he's not here, but on the show, I'm docile and subservient."

"Speaking of which, when does the first episode air?"

"Next week. Thursday night, I think."

"I can't wait to see it. You must be excited!"

Roxy wasn't. She dreaded to think what she would look like.

"You should come over. I'll get Mason to come over, too and we'll have a small little informal get-together." Roxy made a face at Hailey's suggestion.

"No. Please, no." If she was going to watch herself on TV, she wanted to do it in the comfort of her own home, preferably with an entire bottle of wine at hand, in case it came to that, and she couldn't stand the sight of herself or the sound of her voice.

"Are you sure? It's been a while since we caught up."

"I have a fiftieth wedding anniversary event to cater for the day before."

"That's going to be a busy day. Are Mason and the TV crew covering that?"

"No. No way." A TV crew filming her when she was cooking for eighty people. No, thank you. The last thing she needed was a camera in her face and Mason barking orders at her. He wanted to cover it, but she wasn't going to allow it. She wasn't even going to mention it to him.

Even though they had been getting along better lately, she didn't want to push things. The man was unpredictable, and whether she liked to admit it or not, he did make her feel nervous.

Around him, she felt like a fledgling amateur cook, like she did back as a twelve-year-old when she had first started to help her parents out at the diner.

Around him, she had started to question even more whether her interest in the diner was waning. She wasn't sure whether having Mason around was helping. It was too soon to see if his advice, raising prices, changing up the menus, was working, but the diner was definitely busier than it had ever been, and that had to be a good sign.

CHAPTER 18

If Hailey hadn't mentioned it to him, he wouldn't have remembered.

Roxy had kept it from him. Catering for an anniversary party would be something different to include on the show, but Roxy hadn't said another word about it and he knew why. She didn't want him filming it.

Obviously, she had no idea what made for great TV. He did, and he was going to use this opportunity and film it. She could thank him later.

Roxy being busy and running around like a headless chicken, not only tending to the daily diner pressure but cooking for another event on top of it all.

Not one for letting such an opportunity pass him by, he directed his crew to show up at the diner on Saturday without giving Roxy any advance warning. Roxy hadn't discussed much about the catering arm of her business, probably because of tonight's event and the fact that she didn't want him anywhere near it.

He had expected to see her as soon as they walked in, and though the diner was half full, Roxy was nowhere in sight.

"Where is she?" he asked Ella, who had just finished serving a customer.

"In the kitchen. Are you guys filming today?" A worry line stretched across her brow. "Because Roxy isn't expecting you. We've got an event on this evening, so it's all hands on deck."

He glanced over his shoulder, winked at the camera, and strode into the kitchen. Roxy had her back turned to him, so she didn't see him come in.

Trays of food were laid out. They looked like canapés for tonight's event. Not the type of canapés he would come up with.

"It looks busy today." At his words, she spun around, her big eyes widening some more. Shock skittered across her face. It was perfect and he hoped the camera caught it. They hadn't had time to prep. No makeup, or proper lighting, but this was raw television, and he was after the element of surprise from her. She certainly gave it to him, glancing from him to the camera and then back at him again. Poison spewed from her eyes.

"What are you doing here? You never said we were filming today."

"I wanted to surprise you." He stepped to the side, wanting the camera to capture her reaction.

"I hate surprises. You should have warned me." The hiss under her breath was loud enough to reach his ears.

"Then it wouldn't have been a surprise. What are you doing? What are all these trays? What's cooking?"

She moved away from the pot she was stirring, and asked him, her voice low, if she could have a word.

"Sure, we can have a word. What's up?"

"In private."

This was good. She could talk low, she could tilt her face to the side, she could indicate that she wanted to speak to him, but the camera would pick all of this up.

"We're on air," he said under his breath. "Why don't you walk me through what you're doing here?"

She gave him a look that could skewer a pig.

He clapped his hands together, could see the tension in the way she bunched up her shoulders. Could feel her stress. "What's going on, Roxy? Talk to me."

"We have a wedding anniversary to cater for tonight." She got back to stirring her pot, stirring it hard and fast deliberately, her hand gripping the wooden spoon so tightly he could see the white of her knuckles.

"A wedding anniversary? I remember you speaking to someone about it when we had that meeting."

She tilted her head, her eyes narrowing as she glared at him with suspicion. "That was a while ago. You didn't know when it was. But you found out it was today. How?" Her back was to the camera, and she obviously seemed to think that she was only talking to him. It was so easy to forget that everything was being captured on camera.

The camera stopped rolling while someone connected a mic to her clothing.

"What are you doing here?" she hissed, using the few moments of off-screen time.

"Filming," he answered easily.

The cameras were switched back on again.

"How many people are you catering for?"

But she ignored him.

"How many people, Roxy?" The determination etched across her tight brow, the hard set of her lips showing her irritation. He moved away a little, thinking how she would gladly hit him if she ever had the chance were the cameras not rolling. He leaned against the counter, obviously at ease with his arms crossed, surveying her. "Roxy?"

"What?" She turned the salt mill, and then the pepper mill, then shook different bottles of seasoning into the pot.

"Chili?" He leaned in for a whiff. It smelled heavenly.

But she stepped away, ignoring him again. Ella came into view, so he spent a few moments talking to her, finding out from her what was going on. It was an event for eighty people and was going to be held in a barn on the outskirts of town.

"It's been a really busy day," Ella acknowledged.

He motioned with his hand across his neck, telling the cameraman to stop shooting.

"Let's take a short break." It was hot in the kitchen, and Roxy didn't look as if she wanted to talk to him, still the footage that he'd managed to get would be good enough. He was hot and thirsty. Venturing out of the kitchen, he went into the diner and ordered a can of iced tea.

"Oh, hey. It's Mason, isn't it?" A pretty young woman who looked familiar greeted him.

In an instant, he remembered who she was. One didn't forget a smile like that. Wide-mouthed and full. She was tall and beautiful. "Bloom?" he said, thinking of the first thing that came to his mind. She was the florist, and she was hard to forget because she had the most amazing floral displays he'd ever seen. It wasn't something he expected in Starling Bay. This woman had a creative eye and flair. He loved flowers, and he didn't care if anyone thought he was less of a man because he did. He'd filled his condo with them.

"Mackenzie."

"Right." He flashed her a smile. "Mackenzie."

"Are you filming?" she asked.

"Uh... yes."

She looked around as a cameraman sat down at one of the tables. "All of this looks so interesting. I can't wait to see Roxy on TV."

He held back a tight smile. He wasn't sure if Roxy was looking forward to seeing herself on TV. Hailey had asked him to come over tomorrow so that they would watch the first show together, but Roxy had declined.

"Care to sit down?" he asked.

"Now?" Mackenzie seemed surprised by his offer.

"I'm taking a break."

"Are you sure?"

It was the type of response he had grown accustomed to. She didn't know him and seemed slightly in awe. He wanted to sit and talk, only because he spent so much of his time alone. There was nothing more to it than that. "I love your shop, and your floral displays."

"You do?" She looked to be in awe of him, when really, it was the other way around. He loved all things creative, and while he could do wonders with food, anything else, like painting, or writing poetry, or creating something not food-related, like this woman and the magic she could create from flowers, intrigued him. "Tell me how you got started."

The man was a nightmare. A huge, impossible to deal with nightmare.

"Who told him?" she asked her staff, when he was out of sight.

Lewis was the first to answer. "I didn't tell him. I barely get any screen time."

"I only mentioned it now when he came in," Ella said.

Roxy hadn't told him. She'd deliberately kept the news of this event from him. But she had met with Hailey and had mentioned it to her. She facepalmed, disappointment and regret mixing in one heavy, thick, suffocating gasp. "Hailey," she muttered under her breath. It had to be Hailey. She had to be careful what she said around her.

"How are the mini burgers coming along?"

Lewis did a thumbs-up.

"And the crab cakes?"

"All in order," Ella replied.

"The buffalo wings?"

"About to start on those," Lewis hollered.

"The leek and goat cheese tartlets?"

"After the buffalo wings," someone else replied.

"Why don't you take a break, and let me take care of this?" Ella said, coming over to take the wooden spoon from her. "I'll watch the chili."

Roxy felt bad. She was barking orders at her staff, when the real source of her anger had disappeared. "I've got this, thanks." Poor Ella. Roxy had her working front and back. What she didn't need was Mason in her face. Luckily, he'd called for a break and had left, along with his crew. And now she was thirsty.

The food was coming along fine, and within the hour, she could quickly change into a clean outfit and get Lewis and the others to help her load up the van and take everything to the party venue.

For now, she was almost done, and boy, was she tired. She tried not to do too many catering events. They took a lot out of her, especially since she didn't close the diner, and she didn't have extra staff to help with that side of her business. It wasn't ideal to have her day staff work so hard and for so long on days when she catered for parties. Ideally, she needed extra staff, and a bigger kitchen, but she couldn't even think about expansion yet.

Turning the heat down on the chili, she put some oil in the pan to sear scallops, because she was going to make scallop shell pies in flaky pastry, something that was a favorite with the happily married couple.

As she walked over to the fridge to get the scallops, the heat of the kitchen overwhelmed her and she needed something to quench her thirst. She pushed the door open to head into the diner to get a cold drink when she saw Mason sitting at a table laughing and talking. Across the table from him was the florist, Mackenzie. Roxy frowned. Mason didn't laugh and talk with her like that. The other day when he'd liked her new menu, when she had made him breakfast, it was the closest they had come to having a decent conversation.

How he acted with Mackenzie wasn't how he was with her, and it wouldn't have mattered ordinarily, but there was nothing ordinary about her current situation. Seeing the two of them, and contrasting it with her experience with Mason, confirmed what she had always known; that people saw her differently. She was plain and average and nothing more.

She pulled back, foregoing the cold drink, not wanting to be in the diner, but an almighty scream made her jump. She spun around and to her horror, saw a pan on fire. Ella was standing next to the stove, flapping her hands, screaming.

"The scallops!" Lewis cried; he was at the other end of the kitchen.

The pan. She had been getting ready to fry some scallops. She'd poured the oil and had forgotten all about it. Thinking fast, she rushed forward, grabbed the lid from the chili pan and covered the flames. Then she turned off the heat source.

"What happened?"

She didn't need to turn around to know that he was in here. Or that the light that had suddenly lit up the kitchen was coming from the camera lights.

Rage erupted inside her. She refused to look at him. Refused to answer him. She needed to see if her customers were okay. Ella's scream had pierced through the air and she was sure everyone in the diner had heard. She needed to make sure her customers were fine.

She rushed into the diner, the footsteps behind her telling her that Mason was hot on her heels. Smiling, needing to broadcast reassurance, she addressed her customers, telling them what had happened.

"Are you okay?" It was the florist, the woman who had been sitting with Mason.

"A fire. We had a fire," Mason announced, almost too gleefully.

"Can you turn that thing off now?" Roxy hissed. "We've just had a fire. Do you mind?"

"A fire?" someone cried.

"It's all okay now, it was a small pan fire," Roxy rushed to reassure the elderly woman. "It's been put out."

"What happened, Roxy?" Mason was in her face again. Mason was always in her face. Mason was always where she didn't want or need anyone to be.

"I forgot I'd poured some oil into the pan."

"That's not very good, is it?" He was asking these condescending, patronizing types of questions to get a rise out of her.

"It was an accident." She'd been too busy staring at him and the florist woman.

"As long as you're okay," Mackenzie said. She'd come over and was standing by Mason, as if … as if … Roxy wasn't sure what. But she now wondered how long they'd known one another. In the rush of her emotions, she hung her head. In this moment, she not only felt like an idiot, but she also felt like a failure.

She was tired and hot and sweaty, and fretting about an event she was catering for that was only hours away. And not only had she just dealt with a fire in her kitchen, but she'd had to suffer it being captured on camera by this chef from hell who never missed an opportunity to show her in her worst light. The last thing Roxy needed was the gorgeous florist to ask her how she was.

"Can you turn off that thing?" she hissed, indicating the camera which magnified every hurt she felt and would soon enough broadcast it out for the world to see.

She felt useless, and she was sick and tired of it all. Mason nodded, and at once the lights went out, and the cameraman moved away from her.

"I'm sorry, everyone. I hope you're not startled. We've had a small fire in the kitchen, and I have a lot on my plate. Everything is under control now." She smiled, hoping to alleviate the worry of her customers.

Then, without saying anything else, she headed back to the kitchen, putting Mason and Mackenzie and the camera crew out of her mind.

CHAPTER 19

It was way after midnight when she returned from the wedding anniversary event.

It had been a long day for everyone. She paid her staff handsomely, as well as she could at time and a half for the extra hours. By the time they had all packed up and brought everything back to the diner, it was way late. And she had a shift at the diner tomorrow.

Would life ever get any easier?

She showered, and crawled into bed a few hours after that, but still, she couldn't sleep.

The day had been long.

It had been gruesome.

And painful.

And not because of the long hours, or the event she had catered at.

It was none of these things.

Her sleeplessness was due to *that* man.

When she had tossed and turned for a good few hours, she got out of bed, tried some neck and shoulder exercises to get the knots of tension out of her body, and when that didn't work, she decided enough was enough.

There was only one way to solve this. Groggy and overtired, she drove to Forest Heights, to Mason's place, unannounced. She knocked on his door, and then rang the bell.

It was only when he didn't answer right away that she looked at her watch.

Dear god. Was that the time?

It was only 7:00 a.m.

She felt as if she had been up for hours. She barely had time to be surprised or feel the odd twang of guilt when the door opened, and she found herself staring at an unkempt-looking Mason. With his disheveled hair, yawning, and a look of utmost displeasure on his face. He blinked at her twice, then yawned. "What are you doing here?"

The question, and that voice, simply ratcheted up the anger which had been building up inside. "I couldn't sleep."

He hadn't opened the door wider, or asked her to come in. "I *was* asleep."

"How do you like it?" she sneered. "Me showing up here unannounced and you not being ready for it? You looking like that."

"Looking like what?" He ran a hand over his stubbly face, as if this was the thing that he was worried about the most.

"A mess, that's what."

He frowned.

"I wish I had a camera crew here, taking in every wrinkle, every messed-up lock of hair, magnifying your five o'clock shadow."

"Wrinkles? Where?" He opened the door, giving her permission to enter.

Once inside, she spun around. "How do you like it?" She was

done with his silly little comments, his refusal to get angry, his treating her as if she were inconsequential.

"I'm glad to see you. Coffee?" He moved into the kitchen, and she marched in after him. This wasn't going as she had planned. He wasn't taking her seriously.

"What you did was out of order. You should have told me you would be there."

"Oh, that. You're annoyed about yesterday."

She almost choked in exasperation. Did he not have any idea? Could he not see? Or had he been too busy staring into Mackenzie's eyes to worry about her state of mind? He had interrupted her busy day and caused her pan to catch fire, in a roundabout way. If he hadn't been there, she wouldn't have been so engrossed watching him and Mackenzie. "Yes, I'm annoyed. I have every reason to be."

"I had a feeling you wouldn't be too happy about that."

"Really? Could you not take the hint?"

"You should have told me. I mean, you did mention the event before ..."

"You said no surprises."

"Calm down, Roxy. I don't understand why you're so angry."

"You don't understand?" she cried, noticing his bare feet, his sweatpants and t-shirt. Under his formal shirts, she couldn't tell, other than that he was slim and tall, but the t-shirt clinging to him as it did, showed off his biceps, his broad chest, his wide, wide shoulders.

It had been a while. A long while since she had even noticed someone of the opposite sex in this way. The hairs on the back of her neck raised and her stomach fluttered.

She told herself she was tired, hadn't slept, wasn't feeling her usual self. This wasn't natural, but she wasn't being her usual self.

"You don't like me showing up now, this early. Me intruding on you, ruining your sleep."

"I don't mind, now that you're here, and it doesn't matter about my sleep. Coffee?" he asked again, pouring himself a cup.

"I don't want your coffee. I just wish I had a camera crew to show up with me now, and you ... you ..." She paced around his vast kitchen, a part of her in awe that he had so much space. It wasn't fair.

For some people, life was easy, for people like her, no matter how hard she worked, she couldn't find a way out of the rat race. She could never imagine having a place like this.

"Why are you angry, Roxy?"

"Why?" she screamed. "Why?" She tried to compose herself. His reaction was infuriating. She hadn't been this mad until she'd arrived.

"What if you had something going on, like a ... a party or something, and you had to cater for it, and if I showed up and asked you a million and one questions, and forced the camera crew on you, and then something in your kitchen caught fire." She jabbed her finger at him. "You can't make yourself look good at my expense. You can't."

"It made for great TV!"

"That's all you care about. Your TV show. Your ratings. You're the most selfish man I've ever met."

"What is the matter with you? Why the drama? You'll never amount to anything if you can't handle the pressure. Have you considered that this might not be the right career for you?"

She stood speechless, his comment knocking the air out of her lungs. He could see right through her. He could see that she was flailing, and this was a last-ditch attempt to hold onto her dream, and sanity, by coming to him to show her the way.

She was a struggling business owner who didn't even deserve to attend the SBWEB meetings. She wasn't as smart as Shay, or as lucky as Jenna, or as beautiful as Mackenzie. She wasn't confident and in charge like Francine.

She hadn't been so great at school. Numbers scared her. Getting an office job wasn't going to work for her; it was something she'd known in her belly.

The diner was her only way to be her own boss, to prove that she could be *someone.*

But Mason's show had reduced her to a quivering wreck of her former self. He was judgmental, critical and callous, and even though she had been surviving by telling herself that she was doing this to get something out of it, that it was for her own good, it was becoming harder to believe this.

She'd seen a sliver of friendliness in him that day she'd cooked him breakfast, but this latest stunt served only to remind her of one thing; that the man cared for no one but himself.

A tsunami of exhaustion crashed over her, her guard down, her defenses paper thin. And Mason was looking at her with something that almost bordered on concern.

"I'm sorry." He took a step towards her.

She backed away. Forced herself to look out of his window. Felt the tears well up in her eyes.

"I didn't know it had upset you so much."

His voice behind her was soft, so unlike him. She swallowed, but stayed quiet, preferring not to say something, preferring not to tell him that she didn't believe him, that she would never believe him. She had figured out who he was, and she didn't need to know anything else.

She forced her gaze to settle on something in the distance. What was that? Something shimmered beyond the green of the trees.

Lake Ivanhoe.

"Roxy." Mason grabbed her wrist, but she snatched it away as if he'd touched her with a hot poker. "I'm sorry. It was never my intention to upset you like this. I had no idea."

He was right. He had no idea. That's because Mason Brandt

was selfish and self-obsessed. He made his fortune at the expense of berating and ridiculing others. He was emotionally and morally bankrupt, and she had been a fool to allow him to do this to her.

"Say something, Roxy." He touched her shoulder, and she flinched.

"You're cold and calculating, and you're selfish. You think only of yourself."

Her words hit him like shrapnel, the pain of her truth hitting a bull's eye in his chest. Monique had said the same, even though he had spent time with her and showered her with gifts. *For time he couldn't spend with her.* He was young, had reached great heights at a young age, but staying there was harder than reaching the top. Everything came at a price. He wanted one more book deal, one more restaurant opened, one more TV show, and he had worked towards this after they had married. Business deals didn't stop because you were in love. He planned to make it up to Monique later.

But later never came.

"I'm not the monster you think I am."

She had expected him to laugh, to do something more Mason-ish, this she wasn't prepared for.

She spun around. "Don't use me to boost your ratings. Don't make me look like an idiot to make yourself feel better. I didn't volunteer to go on your show to be made to look like a fool."

"You're not a fool."

"Then don't treat me like one. I'll see myself out."

"Stay …"

"Don't." She didn't want to hear it, his apology was just to make himself feel better, and she had no time for it.

"Don't go feeling like this."

"You have that effect on me."

"I … I'm not that bad. Let me cook you breakfast, at least."

"No, thanks."

"Well, how about you cook breakfast for me?"

She gave him a withering look.

"I'm joking. I'm just messing around. I'm trying to get a reaction from you."

"And that's what I hate about you, Mason, you always try to get a reaction out of people and it's always for the wrong reasons."

CHAPTER 20

The Blue Velvet Bar was full. Not full as in people were standing shoulder to shoulder inside, or that a line was forming outside, the way his restaurants often were, but full as in almost every table was taken.

Luckily, he found a table and ordered himself a beer. He'd asked Hailey to come. Just her, because he needed to talk to her about Roxy, without having Jackson around.

She had been close to tears earlier today and the shock of seeing someone so strong, like that, had taken him completely by surprise because it highlighted to him the ogre he was, the monster he could be. He was so driven, so tied up in his own goals and needs, and so desperate to make this show work, that he blindsided everyone around him.

His relationships suffered because of it. Monique had said that he didn't care enough for her. She felt abandoned. He had tried, after that, to make more time, but the sword of success was always balanced so precariously above his head. He couldn't let up. He had always worked ridiculous hours, had barely turned anything down, but he was coming to see that this imbalance in his life was costing him.

Roxy had the same drive, but unlike him, she didn't make people look bad in order to make herself look good. He hadn't been able to get her words out of his head. They stood out, her accusations, because no one had the balls to tell him how he made them feel.

He wouldn't have had these problems with Buffalo Bill, but Roxy was putting a mirror up to his face and making him see things about himself that he would rather not see. And Roxy's words earlier had hit a nerve. She called it as she saw it, and she behaved almost as if she were his peer.

She gave as good as she got, but he had obviously crossed a line somewhere and he'd been the object of her wrath when she had shown up on his doorstep earlier today.

In her, he recognized the same level of wanting to hold oneself to a higher standard. He saw that same ferocity of spirit, and the resilience and persistence. The need to claw oneself up from the depths of ordinariness.

Now, his eyes were beginning to open. He wasn't a saint. He had been guilty of asking the people on his show the most humiliating questions, of speaking to them as if they were dumb. He had often been annoyed with them because many of them were often so unorganized and so ignorant, and so lazy, and didn't want to do what it took to do things properly.

Sometimes people didn't listen unless he made them. He'd convinced himself that this was what he was doing, yelling at them to get them to take notice.

He'd been told to tame things down slightly, and he had. He used to be so much worse before, but even so, Roxy caused him to react. Her attitude toward him and the tone she used when talking to him were something he wasn't used to.

His TV crew were telling him that the first couple of episodes were looking good. That he and Roxy had a good chemistry. It sizzled. He would find out later this week when they all watched the show together. Hailey had talked about having him and Roxy over to her place to watch it.

"Sorry I'm late."

A breathless Hailey came up and kissed him on the cheek, before sliding into the seat opposite him.

"Where's your security detail?" Starling Bay was a small town, but after what she'd told him about the stalker in her hotel room, he was surprised that Jax would let her out of his sight without anyone guarding her.

"He's over there." Hailey looked over his shoulder. Mason turned to find Jax sitting at a table with a few guys.

"He does some work on the side for one of them, and the other guy, the one in the pale pink shirt? He's our realtor, and that guy in the white is Dylan, he and his wife have a gift shop not far from you."

"Is that so?"

"His wife's expecting."

Mason looked at her, wondering why Hailey would think that he cared to know such a fact. He didn't have plans to get to know the townspeople, and he had yet to venture out of his condo and head towards the lake and woods.

"Who's he? The one in the black jacket?" The one Hailey hadn't mentioned.

"Reed Knight. He's from a wealthy family and he has connections everywhere. I'm surprised he hasn't come over and introduced himself to you."

He grinned. "Does everyone know everyone else in this place?"

"It depends on how friendly you are."

"It's not my thing." He scoffed. This town obviously wasn't for the likes of him. He hated anyone to know his business. He wasn't one for partying and talking to anyone and everyone. He had a select few friends, even though his fame guaranteed that he knew a lot of people, and that many of these people considered themselves to be his friends. He could count the number of people he trusted and considered as his close friends on one hand, maybe two, at a stretch.

He had been hoping to catch Hailey on her own, so that he could, in a roundabout way, find out more about Roxy, without Jax being around.

"You'd know us. We'd be your friends," Hailey insisted. "I have a feeling you're getting to like it here. Would you ever consider buying a place here?"

"Hell, no." He laughed and took a big gulp from his beer bottle. "Though you're right. I love my place and Forest Heights."

"It's beautiful around there. Jax had never appreciated the woods or the lake. Lived here all his life and he hadn't spent any time there; can you believe it?"

He shrugged.

"We go for walks and have picnics," Hailey continued.

"Jax goes on … picnics?" He glanced over his shoulder at the tall, tattooed boyfriend that Hailey was smitten over, and couldn't imagine him to be a picnic-loving man.

But people could change.

"I need another drink and let's get some in for you and Jax." He summoned a server over.

As soon as he had placed the order, he asked her the question that had been bothering him all morning.

"Am I callous and calculating?"

Hailey sat forward as if she'd misheard. "What?"

"Do I think only of myself? Would you say I'm selfish?"

Hailey stared at him in disbelief. "No. No way. Why, who said you were?"

He pressed his lips together, not wanting to give away anything about Roxy, but damn it, he needed to know. "Roxy. We had a ..." he exhaled slowly, trying to find the right words. "We had a ... disagreement."

"About what?"

He recounted everything, told her how he had shown up at the diner unannounced, catching Roxy unawares and filming even though he could tell she didn't want to be filmed. Yet he had persisted, adamant in his belief that getting footage of her unprepared would be great viewing. "She was busy. She was running the diner as usual and she was also catering for an event."

"She was stressed about it," Hailey agreed. "She told me these things took a lot out of her."

He should have read between the lines. Maybe if he hadn't been so selfish, if he hadn't thought only of himself, he might have held back. Roxy was right. "A pan in the kitchen caught fire and—"

"What?"

"It's fine, it was dealt with. Roxy dealt with it; it was out before my TV guy got into the kitchen."

Hailey narrowed her eyes at him. "Your TV guy? Really, Mason?"

He couldn't miss the judgment in Hailey's tone. "She was very upset about it all, and she came to see me at 7:00 a.m. this morning to let me know how she felt."

"For her to do that, you must have really outdone yourself."

"I feel terrible."

"This isn't like you. Since when do you care how you make someone feel?"

He lifted his bottle of beer, then put it back down again. Hailey's remark only proved that Roxy was right. "So, the answer is 'yes'? I am cold and calculating?"

Hailey shook her head. "Not like a serial killer cold and calculating."

"Well, that's a relief," he answered sarcastically.

"You're not *evil*, Mason."

"Oh, good. That's good to hear." Being brash and unfeeling was part of his persona, but with his marriage failed, and his life falling to pieces—not that anyone else would know—he was starting to feel jaded about what it meant to be on top. On top of the world, and at the bottom of a heap, which is what it felt like to him lately. He'd slipped. During the course of his short-lived marriage, he had slipped, and both his personal and business life had failed. He could no longer keep up. Younger, more ambitious, ruthless chefs were coming up from Paris and other culinary cities of the world with their nouveau cuisine and different takes on food, and it made him feel as if he was losing his grasp.

"Hey." Hailey squeezed his hand. "You're not a bad man."

"Monique thought I was. She left me."

"For someone else," Hailey told him. "It wasn't your fault entirely."

"But if I'd paid her more attention, spent more time being a husband, we might still be married. I was madly in love with that woman."

"She hurt you."

No matter how much he attributed the blame to himself, Hailey was still adamant that he wasn't fully at fault. But as a man who had lost not just his wife but was also in danger of losing his grip on his success, he wasn't so sure anymore.

"I'm going to be nicer to Roxy. I'm going to take more of a backseat on the show. I can be... demanding at times."

"This is enlightening, you coming to these revelations about yourself."

"What I do is cutthroat." He was almost tempted to tell her about his problems, his worries and his fears. Being number one, staying at the top wasn't easy. But he wasn't a man who shared his troubles. Hailey didn't need to be burdened by them.

"Hey, Mason." Jax had walked over with someone. "One of

my friends wanted to meet you." It was the guy in the black jacket. Mason stood up as the man introduced himself.

"Hey, I'm Reed Knight." They shook hands.

"Nice to meet you." The man's friends were still sitting at their table, but they were looking at him and Reed, and they raised their drinks at him. "They're too polite to come over. They wouldn't see an opportunity if it hit them in the face." Reed chortled. Mason understood this man, who wasn't that much different than him.

Reed told him that he had been to a few of Mason's restaurants and that he was a huge fan and loved his old shows and was looking forward to the new one. He said all the right things, and then said he didn't want to take up any more of his time and told him to enjoy the rest of his evening.

"Nice guy." Mason sat back down.

"He is. He's gotten me a lot of work over the years. The guy has great connections."

"He seems like an ambitious guy."

"Takes one to know one," quipped Hailey.

"He proposed to his girlfriend," Jax told them. This obviously meant something to Hailey, who looked delighted.

"He did?" she cried.

"He's thinking of throwing a big engagement party. So," Jax looked at them both. "What have you two been talking about?"

CHAPTER 21

Had she really marched to his place so early in the morning?

In the cold light of day, Roxy couldn't believe what she had done and now that it was a few days later, and there was filming going forward in the diner, it would be the first time she'd seen Mason since that day. As the makeup artist applied her makeup, her insides twisted at the idea of facing Mason any time soon.

What did he think of her now?

She felt silly. Like a hormonal teenager getting upset at the slightest of things. She had never been like this until Mason had shown up. His presence chipped away at her confidence—the only thing she possessed.

"No interactions?" she heard someone say loudly.

"No." It was Mason's voice, not far from her. If she could only tilt her head and see, but her eyes were closed as she let the assistant do her job. "No meetings, there's nothing to be discussed. You can just follow Roxy around the diner for this one."

"But we need dialog, Mason. We need something."

"Not today." He sounded adamant. "Just film her going about

her daily tasks and you can edit it and fix it later. We have another day's filming later this week. Maybe you can swipe something from that."

"You're good to go," the makeup artist told her.

She thanked the lady as she got up from her chair, and then walked right into Mason's hard chest. Her first thought was concern that she had smeared some makeup over his white shirt. She blinked and peered closer, before looking up at him. "It looks like I missed."

He, not understanding what she was talking about, scowled at her. "Missed what?"

"Your ... shirt..." she pointed.

"Mason," another assistant came running up to him. "Apparently we're just shooting Roxy today."

"That's right."

"No."

The assistant looked at him as if she was unsure and then rushed away. "Don't you want to have any discussions about the menu or anything else?" Roxy asked him. It would be odd for the camera crew to follow her around and not have Mason chasing her and barking orders at her like he usually did.

"We'll keep it simple."

Their eyes met and held, and she wanted to say something about disturbing him early that morning and saying those things to him. Truthful things, no less, but now she felt bad that she had been as blunt with him as she had. There was a softness in his eyes today that she hadn't seen before.

She had prepared herself for anything he might have hurled at her today, but this morning, Mason was the epitome of nicety. Polite and friendly, he asked her how her customers had taken to the new menu options she had introduced, and then asked her if she was going to make any other changes.

"Shouldn't we discuss this in front of the cameras?" she asked.

"That's not necessary."

She was confused by his sudden change in attitude. At times, when Mason had fired questions at her in a busy kitchen, she had felt as if she was on a tennis court, fielding balls coming at her at one hundred miles an hour. This, the way he was today, was something altogether different and she wondered how much of this change had been because of what she'd said to him that morning.

It had been easy enough to do. Standing back, watching like an observer and letting the cameraman follow Roxy around.

Just because she hadn't gone to Paris and sought work with the top chefs in the world, or chased Michelin stars, or the recommendations of the world's elite, didn't mean that she was any less than him.

This realization, that they weren't so different after all, made him see things he had overlooked before. Because Roxy wasn't someone he expected to give a second thought about, and here he was, doing just that. Changing the way he behaved on the show so as to be mindful of her feelings. She seemed all the more relaxed for it and that was a good thing.

Her reaction that day she'd come to his apartment had jolted him. He had cultivated his image as a blunt, hold-nothing-back chef, telling people things as he saw them, but now it made him wonder if he had also been like this with Monique, and with the people in his life who mattered, as few as they were.

At least he was making an effort to change things. He didn't want the people on his show traumatized because of his behavior.

Wanting to make amends with Roxy, he asked her, once the

filming for the show was finished, if she was going to Hailey's to watch the first episode which was going to be aired in a few days' time.

"Watch the show?" She didn't sound at all eager.

"We can all watch it together, Hailey's getting us all together at her place. We can make an evening of it."

"An evening of it?"

"Are you deliberately echoing everything I say?"

She stared up at him. The usual friction between them had now gone and in its place had left space for something more fragile, more tenuous. "She did ask me."

"Good! So, you'll come?"

"No."

He frowned. "Why not?"

"It's going to be weird watching myself on TV."

"It's only going to be us, me, Hailey and Jax. You'll feel at home with them, if not me."

"No, thanks. I think I'd like to watch it alone."

There was no changing her mind.

"Thanks for asking."

It was disappointing. He shrugged. "If you change your mind ..."

"I meant thanks for the show today. For being ... nicer."

She had noticed. "After the other day, I thought it might be better if I backed off."

"Is that the only way you can be nice? Take a more hands-off approach?"

If she was joking with him, he couldn't tell, because she was so close to the truth. Maybe it wasn't in his nature to be nice to people. Maybe backing off was the only way he allowed people to breathe. It would explain why his marriage had failed; Monique didn't want him in her life anymore.

"I haven't had much practice being nice to people when I'm around them."

"And how do you know that?"

"Because some people, like you, tell me."

She bit her lip.

"No one has your courage," he told her.

She grimaced. "I acted without thinking. I hadn't slept, and I was angry, and I shouldn't have said all those things to you."

"You're not the only one who's told me I'm difficult. But you're one of the few I've heard. I have no idea what my producer is going to make of it. No barbed comments, no acidic questioning." He had a feeling that Gerard wasn't going to like it.

He saw something of himself in Roxy, from when he was poor and just starting out, and was determined to prove himself. Her determination and sure-fire persistence to want to make good, to make something of herself, was too close to home.

He hadn't changed. His DNA hadn't magically transformed, but being here in Starling Bay had given him time to think. Roxy's words had hit deep, sinking into the pores of his skin and burrowing deep.

Here, as in LA, he went home to a beautiful apartment, but it was an empty apartment. In LA, life was busy; if he wasn't checking in on one of his restaurants, then he was hustling for a book deal, or negotiating with a show producer.

Now that he was here, he had been forced to slow down. Slowing down had given him a chance to stand still. Standing still had given him the opportunity to reevaluate parts of his life.

She opened her mouth, then seemed lost as to what to say.

"You know where I am, if you change your mind about wanting to watch the show with us."

CHAPTER 22

She looked hideous.

And did she really sound like *that?*

Did she look like that? Have those mannerisms? Was her mouth set that hard when she was displeased?

Roxy squirmed behind her sofa cushion and averted her eyes. Watching the first episode of the show was becoming more painful by the moment.

At this rate, she would suffer from PTSD once it was over.

Mason didn't look any different. He was exactly as she saw him in real life. Loud and commandeering, as he had been in the earlier episodes. It would be interesting to see how different he was in the later episodes, like the one they had filmed a few days ago.

She watched for another five minutes before planting her face into her cushion and screaming.

It was in a moment such as this that she wished she'd taken her parents' advice.

Oh, dear god.

Her phone rang and, grateful to have something to distract her from watching herself on TV, she grabbed it immediately.

"Are you watching this?" Hailey asked.

"I'm trying hard not to scream. I look awful. I sound so bad. Do I really sound like that?"

Hailey giggled. "Relax. We always sound different than how we think we sound in our head."

Roxy was horrified. "My voice isn't husky," she wailed. For years, she'd thought her voice was sexy, raspy even. It had been her one good redeeming feature. "I sound like a man!"

"You do not."

She thought she heard someone in the background asking, "What's she saying?"

"I hate it," she insisted.

"Hate what?" Mason came on the phone. She sat upright, in shock.

"Are you watching the show?" She could just see Hailey, Jax and Mason huddled on the sofa watching the show on Hailey's huge plasma screen.

"You should have been here."

"This is the reason I didn't want to. I ... Oh my god. I look awful. Do I always look so angry?"

"Jax and Hailey were discussing that. They blamed it on me and said it must be my effect, because you don't look that angry ordinarily."

"I hate it."

"So ... do I? Is it because of me?"

"Is what?" she asked, watching her face as she scurried around the diner kitchen checking up on her staff. She recalled the day that scene was shot. It had been a particularly busy day, and it had been hot. Which would explain her greasy face. Maybe she should have taken her mom's advice and treated herself to a facial? Or at least gotten a haircut and color. Both of these things were only-for-a-special-occasion, at least the facial was. But if going on TV wasn't a special event, then what was?

"I wouldn't be so hard on yourself, Roxy. That's what everyone thinks the first time they see themselves on TV."

"But this is bad. Reeeeeeeally bad."

He laughed.

"Don't laugh. I don't think I want to watch any more of it."

"You should watch it. We're very good. We have chemistry. This is what I keep hearing, from the producers, from everyone on the show. From Hailey and Jax."

"Chemistry?" She had no idea what he meant. She remembered that episode. The only chemistry she could think of was the explosive kind.

"I've got something I need to discuss with you."

Were her hips that big? She didn't like the way the camera angle focused on her back. She didn't like it one bit. "What?"

"I can tell that you're engrossed. We'll talk when I next see you."

She hung up and grabbed her cushion again, ready to hide behind it when the need next arose.

CHAPTER 23

"Sixty-four flavors of ice cream?" Mason repeated, when she told him that what he'd read on the signage of Kandinsky's wasn't wrong.

"Yes. Shocking, right?"

"Not shocking. It's a great USP. Come on, let's go."

Her mouth fell open. It was one thing for Mason being nicer on the set, but now he was asking her to go for a walk to the ice cream parlor, and well, no. Just no. "Uh … I've got a lot going on."

He looked around. "Where?"

The lunchtime rush had died down. "I had ideas for more menu options. I want to revamp the entire menu." The uptake on her new additions had been significant enough to make her want to change the whole thing. Why hadn't she done this before? It was a simple enough change to make. She hadn't needed a world-famous chef to come and tell her this.

"Then we can discuss them while we're walking along the beach."

She didn't want to go for a walk along the beach. Not with

him. Not now. His niceness was beginning to make her uneasy, just like his previous behavior had, but for the wrong reasons.

"I'd like to try it." His persistence was beginning to tire her down.

"I can't."

"Can't or won't?"

Her hands went to her hips. She preferred Mason more when he was being cold and nasty. At least that way, she could answer him back, put him in his place, or try. She could say something. What was she supposed to do if he was being all nice and friendly? This, this was too much. "Can't. Please, you go. Take Ella and Lewis with you if you want to."

She hated herself for having said something that had completely changed his behavior. This wasn't normal. She almost wished the old Mason was back.

"I thought we could take a break. Do something different." His eyes never left her face.

"Look, Mason. I appreciate you wanting to make things up for how you behaved the other day, but you don't have to keep being nice."

"I'm not being overly nice. Nor am I after something."

She felt her insides blush, if such a thing were possible. Had he insinuated that she thought he was hitting on her?

"I never said you were." She wished the floor would open up and swallow her. Why was she shying away? He wasn't asking her for dinner for two, or drinks for two. He was simply suggesting that they talk about business matters away from the camera.

Wasn't this what she wanted? Wasn't this good of him? That he was putting her before his TV ratings?

She used work as an excuse for everything. The only time she allowed herself an evening out was to attend the SBWEB meetings or to see Jax, and Hailey, or her parents.

"I wanted to discuss something with you."

Now she remembered. He'd mentioned last night that he wanted to talk to her about something. Was he thinking of replacing her? A dart of worry shot through her, as sharp and as cutting. Maybe that was why he had backed off on the show, on the way he treated her. Maybe he wanted to prepare her for the fact that this wasn't working, and he needed to replace her, or finish her part of the show quickly.

Her imagination went into overdrive.

"Reed Knight called me a few days ago."

She blinked. Those weren't the words she had been expecting. But then again, Reed didn't waste any time when it came to making connections with important people.

"You've met him?" she asked, wondering how and when this might have happened.

"Jax introduced me at the bar one evening."

"Jax?" It surprised her that he met with Jax and she hadn't known a thing about it.

"I do have a life outside of the diner, you know. The Blue Velvet Bar isn't so bad."

He had more of a life than she did, if he was meeting the likes of Reed at the Blue Velvet Bar. She went home every evening to an empty house and TV, and Mason was going out and meeting people. He surprised her.

"He's having an engagement party."

She nodded. "He got engaged recently." Trust that man to not waste any time throwing a party. "They have many parties up at his mansion. I expect this one to be bigger than all the others."

"You've catered for him before?"

She laughed and stared out of the window. "Me? No. Reed has other more prestigious caterers he goes to. I'm surprised he hasn't asked you to cater for his big event."

"That's just the thing I wanted to discuss with you. Reed Knight wants me to cater at his event."

His announcement made her look up. "He does?" But of course. Why wouldn't he want the best? "Reed often does fundraisers and parties at his home." She rolled her eyes. "He has a beautiful place. Wait until you see it."

Reed Knight had used her services before, but only for low-key events. Never parties. She imagined that he wanted something more upscale and what could be more upscale than having Mason Brandt cater at such an event?

Mason asking her to help him made her wonder if this was some sort of challenge. Catering events were hectic and working alongside Mason might be a bigger challenge than the act of catering at Reed's big event.

"Reed said I needed to surprise him. We'll have dressed crab, sea bass on blinis with Ossetra caviar and cream, salmon gravlax with horseradish and lobster risotto—maybe. I don't know. It's just a thought."

Her thoughts offered up simpler things, but she was going to keep her mouth shut.

"No? Yes? You like my suggestions?" He was asking her.

"I … I … I work in a diner. You've cooked for royalty."

"There you go again, putting yourself down. If I say you can do this, you can."

"Caviar? Lobster risotto?"

"It's no different from mushroom risotto …, well, not too different. You'll be fine. You just have to believe in yourself. I know you can do it."

"Are you going to do it? Take Reed up on his offer?"

"I have. He's fired the caterers he had, and he's paying me handsomely for it."

"He can afford to," she pointed out.

"Of course, it's very short notice. The party is this weekend, but since I'm in town … and I don't have anything else to do …"

"You really want me to help you?"

"I'm going to need all the help I can get, Roxy, and I'm going to need all of your staff." He rolled his shoulder.

"He's also got a butler and a housekeeper."

"I expect nothing less," Mason said. "Hailey and Jackson will be there, I imagine."

Yes, they would be, as would countless others who were 'someone' in Starling Bay. She would be there as house help. Kitchen staff. Helper of the great Mason Brandt. "Are you allowing the cameras to film this?" she wanted to know. She couldn't dictate since it was Mason who was in charge, and she was sure that Reed would be okay with it, as long as the filming only happened in the kitchen area.

"Would that be a problem?"

It would be. Tension inched across her shoulders at the thought of cameras over her shoulder, capturing every mistake, every heart-pounding action as she raced to Mason's orders.

He'd want to give it his best, and as nice as Mason was being right now, she had spent enough time around him to know that he had a short temper.

He would want to put on the best event for Reed because he'd want Reed and his friends to look upon him well. She was mere collateral who would be the target of his wrath should anything go wrong.

"I don't want cameras around, but Ella and Lewis, and the rest of my staff don't mind."

"What are you saying?"

"I'm saying that I won't want to be there, but my staff will."

"And if I don't have any cameras rolling?"

She frowned wondering why he would go that far, dismiss the cameras and all because of her. "Why would you do that?"

"So that you could help."

"Why is that so important to you?"

"Because it would be good for you, and I don't mean that in a big-headed way."

"Why?"

"Because I'm not big-headed—despite what you think."

"No, I mean, why would it be good for me? Getting a full eight hours sleep a night is what would be good for me."

"You're not sleeping well?" he asked, peering closely at the dark circles beneath her eyes.

"Mason. Can you keep the conversation on the right track? Why do you think me helping you at Reed's party would be good for me?" The only way she'd ever get to attend an event at the Knight mansion was by being the help. Hailey and Jax and probably most of the women who attended the SBWEB meetings would be there, but she would only get to attend because she was catering staff, and even that was because Mason had asked her to help him. Was he taking pity on her again, or was he looking to get a rise out of making her look silly? This man didn't need a camera to do that and she'd be damned if she was going to let him do that to her.

"Because all of the pressure for this will be on me. The menu, getting everything ready, making sure everything is the best it can be. You get to help and it's my neck that's on the line."

"As long as it's your neck and not mine. I'll help you."

CHAPTER 24

She was nervous as she walked into Reed's mansion with her staff, but Mason seemed at ease, as if he belonged in a place like this. He didn't seem in the slightest bit bothered that he was going to be working.

Just walking into the Reed mansion took her breath away. Luckily, a flurry of activity was taking place in whichever direction she looked, and she was forced to pay attention to where they were being told to go.

"This is ginormous," Ella exclaimed, staring up at the sweeping staircase and the chandeliers.

"How the other half live," Lewis muttered under his breath.

"Shhhhh." She put a finger to her lips. While some people were busy decorating the house with flowers, and others were rushing in and out carrying boxes and crates, she had heard about Reed's butler and his housekeeper having perfect hearing and she didn't want her staff to be caught saying anything they shouldn't be.

Reed appeared and greeted them both, but seemed to talk directly to Mason, rather than her. Which was fine. She preferred to hover in the background and watch everything from a safe unnoticed place. They were shown into the kitchen, and from there she saw the huge tent which was erected in the yard. She heard Reed say that they would have the party there, rather than in the ballroom.

"Let's get started," she told her staff, seeing that Mason was still chatting away with Reed. They'd spent two days in tireless preparation in her diner kitchen, working long hours preparing the delicacies that Mason had decided on.

Reed had left the menu choices to Mason, telling him only that he liked shrimp, and crab, and that Jenna loved salmon and asparagus and lots of chocolate for dessert. They both wanted to be surprised and were eager to see what Mason would come up with. He had also mentioned that there was no limit to the budget.

With most of the cooking already done, with just the final parts to do here, Roxy envisioned an easy night, though every so often Reed's butler and housekeeper would come over to make sure that their precious territory wasn't being damaged.

As soon as Reed had left, Mason issued instructions, and they worked tirelessly, getting canapés prepared for the 7:00 p.m. champagne reception.

The pressure was off her. She wasn't in charge, and she relished the thought that all of the responsibility for this event lay solely on Mason's shoulders.

"It's insane." Ella rushed in, followed by a whole line of servers who had been recruited by Jenna and Reed. She showed them the canapés which had to be taken out to the tent.

Mason made things look so easy. The lobster risotto, the various canapés which looked so pretty to eat. The presentation and display were mesmerizing, a profusion of color, and the very best of ingredients so that everything they prepared not only looked delicious but smelled divine.

At one point, she wasn't sure when it was, sometime after the canapés and just before the main dinner was to be served, Reed and Jenna came into the kitchen to thank them all.

Roxy felt like a mess. In her sweaty outfit, her underarms damp and sweat sliding down her back, seeing Jenna in a beautiful long dress with a sparkling diamond necklace and *that* ring, made her shrink back against the wall where she stood, guzzling down a big glass of iced lemonade.

She managed to congratulate the happy couple, and replied, "Yes," when Jenna told her to come inside and enjoy the party once all the work was completed. Hailey and Jax had come by a few times, until she'd told them to leave because she was working. Couldn't they see?

The work was never done, not until they had packed everything away towards the end of the event. She had no intention of going to the party or mingling with everyone, because she fully understood in which capacity she had been invited here, and it wasn't as a guest.

For the next few hours, they continued to work, preparing the main meal, and making sure everything was perfect as the servers were taking it all out.

It was a few hours later that the onslaught stopped. Even though they had prepared most of the things in her diner, there were many things which Mason wanted to prepare in Reed's kitchen; miniature souffles which had to be cooked just so, in a short time, and pastries which needed finishing touches.

She could feel the sweat along the back of her neck, the dampness in her hair. She fanned her face, stepping outside the kitchen to get some breeze on her face.

"You did well." Mason had slipped outside to cool off.

"Thank you. You were a good lead."

He held a can of pop against his forehead. "I had a great team."

Reed's butler came through. "Reed would like you to come through, sir."

"Who, me?"

The man nodded.

"Go on," Roxy urged him, then, lowering her voice, "He probably wants to have a photo taken with you."

"He would like to thank you publicly," the butler explained.

Mason looked unsure. "That's all right. He's already thanked me enough."

"He would like to thank you in person."

Roxy grinned. "Go on, give him that photo opportunity. I'm sure that's what he'll want. You'll see it in the local paper and hanging somewhere in his study, I expect."

"Sir, they're waiting."

Mason looked as if he would have to be dragged to the tent. "You're coming too," he said, taking her by the elbow.

"No, not me. I'm only here because you forced me." She refused to move.

"Take her, take her," Ella and Lewis chimed in.

"I'm not going." Dread filled every ounce in her body. She did not want to stand in front of all those people and have them staring at her, especially when she was sweaty and sticky and looked like a wreck.

"Yes, you are." He pulled her arm and tugged her towards him. Her insides hardened with fear. She looked at Lewis and Ella as she scurried, against her will, along with Mason, his hold on her too strong for her to break free from.

"Relax." Mason looked over his shoulder. "Relax." But as they stepped into the tent, the sheer splendor and luxury of it took her breath away. Chandeliers sparkled, the floor was solid, with a red carpet pathway leading from one end of the tent to the other. Tables and chairs were dotted around, and the servers stood at the ready along the side. Bunches of glorious flowers, creating a splash of bright color, adorned the center of every table.

She'd never seen a tent like this.

"I can't." Her heart rattled in her throat, as Mason started to walk up the red carpet. She couldn't face these people, looking the way she did, with them looking the way they did, all beautiful and glamorous. She pulled back, tugged her hand away. Mason stopped walking and glanced at her.

"I can't, please …" she pleaded. And just like that, he let her hand go, as he continued to proceed without her.

He strode to the front, overbrimming with confidence, and walked right up to Reed and Jenna, who stood together holding hands. Jenna wore a stylish deep purple dress. She heard applause, saw Mason smile, heard Reed thank him, and even as she watched from the back of the tent, barely inside it, she felt a crippling sense of paralysis overtake her.

That was the difference between people like Mason and people like her.

She could not do this. She didn't want this, having to stand up in front of people. It was still a shock that she had allowed herself to go on TV, but this, standing in front of a crowd, saying something, looking into their eyes, that, she could not do. The TV show seemed easier compared to this.

Reed thanked Mason for adding such a magnificent culinary touch to their engagement party and said he was honored that the esteemed chef had agreed to cook for his engagement. Then he talked about Mason's show and how grateful he was that Mason had decided to come to Starling Bay and film the next season of his show here.

The crowd clapped again then Reed handed the mic to Mason. Roxy's shoulders slumped and she seemed to fold into herself.

"First of all, let me say a huge congratulations to the happy couple." Then he went on to express his gratitude that Reed had asked him to cater here. "I'll keep this short. I've enjoyed my time here. I'm finding out more things every day that I like about Starling Bay. However, tonight would not have been possible without my catering partner, and the proud owner of Roxy's Diner, which is featured on our show. She's standing at the back, and that's fine, but please, a round of applause for Roxy and her team without whom this evening would not have been possible."

To her extreme shock and fear, everyone in the tent, all those hundreds of pairs of eyes turned and stared at her, and people clapped. Mason had handed the mic back and was clapping too.

She froze, not knowing what to do, so she smiled, and bowed her head in some sort of acknowledgment. She hoped it would come across as that and not that she had a crick in her neck. Every movement she made seemed in slow motion, as if time had stopped.

By the time she took a deep breath, and grew accustomed to the applause, and started to feel at ease, it stopped, and Mason was walking towards her again.

"I need a proper drink," he muttered. She turned and followed him out of the tent.

CHAPTER 25

She worked well under pressure, and she'd surprised him. Hailey was right. When he was nicer, he got more from people, and while he had known this basic fact of life, he didn't always apply it. It didn't always work in his cutthroat culinary world.

But it was surprising how well this seemed to work with Roxy. She blossomed when she didn't have to stand her corner or go on the defensive against him.

Because last night had gone so well, and because Roxy had stepped up, he wanted to do something different, something that might get her out of the diner. He wanted to enable her to have some down time because, from what he'd seen and learned about her, she didn't know the meaning of the word.

He had ventured out in the evenings and on the days when he wasn't filming. The lake and the woods were beautiful. They gave him a sense of serenity he hadn't experienced for a while. Going on walks had allowed him to find solace and time to rethink his life.

The more he got to know Roxy, the more he saw of himself in her. He recalled that moment when he'd tried to drag her to the front, when Reed had wanted to acknowledge them. Hers hadn't been the fear of unexpectedly having to face a crowd. No, there had been something more than just the natural dread of public speaking. Roxy's fear went deeper, he knew, because as hard as she tried to hide it, he could see it clearly. It was a fear he'd had himself, that he wasn't good enough, and he didn't belong.

He'd built his career and his reputation on wanting to prove them all wrong, and he had.

One day, after filming was over, he told her that they could discuss Reed's party and the catering, and dissect her and her team's performance, and he had ideas for her to think about, on improvements she could make, new things she could try, for that side of her business.

"Why don't we discuss this in front of the cameras?"

"You're suddenly eager to discuss things in front of the cameras."

"That's because these are safe topics," she threw back.

"Safe topics?" This was a term he'd never heard before.

She wiped her hands on her apron, as if trying to find the right words, but he was most curious now.

"Safe?" Had he ever made her feel unsafe? The thought made him uneasy. In his quest to become a top chef and hold onto that crown, he'd lost what it was to be a respectful human being.

"As in ... if we're going to dissect how we performed at Reed's party, you won't be able to talk down to me."

"I feel bad for making you feel bad, and I'm trying, Roxy."

"I noticed. It's just that ..."

"What?"

"You don't have to keep being nice all the time."

He scoffed. "Now you're accusing me of being too nice. This is a delicate balancing act. I'm trying."

"You are, and I'm grateful."

"But, getting back to dissecting Reed's party in front of the cameras, you forget one thing."

"What?"

"We never allowed cameras into that event, you said you didn't want them. So, it won't make sense to dissect something that the viewers weren't even party to."

She stared back at him sheepishly, and maybe this was where he would get his leverage. "My offer still stands. Come over to my place. Don't look so distraught. I have a surprise."

"I don't like surprises."

He thought back to when he'd allowed the cameras to capture her reaction when the pan had caught fire. "This will be a pleasant surprise."

"Well ..."

"You're not working at the diner tomorrow."

"How do you know that?" she asked, her voice shaky.

"Because I can read and because the roster on the wall tells me."

"Oh."

"And because I double-checked with Ella."

"I see."

"Come over tomorrow at noon."

Go over to his, tomorrow at noon?

He must have sensed her hesitation. "We're just talking business, Roxy. Business. That's all." Something she couldn't decipher flashed across his smooth features.

She wasn't sure about this. Something was off. Mason was too nice, and she couldn't quite handle that. But he had asked her to many times now, and she had always turned him down. He seemed to be making a real effort to be nice and she had to acknowledge that and stop pushing him away.

He'd been so easy to work with at Reed's event, encouraging and supportive and helpful as he had shown her and her team how to prepare the canapés, the likes of which they hadn't made before.

But she would definitely be adding those things to her new catering menu. Mason had talked to her about how she could offer different levels of service for her catering events, pricing higher at each tier.

This made sense. Some people wanted more upscale food, like Reed and his guests. She could now offer that, thanks to Mason.

She noted that he offered business advice in those small moments when the cameras were turned off, or, as he had last week, he came into the diner on the days when they weren't filming and offered her more business advice. She sensed he was eager to help her, and the fact that he chose to do this away from the cameras made her feel more encouraged than ever.

Why not throw caution to the wind and do something different on a Sunday on her day off?

It sure beat going to her mom and dad's house.

CHAPTER 26

She didn't know what to wear. Didn't know how to do her hair. She only had two styles for it. Wearing it down, or in a ponytail when she was at work.

Maybe she should have listened to her mom and gotten her highlights done? She hadn't had them redone for months and now the lightened ends contrasted with her dark hair and looked rather odd. She'd have to get it all sorted out. But she couldn't do it right now.

She'd tried on several different blouses. Was a spaghetti strap top going to make him think she was trying to catch his attention? Would the red one be too bright, and scream 'look at me'? Another blouse made her look too short, its stripes doing nothing for her. In the end, she settled on an orange-colored, short-sleeved top with white polka dots, that and a pair of jeans and sneakers.

She didn't know what to take, and didn't want to go empty-handed, so she took with her a box of chocolates and a bottle of her mom's homemade lemonade.

Only, when she arrived at Mason's place, instead of showing her into his apartment, he handed her a backpack.

"What's this?" she asked in a shaky voice as he disappeared out of view.

"We're having a picnic." He was carrying a picnic hamper.

Oh, dear god, she was going to be sick. Her stomach churned. She had never gone on a picnic before. She had prepared a hamper for Jax and Hailey for *their* picnics. This was the type of lovey-dovey thing that they did, and she had derided Jax for his newfound pastime plenty of times.

She didn't do picnics.

She didn't have time for such frivolity, and now Mason was forcing her to go on one.

He set the picnic hamper back on the floor. "Is there a problem, Roxy? Do you have hay fever? Are you allergic to the sunlight?" His slightly jokey, mocking tone was back.

"No to all of those things." She had turned Mason down so many times, and she had to force herself to have a sense of enthusiasm because he seemed eager.

"Are you sure you want to do this?" he asked, moving his head from side to side as if he was running this life-changing decision by her again.

"Stop it! Yes, I'm fine. It's just that … it's just that I don't do these things."

"Enjoy life, you mean? Give yourself some down time? Take it easy?"

It was true, of course, but now that he put it like that, it made her life sound boring. Uneventful. And it was. The diner was her life. Its success was her beating heart, the very thing she lived for, and one day, when it was a brilliant, thriving success, she would give herself more time off and take things easy. But until then …

"Ready?" he asked her as he grabbed a hold of the hamper again.

"Yes. That looks heavy." It was big, and didn't look easy to carry with its big bulky size.

"I can manage. I'm not a complete wimp."

She could see that. He filled out his t-shirt well. Too well, in fact. Especially because today, he wasn't wearing a shirt over it. Today she could see the wide span of his shoulders, and the bulging biceps of his arms. Today, Mason didn't look like the chef she had become accustomed to. Today, he looked altogether more delicious.

He tapped his stomach, and she averted her gaze, conscious of the fact that she'd been staring at him a little too much. "I need to work on this."

She looked away, hoping he wouldn't see the color creeping along her cheeks. "What's in this?" She strapped the backpack on her shoulder.

"A tablecloth, utensils and all the other odd little things we'll need."

He had taken care of everything. She'd already made her mind up to enjoy this, no matter what.

They walked across a small field. He'd chosen a path which avoided going through the forest; it was probably just as well because carrying that hamper over uneven forest ground was going to be no easy task, not even for someone like Mason.

He seemed to be going to such extreme lengths and she didn't know why. Had he had a seizure? Woken up a different person? This wasn't the Mason she was used to. This wasn't the type of attention and behavior she was used to.

"Don't scowl." He gave her a sideways glance.

She immediately went poker-faced. "I have to tone that down, don't I? I looked awful."

"Like I said, Hailey and Jax said this was a new face for you. You tend not to frown so much."

"It's not easy being on TV," she replied, glancing at him, but her gaze slipped down to his shoulder, then his arm, and she blushed, because he caught her checking him out. She coughed and stared directly ahead of her.

"I'm not an easy person to be around."

"You've changed a lot lately. Did my meltdown have something to do with it? When I showed up on your doorstep?" Because the way she saw it, things had definitely changed since that moment.

"Hailey said some things that made me think."

"Hailey?" Now she was doubly curious.

"About my ex-wife, about things I could have done better."

His ex-wife? Something pinched at her insides.

"I thought this would be a good spot," he said, setting down his heavy load. "Do you like it?"

"It looks like it's taken." Someone had left what looked like a folding table and some chairs on the ground, which was a shame because this was a lovely spot. She looked around for signs of others.

"That's ours," he told her. I left them there earlier, just before you arrived."

"What?" She set the backpack on the ground.

"I rushed over and put these here. It would have been too much to carry it all."

She couldn't find the words. Couldn't get over his planning, and thoughtfulness, and his preparation.

"Don't you like it here? We could go someplace else—"

"It's perfect." He had mistaken her silence for disapproval, when the real issue was that her heart fluttered inside her chest, giving her palpitations such as she had never had before. "It's perfect," she whispered, but he didn't hear her. He had set down the hamper and was checking inside it.

This was too much. She wasn't used to being wooed. It had been a while. She couldn't remember the last date she had been on. Now Mason, a famous man, a wealthy and successful man, a celebrity chef, for goodness' sake, had put on a picnic for her.

"You didn't have to do all of this, Mason."

"I wanted to. It's something different."

Her stomach felt all funny and fizzy. A lightness settled over her and everything looked brighter and more beautiful.

They had a perfect view of the lake. Behind them, the forest, and all around them, peace and sunshine. He could not have picked a more perfect spot. "This is perfect." She gazed at the lake, felt the sun gently kiss her skin. She savored it, closing her eyes and immersing herself in it fully, losing herself in the moment. When she opened her eyes, Mason was staring at her, a curious expression on his face.

"I knew you would like it."

She smiled.

"Come and give me a hand with these, Roxy."

They worked together, opening up the table, and setting up the two chairs, and he told her how he'd woken up early and put together the food for the picnic. She laughed, feeling spoiled and frivolous, and unsure of what to say because she had never been in this position before.

"This is … this is very sweet of you to do this, Mason."

"I discovered this place while out walking. I'm doing a lot more of that. We don't walk much in LA. I've come here a few times. I like eating outside and this view is gorgeous. I'm aware that you don't always want to discuss things in front of the camera. We're not going to be able to sit in your diner and discuss anything, because you're going to get a lot of interruptions. You won't go out to dinner with me because…well. ... it might not seem appropriate. You don't want to come over to my place, even when Hailey and Jax are over, so this is my way of enjoying the day, enjoying the food, and getting the business matters out of the way without you turning me down."

She gasped. "Wow. You've thought of everything."

"Every get-out clause you could come up with."

"I'm impressed."

"I'm humbled that I could impress you."

She frowned, not understanding what he meant. She wasn't a high-maintenance woman. She didn't ask for much, so impressing her was easy enough to do. If he'd bought her an ice cream, she'd have been grateful, because she had come to not rely on anyone for anything and she had no expectations, especially when it came to the opposite sex. But then she remembered. Mason had tried to get her to go for a walk, and she had turned him down on every occasion.

He opened the backpack and pulled out a tablecloth. The man was so organized, she had to give him that. He spread the cloth over the table, and she got busy taking everything out of the hamper.

He had thought of everything. He'd packed plates, and glasses, utensils and napkins. A cutting board and knives. A variety of cheeses and crackers. Ice packs, paper towels.

And then there was the food, not too much food, just enough for the two of them., miniature sandwiches, some of the canapés they had served at Reed's party, tiny bowls of salad, hard-boiled eggs, little tarts.

"This is a feast, Mason."

"It's just something I threw together."

"You made these?" It was her turn to be impressed. It had been late by the time they had finished at Reed's. She'd crawled into bed and woken up late today. To think that Mason had been busy putting all of this together while she'd enjoyed sleeping in then getting up late with nothing to worry about but deciding on what she was going to wear.

"If you're going to do something, you should do it properly or not at all. I like picnics. Don't you?"

She stared at him blankly.

"When was the last time you went on a picnic?"

"A while."

"Define 'a while.'"

"Uh…." Would the picnic she'd had on a school trip to count? "Lemonade?" she asked, pulling out her own contribution to the picnic.

"Please." He offered her his glass. "I'm still waiting, Roxy. Define 'a while.'"

She kept her eyes down, choosing to focus hard on pouring the lemonade, and when she handed him his glass back, their gazes met and locked.

"I'm guessing never. Am I right? Do you ever get to relax, Roxy?"

He might as well have asked her if she had flown to Mars and back. No, of course not. She never relaxed. She sensed that he was peeling back the layers of protection that kept her safe. He was slowly pulling them back one by one.

"Relax?" she asked.

"Yes. Sit down," he instructed, pulling out the chair for her. She wasn't used to this level of chivalry. It felt odd, all of it, to be here, with Mason, sitting outside with the sun shining and the promise of a perfect day staring her in the face. He was indulging her. She would never ever in a million years do something like this and she had never had anyone do something like this for her. Ever.

She wondered why he had divorced, and how Mason would have been like with his wife. The woman was beautiful, on a level with Hailey. She had the type of beauty that made people famous. If Mason was going to the trouble of doing this for her, and she was no one, then what would he have done for his wife?

"I get to relax on my days off, but this is very kind of you. Very thoughtful. Thank you."

"You're welcome. It makes a change from the diner, and goodness knows I can't get you to come to my place."

"I'm fine with wanting to talk away from the cameras, but don't you need things for the show?" While she liked the new easygoing episodes, Ella had commented, confirming her own sneaky suspicions, that it didn't make for such exciting TV. She wondered if the viewers might get bored.

"We have plenty of content for the show. This way it's easier on you."

"But you don't have to go easy on me."

"That's not what you said the other day."

"You went too far."

He nodded. "I upset you."

"I have a tough skin, Mason. You didn't upset me that much."

"But it's nicer to not have a camera in your face when the pan catches fire, and you're already stressed out because of an event you have to cater for that evening."

"This is nicer," she agreed, then, wanting to answer his question, "I work hard and there's not enough time to relax and enjoy life yet."

"It will pass you by if you don't stop. The diner, everything it takes from you to run it and keep the business ticking over. That will never stop. You'll never have a day when you think you'll be satisfied that you've finished everything. You'll never get on top of it all."

Mason understood. She often went home with her head racing with all the things she had to figure out and think about and fix.

Her mind was never free. There was always something to think about, something to worry about. "It must be easy for you, now that you've made it." Mason had it all. The fame, the fortune, the lifestyle. Not a care or worry in the world, except maybe sadness over his divorce.

"Made it? I don't know if I've made it."

"What?" She almost choked on the grape she had popped into her mouth. He didn't think he'd made it. If he hadn't made it, if he didn't consider himself to be a success, then who had? "But look at you."

He picked up a small tart and examined it. "Yes, look at me." His voice was flat, dull, as if he didn't buy into the vision of his success that was so apparent for everyone to see. In that moment, he looked the saddest she had ever seen him. He took a bite of the tart.

"Mason?" In this moment, he was stripped bare, and it was only because his mask had slipped and she saw his forlorn expression that she realized it had been a mask at all.

He looked at her.

"You are what I'd call successful. If you're not, who is? If what you have isn't the epitome of success, then what is?"

"There are many definitions of success."

"And you are definitely a walking, talking version of it."

His sad eyes seemed to imply that he didn't agree. "What do you see?" he asked her.

She shuffled in her chair, the desire to need to be careful about what she said utmost in her mind. "You've got it all, the …the… TV shows, the restaurants, the books, the fame, …." Did she have to spell it out for him?

"What do you want, Roxy? What would constitute success for you?" He hadn't answered her question, rather, he had deflected and pushed the question to her.

"I want my diner to thrive. I want it to be bringing in more, much more than it currently is. A decent profit margin would be good. It would be more than good … "

"But why do you want all of that? You have those things."

"My diner barely breaks even, some months, I worry. I have sleepless nights. I work all the time. I want to have fun."

"Everything you've talked about is related to your business."

"What else is there?" She was still trying to break out, to find that elusive success. He wouldn't understand, he couldn't because he had it all.

"What else is there? My marriage failed because all I did was work, work, work. I thought I was doing the right thing, becoming successful and then staying successful. They are two different things. The climb to the top isn't as hard, in comparison, as keeping that hold on the top. Monique deserved better."

Monique.

The exotic name tripped around in her brain, and she at once had visions of a beautiful woman, stunning and accomplished. Nothing like her.

"What's this?" She held up what had looked like a sausage roll, but it was thinner, and longer and when she bit into it, she couldn't immediately place the sweet, nutty flavor.

"Apricot and pistachio sausage rolls."

"What's wrong with the normal sausage rolls?" And how did he happen to have apricots and pistachios in his kitchen?

"There's no harm in making something plain more interesting."

She disagreed. "I prefer getting exactly what I asked for. If I eat a cracker with cheese, I expect to taste a cracker with cheese."

"Isn't that different and tasty?" He nodded at the sausage roll in her hand.

"Oh, no, that's not what I meant. It is tasty. It's beyond delicious, but it's just not what I was expecting." She took another bite to confirm, now that she knew what it was. Mason was right. It was luscious. Delectable, and definitely *different*. Yummalicious. It was different. It was a whole other flavor. It just wasn't a sausage roll as she knew it.

"Is it too fancy? Too dressed up?"

"I..." She didn't want him to think she was ungrateful. She was extremely, completely grateful and the enormity of what he had done for her was taking time to sink in. "It wasn't what I had expected. You do that a lot. You like to pretty things up."

He raised an eyebrow, as if she'd unveiled a secret about him. "Sometimes, it's better to go out of your comfort zone, and try things you wouldn't ordinarily try."

"But there's a difference, Mason. There's trying something that I haven't tried before, like those blinis with that oss…oss—"

"Ossetra caviar."

"That's the one. Those things you made for Reed's party."

"The things *we* all made for Reed's party."

She stared at him, wondering how she'd never noticed that that his eyes were so green. Or that she could easily stare into them for hours. "You were saying?" he prompted.

What was she saying? "The … the …" Her brain short-circuited for a split second. It could have been any number of things, like the sun, or the food, or his eyes, or the fact that they were talking like this. The realization made her heart trip. "I … uh … I've forgotten what I was saying."

"That there's a difference in trying something you haven't tried before …" Even with his prompting, she couldn't remember. But clearly, he wasn't struggling to keep up with the conversation. "Uh … there's a difference in …. Oh, yes, trying something you haven't tried before and biting into a sausage roll and expecting it to be a sausage roll."

"That," he pointed to the fast-disappearing sausage roll in her hand, "is a sausage roll. Your definition of it differs from mine. I like to experiment and try different things, and that's what I suggested you do."

She wiped a napkin over her mouth and hoped it didn't leave crumbs. "You did, and that's already made a difference." Her customers liked that she was changing up the menu, and her figures looked better for her having increased her prices.

"Despite what you think, to me it looks as if you have the world at your feet."

He dipped a breadstick into a dip. "The world at my feet," he murmured. "Do I have the world at my feet? Hmmm."

"That's what it looks like." Why did it sound as if he was going to share something contrary to her opinion of him?

"Is that what you think?" he asked her. She was missing something. He was being vague, and this was his most vulnerable moment.

"I've never been good at anything. My teachers thought the same."

"Your teachers told you that?"

"They didn't say it in those words, but they implied that I was useless, and wouldn't amount to much."

"Those idiots."

She wanted to change the subject. "I'm impressed that you had apricots and pistachios in your kitchen cupboards." These weren't things she shopped for weekly.

"I went to a farmers' market last weekend. It was only a couple of hours' car ride from here."

"Was it on the way to Whisper Falls?"

"That's it. That name sounds familiar."

She was intrigued that he'd gone at all. "What was it like?"

"It was magnificent. On par with some of the farmers' markets in Paris, if not better."

"I see we're in good company then."

"I didn't mean to sound snooty. I bought a whole heap of things. Have you been?"

She shook her head.

"You live here, and you've never been? Why not?"

She could hear the judgment in his voice. "I run a diner ..."

"Roxy. Roxy I-Run-A-Diner."

She tried to suppress a laugh and failed.

"You should hear yourself sometimes. It's as if you define yourself by what you do."

"Once my diner is doing well and making serious money, I'll be ..." She looked at him and managed to hold off the word that was on the tip of her tongue. 'Someone.' She would be someone. "Happy," she said instead. She wasn't pretty or rich, or bright, and she was far too stubborn and headstrong to hold down a job and take orders, so this, her diner, and its success were crucial to who she was. Her business was her route to success, it was her goal, her purpose in life.

She felt something land on her hand. She looked up. "Is that ... rain?"

A few more droplets landed in quick succession.

"Darn it." Mason stared up at the sky, his face twisting.

"Oh, no!" The drops landed faster. They looked at one another for a moment, then waited, hoping it would stop, but the rain came down faster. "Oh, no!" she squealed.

"Oh, yes." Mason jumped up and started gathering everything. She reached over for the hamper, and under the falling raindrops, they quickly stacked everything away, the need to pack everything tidily giving way to the onslaught for the rain.

She was devastated. On this rare occasion, she'd let down her guard and started to enjoy their conversation. It wasn't just Mason and the advice he dispensed, or the glimpse into his life that he allowed her to have, she had enjoyed all of it. The food, and him, and talking. Being with him out here had filled her soul in a way that nothing had, for a long, long time.

"What a thing to happen," she cried in despair.

"Life happens." Mason seemed to take it all in his stride.

"But it's not fair." The skies had been a perfect blue, and white cottony clouds had been few and far between. The sun had shone so brightly, she'd felt it on her skin. It had been a perfect day. Until this. And it sucked, yet Mason seemed to be calm about it.

"Ugh." Now the rain was really crashing down.

"I feel so bad," she whined. What a waste. He had gone to such effort to put this together and the rain had ruined everything.

CHAPTER 27

By the time they got back, they were both soaked through. Water dripped off Roxy's face and down her neck. Her short-sleeved blouse clung to her like a second skin and he would have offered her something to wear, but he hadn't taken anything with him, no jacket or sweatshirt. The day had been too glorious and the ensuing downpour had been as unexpected as it was unwanted.

"Just put that here." He cleared space at the kitchen table, the telltale signs of his preparation in full evidence.

"You worked all morning on this," she cried, her gaze taking in all of the dirty plates and utensils, and the mess.

"Okay, maybe I lied a little. I didn't just throw it all together."

"He is not a god," she said rather dramatically.

"As you are finding out, no doubt."

They had left the table and chairs under some trees, because it was too much to carry back. The rain had pelted down, and it had been a trek rushing in the downpour with the hamper and the backpack. He would go back later to get the table and chairs. He stared in dismay at the trail of puddles on the floor.

"I'm sorry today was cut short," Roxy said, as she started to unpack the items from the hamper.

"You say that as if you enjoyed it." He was glad, because this had been his goal. "We can't control the weather, Roxy. It's just another thing that's out of our control. Stop apologizing."

"I feel bad."

"Don't." He couldn't help but stare at her. "You're soaked through."

She pinched at her blouse which now stuck to her like a second skin. "I should go."

"And what about all of this food?" He didn't like to waste food if he could help it, and they had managed to put it away quickly so it hadn't been ruined. Besides, he had enjoyed talking to Roxy, and he didn't relish the idea of spending the rest of his day by himself.

"We can't go out in this." She stared at the floor, then disappeared quickly, returning with a mop. "Sorry … I snooped around but it wasn't hard to find. I hate wet floors." She started to mop the floor.

"You don't have to do that." He attempted to take the mop from her, but she was too nimble for him.

"I've almost finished." Drops fell from her wet clothes and still contributed to the wet droplets on the floor.

"You're soaked, Roxy. The drops are still falling."

She mopped those away too, making him laugh. "All done." She set the mop down by the wall. "Thank you for a wonderful day, Mason. I should get going."

"To where?"

"Home."

"To what?"

"Home," she repeated.

"But to *what*, Roxy?" As far as he understood, she lived alone. She was going home to what? Like him, to nothing and to no one. "Stay for dinner. I promise nothing extravagant. Something simple."

"You're making dinner, Mason?"

"You're going to eat when you get home, aren't you?"

She gesticulated to the picnic food she had taken out of the hamper. "What about all of this? We can't waste this."

"Then stay and help me eat it. We weren't even halfway through." He wasn't ready for her to go and he hated having to cut this day so short. They'd been having a nice time of it so far, and he wasn't ready for it to end.

She smacked her lips together as she surveyed the picnic food. "I was enjoying those sausage rolls."

The rain had slowed down, and now it was drizzling. He opened the doors of the veranda. "We can continue here."

"I'm soaked."

"I can lend you some of my clothes."

"You're going to lend me your clothes?"

"Unless you want to stay in wet clothes all day. I can't imagine anything more uncomfortable. I'm getting changed."

She looked at him, uncertainty swimming in those dark-as-chocolate eyes. "I should just go."

"Why not do something different, Roxy? It rained, so what? Are you going to let a bit of water derail your day?"

But going home probably made the most sense. What was he doing, what was he thinking, resorting to giving her dry clothes? It made the most sense for her to leave, but he didn't want her to go. "Do you want to? You can, if you want to, if you've got something planned. I'll pack you some food."

"I don't have anything planned. I'll stay. It would be a shame to waste the day."

Her surprise confession was music to his ears. He told her to use the spare bedroom, then gave her a clean towel to dry off with and a pair of sweatpants and a t-shirt which both looked way too big for her, but he had nothing else. He prayed that she wouldn't change her mind and leave.

He got changed himself, dried his hair, and felt better for being in dry clothes. In the kitchen, he cleared the table, moving the food to one side and putting the dirty plates and glasses away, before getting clean ones out.

"How do I look?" She gesticulated, moving her hands as if she was modeling clothes. The t-shirt came down to over her thighs, and she had rolled up the sweatpants at both ends, folding them at the bottom, and bunching them up around her waist. He couldn't help but smile. Then she did a twirl, asking him if liked this season's latest designer creation.

She seemed comfortable, happy, and it made his heart full. "I like it very much," he told her, and as their gazes locked, she looked away first, scratching the back of her neck, telling him more than her words would have.

He cleared his throat, not wanting her to feel uneasy. "Shall we continue? We have a lot of food here."

They sat and started eating again and talked. When the rain stopped, they stepped outside and admired the view.

"You can see the lake from here," Roxy said, peering out.

"It's one of my favorite views. I like to stand here in the mornings and have my coffee."

"Did you know that Reed Knight had a hand in the development of Forest Heights?"

"He did?"

"He has a hand in most things. The Knights go back a long time in Starling Bay."

"And the movie theater. His company refurbished it, and now it's named after the Knights. The Knight Movie Theater is what it's now called."

"Fancy that." As nice as Reed was, from the little he'd gotten to know him, his wealth had been handed down to him. Mason didn't doubt that the man would have eventually built up a sizeable fortune himself, but Mason prided himself on the fact that he was a self-made man. Maybe this was what Roxy thought.

"It's not always easy for the rest of us." He stared at the lake, his belly full, his heart content. Today had worked out better than he had hoped. Getting to know Roxy, talking to her away from the diner, away from people, had been wonderful. The rain hadn't ruined things, if anything, it had changed things up a bit. Life had thrown many curveballs and he had always adapted and switched and made things work.

The picnic getting ruined was an analogy he could apply to many periods of his life, but this time, it felt as if him bouncing back wasn't going to come as easily. Maybe he had ridden out his luck.

But he was also content, as he now realized, to slow down. Quitting the race to always be on top no longer seemed a worthy goal.

"No." Roxy's voice was soft.

"My parents weren't rich, but luck and opportunity helped me on my journey. I loved cooking. I loved helping my mom in the kitchen. She got fed up with me and my dreamy 'idiot ideas', she called them, but after I left high school, I worked in restaurants washing dishes at first, before moving up in small, small steps."

"Washing dishes. Imagine that."

"It's true. For a while it, felt as if all I would ever do was wash dishes for a living."

"But clearly, you moved on. And then what?"

"Then I looked for work wherever I could find it. I managed to save up enough money to get into a culinary institute and there I trained some more. And then I got my lucky break. I entered a competition which I won. It was through sheer luck."

"It can't have been sheer luck. You must have had something that they could see, some of your talent, even at that early age?"

"It was hard work, too. A heck of a lot of hard work, but you know that. You work all the time. Trying to get you to spend a day taking a break was hard work."

"But I'm here now," she protested, albeit weakly.

"But hard work, luck, opportunity, whatever it was, it enabled me to work abroad in Paris for a year, under a top sous chef. Later that year, the restaurant was awarded a third Michelin star. Again, it was luck that worked for me. I was in the right place at the right time. Imagine me, a nobody, ending up in a three-star Michelin restaurant in the heart of Paris."

"It can't have been just luck, Mason. You have talent." She made a face. "This is like role reversal, me trying to boost you up."

"Sometimes you have to lift yourself up by your bootstraps and make a name for yourself against the odds, and then you have to defend yourself against people who think your success was handed to you on a plate."

"Who thinks that?"

"People do. People who don't know me. Are you glad you stayed?" The day was slipping away, and it was only because the sun was starting to set that he had an inkling of how many hours had passed.

"Yes."

"It's important to play sometimes, Roxy."

"To play?"

"I had to almost drag you to this, and even now, the splash of rain scared you enough that you were going to rush back home."

"It wasn't a splash of rain. I was soaked."

"And we fixed it. Now you have dry clothes."

"Your clothes." She stared down at herself.

"That suits you, by the way."

"I look like a clown."

He disagreed. "You look nothing like a clown."

"I should go now. Thanks for a really nice day."

"I'm honored that you could make it."

"I'll have to do something nice for you," she said, turning to go.

"You don't have to feel obliged. I didn't want to spend the day alone again."

She turned and gave him a wistful look. "It sucks, doesn't it?" His heart did a little jig. She felt the same. Two lonely people who understood.

He was about to suggest that they go to the farmers' market when she was next free, but he decided against it. She might find that to be too much.

CHAPTER 28

Filming for the show continued smoothly. Roxy found that she didn't even notice the camera, or the crew as much, and she and her employees were used to having Mason dip his head in and out of the kitchen on those filming days, asking questions, shaking things up.

But it was more than just getting used to things. Something had changed. Mason wasn't only kinder, he was *gentler*. There was no more of the sniping and jibing and what she had previously perceived to be his concerted efforts in making her look bad. Because of this, she now felt more confident in the decisions she made regarding her business, and she was more willing to try new things.

This change had become even more pronounced after they had worked together on Reed's party. The picnic the next day cemented this new change in their relationship.

She wanted to repay the favor. This Mason, the 'nice' Mason, she could handle. The abrupt change in his character made her feel safer around him, not safe as in she'd feared for her life, but safe as in she could ask him anything. He had even opened up to her about his past, and she felt as if she'd joined a club for select members, because she sensed that he, like her, didn't voluntarily divulge his personal information.

He had even opened up about his wife.

She couldn't *not* do anything for him, and there was also the matter of returning his clothes. She racked her brains, trying to think of something different, something special, something fun to do, something like he had done for her with the picnic, but she couldn't think of anything appropriate.

She had considered dinner at The Olive Tree or even Fellini's but decided that it would be too intimate. It was a silly thought to have, but she sometimes felt a little self-conscious around him.

Unable to think of a way to repay his kind gesture, she pushed it to the back of her mind. She was getting exactly what she needed from him, business advice and mentorship, and the exposure from being on his show. This was the basis of their relationship, was it not? There was no use in getting other ideas.

She had also started watching herself on the shows as they slowly aired every week and was getting used to her voice and mannerisms. The more she watched herself, the more she started to accept that this was how she came across in real life.

Her business was slowly reaping the rewards, but only time would tell if the busyness of the diner was due solely to Mason and his TV crew filming there, or if indeed it was due to her newfound fame, or her new and exciting menu.

She was going to move forward with her plans for offering discounts to elderly patrons one morning in the week, and she was also going to get better prepared for holidays and celebrations. Before, she'd only made a half-hearted and often late attempt at celebrating special days, such as Valentine's Day. At Mason's suggestion, she'd decided to plan these days in advance. He had given her strategies for being more effective and organized and for planning ahead.

As for his clothes, she would return his clothes to him at the diner one day, if she remembered to bring them in.

She didn't need to do anything special for Mason. He might think she was starting to have feelings for him, and well, it couldn't be further from the truth.

~

"What do you mean, it lacks chemistry?"

"It's tame, it's boring, and you're being nice," said Gerard. "Nice doesn't pull in viewers, Mason. The ratings of the last few shows aren't as strong as the first ones. The audience figures are going to plummet if this continues."

This news didn't come as a surprise to him. He'd had an inkling that something was wrong when he'd seen the last two episodes that had aired. He and Roxy were different around one another and even she had commented on it.

"Is it really so bad?" he asked, heading towards the diner. Today was a non-filming day and coming here seemed like the most natural thing to do.

"Yes. It's really that bad. Spice it up, Mason, otherwise this isn't going to get a second season. This was supposed to be your comeback."

"It *is* my comeback."

"Murphy confirmed that Buffalo Bill is moving forward with his lawsuit. It doesn't sound like much of a comeback to me."

Mason's gut tightened. "Whose side are you on?" he growled. Trust Gerard to put a dampener on his day. He pushed through the door of the diner. Ella greeted him with a friendly smile, and Roxy sailed through the kitchen door, a tray of food in her arms.

"Do you even want this?" Gerard shot back.

"You know I want this."

"Then fix it. Don't be too nice. Nice doesn't sell."

He hung up. Despite Gerard and his thinly veiled threats, Mason felt a wave of comfort roll over him. This felt like home. Familiar faces, friendly faces. He slipped his phone away and prayed that he wouldn't hear from the man again.

"Good morning," Roxy's wide smile suddenly made everything better. His heart fluttered again. It was something he hadn't experienced in a while. "I'll be with you in a moment."

While she set about seeing to her customers, Ella came over and asked him for his order but he wasn't yet ready to order. She told him to let her know when he'd decided.

"Hey." A beaming Roxy didn't hover around his table, didn't ask him what he would like. Instead, she sat down. "Is everything all right? You didn't look so happy when you walked in."

He couldn't tell her what Gerard had said. "The guy who you replaced, the guy who was going to be on the show, the one I had signed up before I met you, he's threatening to sue me for breach of contract. My producer was getting all riled up about it."

She looked worried. "I'm so sorry."

"There's nothing for you to be sorry about."

"But he's suing you because you picked me."

"And it was the best choice I made." Funny how that had just tumbled out of his mouth.

"Was it?" she asked breathlessly.

Her eyes twinkled, and he couldn't look away. Didn't want to look away. Buffalo Bill could sue him ten times over, he didn't care.

He nodded, loving her smile. He could bask all morning in that smile because it made all of his problems melt away. Why hadn't he ever noticed the way her lips turned up at the corners or how her eyes lit up?

"Are you two going to sit there smiling at one another, or did you want to order something?"

Roxy's expression turned blank. "Ella." Her stern rebuke burst the bubble the two of them had been caught up in. The other people in the diner might as well have disappeared for all that he had noticed them.

Ella's face flushed. "I'm sorry, but you two have been grinning at one another, and this place is getting busy."

There was truth in what Ella had said. He glanced at Roxy, to see if her comment might have elicited a reaction from her. So much had happened lately and the dynamics between them had shifted.

"I'll have a breakfast burrito," he said, then looked to Roxy.

"I have a busy day ahead of me. I'm not hungry." But she made no move to get up. He liked that.

"Just the burrito then?" Ella put away her notepad.

"She often speaks without thinking." Roxy rolled her eyes. "She always has her nose in a romantic book during her breaks. She sees romance everywhere."

Roxy's dark eyes seemed to burn into him and something bubbled over in his chest, like soda pop fizzing and rising. "She does?"

"Even when there's nothing romantic to see," Roxy replied. He could almost see her defenses going up again.

"I had a nice time at the picnic and afterwards."

She looked around, then put a finger to her lips to silence him. Now wasn't the time to be talking to her about such matters. "How would you like to come over and watch the next episode of the show?"

"Me?" he jabbed a finger at himself. "Come to your place and watch the show? Are you sure?" This was unlike Roxy. Maybe she was starting to feel differently about him.

"Yes, why wouldn't I be?"

For someone who positively hated watching herself on TV, this was a huge advancement.

"You did something so nice for me, with the picnic." She

lowered her voice as if she didn't want anyone to hear. "So, I wanted to do something nice for you. It's not as grand as what you did."

"The picnic wasn't grand, Roxy. It was just a picnic."

"It meant a lot to me. I don't do things like that."

There it was, in her voice, the admission that she didn't do anything to recharge her soul or to replenish her batteries. She was battered, and worn out, and she deserved more.

"I would love to watch the show with you."

"Thursday at six, then."

"This is nice."

Mason looked around her kitchen, and she didn't believe him. What was nice? The tiny space that was so small? Her worktops and cupboards had none of the silver and black slickness of the shiny new appliances of his rented condo, or its stylish décor.

He was being nice and polite.

She handed him a bag of the clothes he'd lent her. "All washed."

He peeked inside the bag. "Glad to have been of help."

"You have helped. You've helped a lot." She shrugged, "I have to tell you, I didn't know how to outdo you. The picnic food you came up with was amazing."

"You don't have to outdo me, it's not a competition."

She pulled out her tray. "I made sea bass and vegetables."

"Now that," he pointed at the tray, "I would say that's you outdoing me and succeeding. Not that we're competing. I brought wine and lemonade."

"I have wine, too. The show starts soon. Shall we eat and watch?"

He helped her to set the table and take everything in. Then they sat down to eat. "Are you sure you're ready to watch yourself on TV with me here?"

She had been worried about this very thing, not about physically throwing up, but about baring her soul, making herself watch this with Mason of all people. She hadn't even been able to watch the show with her family, and they had invited her over every week.

Yet, it seemed to be a sign of things that it didn't seem to bother her as much as she thought it might. But as soon as the opening credits stopped rolling, and she saw herself on TV, she squealed.

While she had been slowly getting accustomed to seeing herself on TV more, during the episode that was now airing, she had looked a real mess. She took a big gulp from her wine glass.

"I like this." Mason thankfully lifted up his fork, indicating the sea bass.

"I cooked it with lemon butter and parsley with a hint of chili oil."

"It's perfectly done."

"Thank you."

They turned and stared at the screen again. As she watched, she couldn't help but notice that she and Mason weren't bickering anymore. They were being *normal*. He was the mentor, and she the mentee.

"It's noticeable, don't you think, the change in how we are around one another in front of the cameras, compared to how we used to be. Did you feel it, too?" she asked. Or had it just been her?

"I felt it. You can't miss something like that. My producer—"

He stopped, then lifted his wine glass to his lips. She waited.

"Did you pan fry these vegetables?"

"I roasted them in the oven with a touch of olive oil."

"They're very good."

"You were saying?" she prompted. "The producer. You were going to say something about him."

"Gerard. Oh, him. He told me that the other guy is suing me."

"You already told me." This had been the reason why she had decided to have him over despite having decided against it.

"It's almost like a different show," she said, waiting to hear his opinion but he was silent. "What do you think?"

"What do I think? The truth? My producer thinks we're lacking chemistry. He wants it back; the sizzle, the cutting remarks, me demeaning you. He said being nice doesn't entice people to watch."

She slumped back in her chair. "Is that what he said?" She had been blaming Mason about the ratings, thinking he was solely concerned about the audience size, but it wasn't just him. Others had their own vested interests.

"What do we do? Do we go back to that?"

"To how we were in the earlier episodes?" he asked softly. "I'm not going to do that. I told him I won't go back to that."

"But isn't your show based on that? Isn't that your trademark style? Being blunt and obnoxious."

A laugh hurtled out of him. "Obnoxious? Was I obnoxious to you?"

"A little." She was always on the lookout for validation, for kind words, for words that told her she was doing good.

He rubbed his hand across his brow. "I thought I had softened a little. We were supposed to tamp it down. People didn't like coming on shows to be humiliated."

"And now your producer thinks you've become too soft."

"I'm not going to be blunt and opinionated. I won't give him that."

She hadn't felt comfortable with the earlier shows, but now she felt as if she could learn because she wasn't always dreading what he might say to her. It hit her like a boulder, that the show was designed not to help people, but to show them to be failures, and that only the almighty Mason Brandt could save them.

He lifted his wine glass to his lips, his brow creasing as if he didn't like the thought of bowing to his producer's pressure.

"But the ratings, aren't they important? Don't they determine if a show gets axed or not?"

"I don't know what's important anymore, Roxy."

From his contemplative expression, she wondered what he was thinking about. She made a thoughtful noise, and didn't say anything.

"I'll revert to form with the others."

"Why not with me? If it helps your show, and … you have that other problem with the guy suing you."

"I'm not going to do it, Roxy."

"But if it helps with the ratings …." She hated that his ratings would fall because of this. It didn't seem right. She had been worried about getting her diner to be more profitable, and she hadn't for once considered that Mason would have problems of his own. She'd never seen him as someone who had problems, and now she was getting to see into his world, and that it wasn't all easy.

"To hell with the ratings." He set his cutlery down. "I couldn't do that to you." He stared at her for a moment longer than usual. It was on the tip of her tongue to ask him why, but she didn't.

Couldn't.

It would make it all real then. The tenuous feelings which kept her awake at night. The snippets of dialog between them which she replayed and analyzed and went through with a fine-tooth comb.

An electric current buzzed in the air between them, but she wondered if she was in an alternate universe and was the only one who felt it. It could not be real. Mason belonged to a different world, and soon he would be gone.

She waited for him to elaborate, and when he didn't, she thought it best not to ask him any more on the matter.

They finished the meal, skimming around the edges of the conversation she couldn't stop thinking about. Mason was going to treat the others with contempt, to boost his ratings, but not her.

That told her something, didn't it?

When the show ended, she heaved a sigh of relief. "That wasn't so bad."

"You get used to watching yourself on TV, I told you."

She rose and reached for his empty plate, but he didn't give it to her. Instead, he helped her to clear everything up.

She'd made crème brûlée, and they had their dessert sitting in her back yard, watching the sun set.

She lifted her shoulders, feeling that crick that always seemed to stick in the side of her shoulder, rendering it stiff. She was about to turn her head and do the head and neck exercises when she caught Mason staring at her.

"Stiff neck?"

"I get it sometimes."

He set down his glass and got up. "Mind if I try something?"

He stood behind her chair, while her heart hammered against her chest and she wasn't sure if her mind was playing tricks on her. "What … what are you going to do?" Her voice was shaky, and so unlike hers that she didn't recognize it.

"Tell me if it's too much." He placed his hands gently on either side of her shoulders, the touch making her almost sigh with something that wasn't relief. More like longing. He pressed down, not too hard, but with slight pressure, his thumbs kneading into her stiff muscles and making them malleable again. She shivered, but it wasn't from the cold, not on this warm summer's night.

"Aaahhh." The sigh escaped before she had a chance to stop it, Mason was finding every knot and undoing it with his magic touch. Her tension vanished with each press of his hands and fingers into her flesh.

"Good?"

She'd closed her eyes, her head starting to roll back as she felt the stiffening in her body disappear. "It's good," she murmured. "So, so, good."

He laughed. "Want me to keep doing this?"

"Uh…" She didn't want him to stop. Ever. And yet she couldn't bring herself to tell him she wanted more.

"I'll stop when you tell me," he said, making it easy for her. Probably knowing her better than she gave him credit for.

She didn't want him to stop. His movements loosened her up, softened the hardness that kept her together; his fingers unraveling the walls she kept up, bringing them down brick by brick.

"Is it helping?" His hands stilled on her, the heat from them making every cell in her body dance for joy. She didn't want him to move away. How could she have this man do this for hours?

Shameless thoughts tempted her. "It's so good, Mason. I can feel the tension unwinding."

His hands were still, and silence filled the night air.

She forced a giggle, because laughing seemed the best defense against telling him in this moment that the wine had loosened her tongue, and his fingers had removed the knots. She wanted him. She wanted more of him. Was he waiting for her to give him more instruction? She chewed her lip, contemplating how to. It was easy enough to hurl instructions at work, but to tell this man that she loved what he was doing? She couldn't bring herself to.

He started to massage her shoulders again and she sank back in her seat, her head flopping back slightly as her body turned boneless from head to toe.

This, wine, dinner, dessert, two chairs under an indigo night, this was the most perfect balmy summer evening she had ever had. The best thing about it? This man taking away her troubles, not only at work, but here, in the flesh. Easing, teasing out the things which pained her.

When enough time had passed, she, not trusting her voice, raised a hand and put it over his, stilling it.

"Is that enough?"

She nodded. Emotions twirled inside her, rising like a gentle breeze and threatening to turn into a cyclone if she didn't keep them in check.

Mason cleared his throat. "I should go. We're filming tomorrow," he explained, as if the two were related. It wasn't late, but he seemed to be justifying his need to leave.

She didn't want him to go, but she would have to say something to keep him here and saying something might mean having to tell him how she felt. How could she do that when she wasn't sure? Just because he'd taken a few knots out of her shoulders didn't mean he cared.

The man had been married to a woman who looked like a model. Why would Mason ever be interested in someone like her?

She stood up a little shakily, not because she'd had too much wine, but because he'd made her go weak at the knees.

"You okay?" He came over and reached for her arm. He stood in front of her, with his hands on her elbows, making sure she didn't buckle and fall back in her chair, and all she wanted was to throw her arms around him and beg him to stay.

But she wouldn't. Of course not. "Let me give you your clothes," is what she said instead.

"You already did, when I got here, remember?"

"I did?" Her fingers went to the back of her neck, getting ready to scratch an itch that was never there. "Oh, yes, I did." Was it too much wine or too much Mason that was fogging up her brain?

They walked back into the house, and he got his belongings. She walked him to the door.

"Thanks for a lovely evening."

"You're welcome."

The light from the lamp above illuminated his face, and his gaze held her captive. She couldn't move, didn't want to move, or look away. Wanted to hold onto this evening and cherish it for a moment longer.

Awkwardness settled over them like a thick blanket.

"I'll … uh … I'll see you tomorrow." She shoved her hands behind her, and clasped them, as if she was scared of doing something foolish. Like reaching for his hands, or putting them around his neck.

She would never, but the thought was as vivid in her mind right now as if it were real.

"See you tomorrow."

He leaned towards her, she wasn't sure what for, and by the time she realized that he was going to kiss her on the cheek, the shock of his nearness confused her completely. She forgot to turn her face and ended up kissing him on the lips.

It was short, and quick, and shock filled.

"Sorry," she mumbled, her lips ablaze with that one-second press of his lips. "I was trying to …"

"I know." She didn't need him to spell it out for her. Embarrassment stunned her into silence, so that as he walked down the steps, giving her a backward glance, all she could do was lift her arm to wave.

CHAPTER 30

He couldn't stop that smile from setting on his face. It was permanent.

He had intended to kiss her on the cheek; a normal, regular, safe-as-a-security-blanket peck on the cheek. A thank-you-for-this-evening kiss.

He hadn't intended to do *that*. Even though the thought had crossed his mind.

Massaging Roxy's shoulders, feeling those itty-bitty tight knots and kneading them away, he'd wondered if he would ever get a chance to kiss her.

Properly.

He had missed her cheek—because he'd taken her completely by surprise—and he'd ended up with a peck on the lips.

The lips. But it was the sort of short and hasty kiss young children would give to their grandparents.

Or the type of kiss a husband and wife who'd been married for decades had before they left for work. The type of kiss Monique had started to give him long before he had realized their marriage was in trouble.

He shook his head, wanting to get every annoying thing about Monique out of his brain.

He was still gliding on air the next day when he saw Roxy at the diner. He and Roxy said nothing about 'that' kiss, even though furtive glances and knowing smiles passed between them.

Later, as the cameras rolled, and their interactions were fused with more knowing, he wondered if the audience, if Gerard, and others, would be able to tell.

He could.

But it was a telling that couldn't be explained in mere words. It was defined by a myriad of emotions and feelings. He now hung his head in shame when he remembered the way he had treated Roxy in the early days.

As the week passed, he met with Hailey and Jax, and one evening, on a Thursday, Roxy agreed to watch the next episode at Hailey's place.

If Hailey and Jax noticed anything different in the show, they didn't say.

Roxy maintained an air of detachment in the diner, and in front of her brother and his girlfriend.

It was only in the car, when she later drove him back to his place, that the veil dropped.

The air was lighter, freer. The pretense—previously all business-like—vanished.

"Are we different on the show again?" she asked as they reached the parking lot in Forest Heights. She turned the engine off.

"Do you think we're different?"

She giggled. "You can't answer my question with a question."

The sky was inky, and as he turned to her, he couldn't see her face. He wanted to take her hand, but he couldn't decipher her expression clearly, and he didn't want to make a mistake and read something that wasn't there.

What if that accidental kiss was what Roxy wanted and nothing more? Aside from his own feelings, he had no way of knowing how she felt and until such a time as they discussed their feelings—if such a time would ever come—he would always be none the wiser.

"Yes, I think we're different. It's been like that a while now."

"Is your producer handling it okay?"

"I don't know." He didn't care to ask Gerard, and Gerard hadn't said anything to him, but he expected to hear some grumbling from him soon. "I was going to go to the farmers' market this Sunday. Would you … are you … I mean …"

"Yes."

"Yes?" That was fast. He'd bumbled his way into asking her —he could woo a woman he didn't know with more confidence than he needed—and he had struggled to ask Roxy if she would want to come to a farmers' market with him. "You haven't even checked your roster."

"I'm working that day, but I can fix it. I'll get someone to cover for me."

Now that was an answer he hadn't expected.

CHAPTER 31

It was a good long drive to the farmers' market near Whisper Falls.

Roxy couldn't believe that Mason had driven all this way before just to visit it, but now she was overjoyed that he had asked her to come along. She had never asked anyone in years to take her shift on a Sunday. It was usually the other way round; she was the one who filled in for others.

The last time she had, Jax had filled in for her when she had fallen ill with the flu.

That she had jumped at this chance when Mason had asked her was telling in itself. Life was no longer centered around work because Mason was giving her something else to be excited about.

He had offered to drive and had picked her up. Along the way, they talked about her business and the progress she was making. It wasn't a monumental shift, but it was enough for her to see that the things she was implementing, the changes he suggested she make, were having a positive effect. She had more customers, more income as well as more bookings for the catering side of her business.

She had plans to look for extra staff, specifically moms of young children who wanted on-call work to do once in a while, who could help out so that she and her diner employees wouldn't end up doing twenty-hour days on those days when she had events to cater for.

She was also planning to get the diner revamped. A fresh lick of paint, new furniture, new signage. And an overhaul for the kitchen, which would be her costliest expense.

These were just some of the things that Mason had suggested.

As he drove, during long stretches of silence, she wondered if he ever thought about that night at her house, the night he'd massaged her shoulders and had accidentally kissed her.

She wondered if that night would be turn into a fading memory, or whether it had the potential to lead to something more. She hoped it would, but she held back from ever doing or saying anything, rather, she waited on the sidelines, hoping and dreaming. And every time she dared to dream, she forced herself to remember his ex-wife, the tall and beautiful Monique.

And Mackenzie, also tall and beautiful.

It was as if she purposely fed her mind these magazine-cover images as a self-preservation tactic; to remind herself of who she was. And, who she was, was *not* like those women, and therefore not someone that Mason would be interested in.

That accidental kiss had been just that, *an accident.*

But why had he asked her to come to the market with him today?

"To buy apricots and pistachios."

"What?" Mason looked at her as if she'd lost her mind. "What did you say?"

Heat burned her cheeks as she realized that she had said this out aloud. "This is where you bought the apricots and pistachios from, wasn't it?" The art of smooth deflection was one she had honed over the years. "For those sausage rolls you made."

"Oh, yes. They were from here. Did you want to get some?"

"Sure." She'd have to now.

He frowned. "You okay?"

She laughed nervously. "Yes. I'm curious to see what it's like. Shall we listen to some music?"

"Yes." If it sounded rude for her to suggest it, he didn't show it. He turned on the radio and she was grateful to have some noise to fill the quiet and give her something else to think about, instead of that evening when he'd come over for dinner.

Wide streets lined with trees were dotted with rows of small tents, all lined up neatly with brightly colored produce on display.

They pulled into the parking lot. "This is a big market."

"It's going to take us all day to get through this."

She couldn't think of a better way to spend the day.

They stopped by each and every stall, but she was enthralled watching Mason handle the fruits and vegetables, picking them up and smelling them, feeling them, checking the texture, the size, examining them and taking so long doing all of this that sometimes she'd slope off to a nearby stall only to come back and find him looking at other things at the same stall.

They both bought things, herbs, fruit and vegetables. She, for the diner, but Mason for himself. He bought so many things.

"How many people are you cooking for?" He had two bags of food, one in each arm.

"I love to cook."

"For an army, it looks like."

When they both had too many things to easily carry, they returned to his car and offloaded their bags. Being the super-organized person that she was beginning to discover he was, he had brought the hamper complete with cold packs in it, so that they were able to keep the food cold.

Then they wandered around, bought hot food, freshly cooked

right there on the street. A delicious chicken and veggie wrap for her, an artisan bread and beef sandwich for him.

Strolling around the market like this was such a wonderful way to spend the day, she wondered why she hadn't ever done this before. In time they walked the full length on either side, not missing a single stall and by the time they came to the end of the street, having doubled back, they'd been through the entire market.

"We don't have many episodes left to film," he said, a touch of wistfulness in his voice.

"I feel sad thinking about it, and I never thought I would ever feel sad about it."

They wandered into a park; the grass had been freshly cut and it smelled like summer.

"That's pretty."

In the distance a gazebo decked in fairy lights twinkled near a clump of trees. It looked like a grotto, so pretty that it almost didn't look real. She was drawn to it. "Can we take a look?"

"We can do whatever you want."

She walked up the two steps and into the gazebo. It was too picturesque not to capture on her phone. She pulled out her cellphone and took a picture of it. "Mind if I take one of you?" Mason had his back to her and seemed to be surveying the park outside. Taking a picture was so much better if there was a person in it, and a picture of Mason would be all she'd have left once he was gone.

He turned around and whipped out his own cellphone. "We should both be in it."

They positioned themselves near a wooden pillar around which fairy lights were draped, but standing together, they lost the fairy lights in the background.

"This way," she angled her face just so, but it still cut out the lights.

"Do you need the lights?"

"I have to have the lights."

"Try this." Mason put his arm around her and pressed her gently towards him. This way she could see more of the lights. They twisted and turned, moving their heads this way and that, until the image was perfect; just the two of them, looking so happy, and a string of lights all around them in the background.

He snapped a few pictures, and she asked him to send them to her so she would have copies.

"Better, no? With both of us in it?" He showed her the images.

She smiled, agreeing. These photos said so much more. They looked like they were together. She looked up at him, and his gaze dropped to her lips, before he quickly loosened his hold on her. Then he pressed some buttons on his phone. "You should have them. Check."

She didn't need to check. She heard the notifications pinging on her phone. She wanted to linger in this moment and have it be etched on her mind forever.

"Was it worth it?" he asked her.

"Coming here? Yes, for sure." Just like the other day at her house, this one would also be a memory to cherish.

"And coming on my show?"

"It was one hundred percent worth it. You've changed so many things for me."

"Good." He nodded, his eyes searching hers for answers, as if there were other meanings hidden beneath his questions. "That's good to know. I'm glad I helped a little."

"A little? You helped a lot."

"No," he shook his head. "It was all you. I merely steered you."

"You're nothing like how I thought you would be." Her voice was almost a whisper.

"And you," her eyes widened as he shifted an inch closer. "You're not as hard as I thought."

"No?" She could barely breathe. Not because he was suffocating her, but for another reason. Confusion mingled with yearning as his scent, his closeness, the memory of that night, of the press of his lips on hers spun around her like a web of seduction.

"It's a front. Your granite armor. Inside, you're all soft and fragile, Roxy."

"Keep that thought to yourself. It wouldn't do for my staff to know I'm soft. I'm hoping that some of your success has rubbed off on me. Even if it's a teeny bit, it will make a big difference. If I forget to thank you later, I'm really thankful for all the advice you've given me."

He looked into her eyes, and her heart almost tripped a beat when he cupped her face, his warm hand a welcome touch to a face that hadn't been touched by anyone else in years. She had forgotten what it was like.

"You have to know something about me, Roxy. I'm not the success you think I am. My ex-wife is getting half of everything I worked for, my restaurants aren't doing as well as they used to and if I don't figure things out, I'm going to have to close some of them. I haven't had a book deal in years, and I'm already considered a has-been. That's why my TV show has to do well. It's my only chance of making a comeback."

She almost slumped with the weight of his confession. Words she hadn't expected, words she didn't quite believe sank into her, changing all the things she thought she knew about this man. She placed her hand on his hand and reached for the other one. He looked so deflated that it shook her, because she had never seen him like this, and she wondered if he'd kept that inside him the whole time.

"You're not a failure."

"I'm not the success you think I am."

"You're a man of high standards. You're a success in my books."

One moment she was looking into his eyes, and then the next their lips were joined. She fell against him, the sudden melding of his body against hers not fully hitting her until his hands slid around her waist. His mouth was sweet, his kiss unexpected, like a burst of sunshine during autumn.

He was just a man, stripped away, he was like her, he had his vulnerabilities. She had assumed him to be superman, but he wasn't. He was just a man.

And she had kissed him.

CHAPTER 32

She lost track of time as they kissed in that gazebo, and only when the sky turned dark, and the lamp lights came on in the park, did they realize they had spent the entire day out.

He drove her home, and they kissed again in the car before she got out. He waited until she had turned the key and gone into her house before he drove away.

No sooner had she walked in when someone knocked on her door. She opened it to find Mason standing there with the picnic hamper.

They had forgotten to sort out the food.

Did this man never forget anything? She pulled out her shopping from the hamper, and he was soon on his way.

That night, she didn't sleep well, but this time it wasn't from fretting about worrisome things, it was because Mason Brandt had changed the trajectory of her mundane life. For now. For as long as he was here.

During the week, it became even harder for her and Mason to hide their true feelings for one another.

At one time, she'd flinched when they were discussing

something, and he'd looked at her knowingly, a sexy smile on his lips as he waited for her to finish glazing the chicken pies.

She tried to imagine it, how he would have been if he had still been the old Mason, but that man now seemed like a ghost.

She no longer waited to catch a glimpse of Mason, hoping he would pass by on his days off, because they saw one another for dinner every evening. A few times, he would come to her place, or she would go over to his, or they would eat out. She went to Fellini's with him, on a proper date to the place which had once been reserved strictly for important family occasions.

One evening, she was summoned to her parents' house for dinner. Having put them off for so long, she decided she could no longer keep avoiding them.

Luckily for her, Jax and Hailey were also over.

She had been meaning to tell Hailey of the new developments in her life, but she hadn't had a chance, and she wasn't eager to discuss that at her parents' place where her mother's keen hearing would pick up even the minutest of exchanges.

"Pass the sauce, please, honey." She did as her mother asked.

"We watched you on the show the other night." Her father declared. "I'm not sure I like that man."

"Mason is a lovely man." Hailey jumped to Mason's defense without hesitation.

"He's a great dude, Dad," Jax chimed in.

Roxy's mom set down her cutlery. "But he's so rude. I hate the way he's so disrespectful to Roxy."

"It's nothing I can't handle, Mom. He's better now though." Then, desperate to change the subject, "Have you watched all the episodes?" She was anxious to find out if they had seen all the ones that had aired.

"Not all of them. We're running a bit behind. We've got them recorded though."

Roxy didn't know whether to be relieved or indignant that her parents couldn't even be bothered to keep up with her TV show.

"He seems calmer now, but oh, my goodness, that fire in the kitchen. The way he treated you was so wrong. If I ever meet that man," her mother stabbed a fork in her direction, using it like a weapon.

"He's really not that bad, Mom."

Her father pointed a knife at her. "I told you not to do it."

"I'm glad I did. I've learned a lot from him," She turned to Hailey and Jax for backup.

"Some of the things he said to you, Roxy," her mother continued. "I'm surprised you didn't throw something at him."

"He can be short. It's his style, Mom."

"Pfft. Style, hmph," her mother scoffed.

Roxy looked at her plate and couldn't help but smile. From the corner of her eyes, she detected Hailey looking at her.

"He's very easy on the eye, I'll give him that. I could find myself warming up to him."

"Mom!" Jax cried.

"Warming up to him?" Her father lifted his glass of water to his lips. "What are you talking about?"

"He is easy on the eye. I'm only saying what's right. Don't you think he's easy on the eye, Hailey?"

Jax put his arm around Hailey's shoulder, an odd and rather protective feat, given that they were both still in the middle of eating their dinner. "Mason's a lovely man."

"He gets better, I promise." Roxy tried to swallow the piece of chicken that she had been chewing for a good few minutes but was having trouble getting down.

"He'd better," her father threatened. "I can't have him treating my daughter like that on national TV."

Later, when they were clearing the table, and Jax was loading the dishwasher, Hailey pulled her to one side.

"What's happened to Mason? He's acting very different. I wonder if he's depressed. Does he seem down to you?"

"What? No." She was surprised by Hailey's conclusion. Setting down the dirty plates in her hand because they were so heavy, she motioned for Hailey to follow her out of the kitchen again. Their parents were thankfully watching TV.

"Why do you think he's depressed?" Could Hailey not see how happy he was?

"He didn't take too well to the divorce. Mason has always been about winning. The breakdown of his marriage has hit him hard."

"Are you helping me or what?" Jax cried out.

Hailey rushed away, leaving Roxy to ponder over the last few weeks, some of the best of her life, in order to see what she had missed.

CHAPTER 33

*R*oxy was avoiding eye contact.

They had the usual easygoing conversation in front of the cameras, but lately they'd had to be careful. A couple of times they had slipped up. He'd almost reached for her hand as she was passing him a tray of tarts, and he had almost tucked a lock of hair behind her ear when it had snuck out and dangled in front of her face as she had rolled out pastry.

Today she was different. Avoiding him. And the jokes and chemistry of late had vanished.

When the camera crew had left, he knocked on the door of her office, where she had snuck off to. He opened the door and poked his head in. "Got a minute?"

She wasn't doing anything as far as he could make out. Her screensaver was on, indicating that she hadn't touched her keyboard for a while. Her desk looked clear.

"Come in."

She lifted a hand to the back of her shoulder. Maybe she had been about to do those neck exercises he'd caught her doing once.

"Are your shoulders tight again?" He was ready to relieve her tension and put that to right at once, she just had to say the word.

She immediately dropped her hand. "No, I'm good."

"So," a humorless laugh escaped his mouth. Something was off. The tempo, the mood, the vibe. He racked his brains, trying to think what he'd done wrong.

"What did you want to see me about?"

He stood on the other side of her desk, placing his hands palm down on the surface, his eyes pinning her. "What just happened in there?"

"Where?"

"During filming. You barely looked at me." He hadn't meant for it to sound like an accusation but it had. He didn't like playing games. Life with Monique had turned out to be one big game which he had lost. He didn't want that anymore. Roxy was down to earth, what you saw was what you got. She didn't hide behind fancy airs and graces. So her distance earlier had come as a shock to him. "You're closed off. It's like the last few weeks didn't mean anything."

"I was about to start planning for the next month," she offered, her voice dull, but he could see right through her. They had been spending a lot of time together, and this was pure deflection.

She wasn't about to start strategizing about how to grow her bottom line, right now, in the middle of a busy day. She had plenty of time to do that in the evenings, and when they'd talked over dinner. He had gone through her goals, and given her actionable advice, telling her of the small things she could do that, over time, would lead to greater returns.

The worry in her eyes ate away at his heart and he wondered if she was having doubts about him. He was also aware that the show was coming to an end, but it didn't mean that his time here had to. He had no desire to rush back to the location for the next shoot.

"Do you ..." her voice tapered off.

"Say it." She looked so fragile, so unlike the Roxy he had come to know, that he was suddenly scared. "What, Roxy?" He bent down, his face level with hers. "You can tell me anything, you know that." He took her hand, but she pulled hers away.

"Are you still in love with your wife?" Her eyes searched his face frantically.

He hadn't seen that question coming. At all. And now he wondered what could have possessed her to even think it.

Monique had been so far off his mind that she might as well have been a stranger. Curiosity got the better of him. "Why are you asking this?"

"I don't want to be a rebound relationship. If you're using me because you're lonely, or because you—"

He pulled her to her feet and kissed her hair. Held her to his chest, his arms snug around her waist. "Using you? Roxy, really? I haven't thought of Monique until you mentioned her. She'd been gone from my life way before we divorced."

Roxy chewed her lip.

"You are not a rebound anything. I am not using you. I'm with you because I want to be, and because you've let me in, at last."

She gazed up at him, a flicker of disbelief crossing her face. "Do you mean that?" Her voice was shaky.

He moved away a little, giving her space so she didn't need to arch her neck too much, and because he wanted to look at her. Hers was the face he saw in his mind's eye before he went to sleep, and it was also the first he saw when he woke up. The reason he had come to Starling Bay had slipped into the background, and the only reason he wanted to not leave was now in his arms, wondering if he cared about her.

"Can you not tell? Everyone says I've changed, but I'll be the same with the others. I'll be the same rude man shouting orders and humiliating the people who dare to come on my show. I just can't do that with you. I don't want to. I can't see you upset. And if I'm different around you, it's because I feel different around you. You've changed me."

He dipped his head lower, desperate to kiss her, but conscious of where they were. Her eyes narrowed, even as she slid her hands around his back.

"I want to kiss you," he murmured.

"Then you'll have to come over for dinner."

"How about this time you come to me? I'll make dinner and work those knots out of your shoulders again." Her eyes widened briefly, a flicker of anticipation dancing across her irises. His heart bloomed inside his chest. He could get used to this slower pace of life, with Roxy, watching the sun set in the back yard.

She'd worried for no reason.

How this was going to turn out wasn't something Roxy wanted to think about, but Mason had told her that he didn't think about his ex-wife.

That was good enough for her.

She had to believe in herself the way Mason believed in her. She compared herself to people like Monique and people like Mackenzie—even when the poor girl hadn't even done anything and had no idea that Roxy was even getting worked up about her. For too long she had placed her measure by others and it had to stop, because it didn't serve her.

Mason was interested in her, for *her*.

Next weekend, she had a small house party, someone's fortieth, that she was catering for. It would be an easy one. Having helped out at Reed's engagement party had prepared her well.

Her new tiered menu was a hit, and the hosts had—to her surprise and delight—opted for the upscale package. It didn't take her any longer to make shrimp cocktails—something which had been a staple on her menus—than it did to prepare sea bass on blinis with Ossetra caviar and cream.

Thanks to Mason, she not only had new and different dishes she could offer, but she could charge much more for them.

He had offered to help her at this event but she needed to stop getting used to having him around. It was something that had preyed on her mind lately, more and more as their time together was coming to an end.

How she wished they had started from the beginning like they were now. It didn't seem fair. She had finally met someone, had allowed herself to trust and open up to someone, and they didn't have long left together.

Mason would leave soon enough and she would be left with nothing but memories of a summer romance.

CHAPTER 34

He met with Gerard at the Blue Velvet Bar on Saturday night.

It was more to kill the time than a great desire to see his friend. Roxy was busy catering for a fortieth birthday party and had told him she didn't need him to help out.

"What's going on, Mason?"

Distracted, he finished off sending a 'Good luck' text to Roxy. "What do you mean?"

"You're not sniping at one another."

"I don't see why I need to. The ratings aren't as bad as you're making out."

"But there's definitely something else. A spark. Something new and different from the early edits I've seen of the latest shows."

"Shouldn't you be happy, then?" Mason rested his head against the plush leather of his seat. Glasses clinked, laughter rippled, and chatter flowed around the bar.

"I am happier. Honest to goodness, Mason, you're all over the place with this. I'm not sure if it's the format, or something else.

This show seems to be less about the cooking and more about the metamorphosis the candidate is growing through."

"The candidate?" Mason's voice was serious. "Don't call her that."

"Roxy, then."

"And don't say it like that." A newfound sense of protectiveness was growing in him. Gerard looked at him for a moment that stretched out uncomfortably.

"Is there something going on? Is that what the camera's picking up?" Surprise glinted in Gerard's eyes and he raised an eyebrow.

"Does the 'spark' work for you?"

"Oh, it works, it definitely works."

"Good." He wasn't about to give anything away. What went on between him and Roxy was no one's business but theirs.

It was a crazy world he lived in, one in which he spent some time letting the camera share a part of his working life, while the rest of the time he wanted his privacy.

For Roxy's sake too, he wasn't going to discuss what they had with anyone.

"I'm not asking anything, Mason. I'm just letting you know that this new chemistry of yours is working. Whatever you're doing, keep doing it."

"Yeah." He checked his phone to see if Roxy had replied. She hadn't, and he assumed that she was too busy.

"Buffalo Bill is in discussions with us again." Mason lifted his head at this new announcement. "He's considering holding off on the lawsuit if he'll be the next one on."

"Sure. He was next on the list anyway. I don't know why he jumped up and down when we replaced him with Roxy."

"He jumped up and down," Gerard said tightly, "because we'd signed and everything was ready to go."

"Aren't you glad we switched?" He saw Reed walk in with his fiancée and raised a hand in acknowledgment.

Gerard popped a couple of peanuts in his mouth. "Hell, I'm glad we switched. She works, and the location is great. It's different, but she works."

"Her name is Roxy."

Gerard studied his face for a moment, opened his mouth as if he were about to say something, then thought better of it and popped another peanut into his mouth again.

"Roxy is a great start to the series," he said, finally. "As always, we're going to need to end with a bang."

The cliffhanger. A dramatic way to close the last show. Gerard wanted tears and emotion, with the restaurant owner proclaiming how Mason had changed their life. He wasn't eager to give Gerard the drama he wanted.

It wasn't so much the case that he had changed things for Roxy and her diner, but that she had changed things for him.

The series drawing to a close was something he didn't want to think about it. Shooting would take place in New York next, but it could work; traveling back and forth between Starling Bay and New York on weekends.

Whatever it took.

Whatever this was between him and Roxy.

With Monique, it had been different. Theirs had been a heady, dizzying romance. Their eyes had met across the room of a decadent Parisian restaurant. He'd sent a bottle of champagne over. She'd asked to speak to him privately. They'd started seeing one another a few days later.

With Roxy, it was all so different. It had been a journey of discovery. Slow going, getting to know her first, understanding her fears and her hopes, understanding her. He felt confident that this was the start of something beautiful.

~

Later that evening, as he got changed into his PJs, he was about to text Roxy to see how she was doing, but he was interrupted by a persistent knocking on his door.

It was a déjà vu moment, reminiscent of that last time she had come knocking, only then she had been outraged. Hopeful that it was her again, he rushed to open the door.

But he jolted back, shock jump-starting every cell in his body.

"Mason, darling." Her hair was immaculate, her makeup perfect, and she was dressed in haute couture, completely out of place for where she was. Monique at his door knocked the breath right out of his lungs. She walked into his stunned silence, hooking her arm around his neck and was about to kiss him on the lips. He moved his face to the side and her lips planted on his cheek.

He stepped back. "What are you doing here?"

"I missed you." She sashayed in, with her Louis Vuitton wheeled trolley bag.

"What. Are. You. Doing. Here?" he repeated. What in the world had possessed her to come all this way?

They were so done.

So over.

He had no space for her in his heart let alone his mind.

She kicked off her stilettoes, slid off her jacket, gazed at him with puppy dog eyes. "I want to try again. I want to make this work, Mason. I miss you. I made a mistake."

"Does Remy know you're here?" Remy, the friend in whose arms she had sought solace. Mason didn't fully know the ins and outs of their relationship, but he did know that he would never have sought comfort in the arms of another woman, even if, as Monique had claimed, he listened to her.

She shot him a hard glance. "You worked all the time, Mason. What did you expect me to do?"

"Going running to one of your past lovers would have been a good thing *not* to do."

"If you had been around, I would have gone to you," she said sarcastically.

"I've moved on. This is a bad idea you coming here."

"Can't we at least talk?" She wrung her hands, her long and perfectly manicured talons another confirmation of her high-maintenance life. A life he wanted no part of. The shock of her sudden appearance numbed him to the point that he didn't know what to do.

He shook his head. "Nothing to talk about."

"I've had too much time to think. I'm so lonely, Mason. I need you back."

He'd given her three years of his life, even if the last one had been spent in separation while he had tried to make her see that he could be different. While he had pleaded with her that he would make it up to her, that he would spend more time on *them*. In his desperation to fix their marriage, he had slacked off working, hadn't pursued the things that kept his business ticking over. His opportunities had dried up, and he had suffered, but she hadn't relented.

Her showing up now wasn't going to change a thing.

"I'm not coming back, not to France, not to you. I've moved on," he said softly.

"In this place? You who could live anywhere, and you come here?"

"I don't stay in one place for too long, wasn't that one of the problems you had with my career?"

"My father says you are stubborn."

He tilted his chin, curious to know what that old dinosaur had to do with any of this. "Your father is right."

She walked towards him. "He also told me that I hadn't been supportive."

The man had just gone up in his estimation.

"You worked hard for us, and I didn't see that." She reached up and touched his face. He shuddered at her touch. Her cold hands were not the ones he wanted on his skin. Her perfume, sickly sweet and cloying, assaulted his nostrils.

"With his patronage, you can set up again, somewhere near the Seine. Think about it, Mason. You are so talented, you can earn a Michelin star, even two, or three."

That she considered earning Michelin stars to be as easy as that made him stifle a smile.

"Wouldn't that pose the same problem? Me working all the hours and not having enough time to spend with you?"

"But I would learn to live with it. I would understand why you do what you do. You're a talented man, Mason. I can't hold you back. I shouldn't hold you back. And if we have children ... I would be busy raising them."

He almost recoiled. The idea of having children with Monique repulsed him. Now that he had truly spent time away and the divorce was final, he could see that they hadn't been right for one another from the start. No amount of her father's help—which he would never have agreed to—or her suggestion to try to make their relationship work, would fix what was fundamentally wrong in the first place; they were two different people who had nothing in common aside from good looks and an appreciation of the finer things in life.

And even that had changed, for him.

Fancy restaurants weren't as appealing to him now. He loved the outdoors, he loved nothing more than strolling around a farmers' market with Roxy, eating a wrap, or going on a picnic.

He had a different outlook on things now that he had been forced to slow down.

Monique wasn't the answer, and the truth was, she had never been.

She moved forward, taking his hands in hers. He removed his hands from her grasp and placed them on her arms, maintaining a distance, his eyes leveled with hers.

"It was a mistake for you to come here. I don't want to try to make us work. I don't think we were right for one another in the first place and I have no desire to make the same mistake twice."

Anger charged in her heated glance. "You don't even want to try? You who begged me for so long to make it work?"

"I did try," he said, remembering. "But you weren't interested."

"I told you, I made a mistake."

"You deserve to be happy, but we can't make one another happy and it is wrong of you to think we have a future together."

Her eyes turned glassy. "I was ... I was broken, Mason. You seemed to love your work more. You didn't give me any attention."

"Remy did, though."

"It was nothing. We were good friends."

"I was your husband."

"But you weren't there for me emotionally or physically," she wailed.

"I tried to be, after. I slacked off and I tried. You're the one who gave up on us first."

"And I'm here to tell you that I won't give up again. I want to try, and I want you to still be my husband."

"I don't want to be your husband," he threw back, his voice quiet.

She was quiet for the longest time. He could almost hear her brain whirring, spinning a reason for his reluctance to entertain her request. A laugh erupted from her. "You've met someone."

"You should go."

"You have met someone."

"You should leave, Monique." He didn't want to give her the chance to hook her claws into Roxy.

She started to unbutton her dress. The shrew. She'd carefully considered her outfit for this event. A flimsy summer dress with tiny buttons in the middle along the front which she could tantalizingly undo and which would cause the dress to fall off easily.

He grabbed her wrists, stopping her from undoing the third button. "Don't." Aware of his hold on her dainty hands, he loosened his grip. "I am not in love with you. I have no intention of spending my life with you, and I don't want to waste my time even thinking about it."

Harsh words, but true, because that was the only thing she would understand. She stared at him blankly, as if she had lost everything.

"How can you be so cruel? I've come all this way."

"I didn't ask you to."

"But I'm here now."

"Leave."

"And go where?" She buttoned up her dress, her angry face staring back at him. She had brought this on herself, this mess, this unnecessary journey and he hated that she expected him to deal with it. He had a different life now,

"Sleep in the spare bedroom, But I want you to leave first thing in the morning." He couldn't throw her out, but he could leave. He would leave, if it came to that.

CHAPTER 35

The next day, Roxy woke up later than usual. With no shift at the diner, she decided to do something spontaneous. Something with Mason.

She sat up in bed. She would prepare a picnic and show up at his place. They could go back to the picnic spot by the lake and hopefully this time there would be no rain to ruin it.

The idea so grabbed her that she jumped out of bed, and within the hour was showered and dressed and had started to prepare a picnic that would be something like the one Mason had.

It was ten thirty by the time she arrived at Mason's place. She was torn between leaving the hamper in the car, where it would be easier to grab before heading towards the lake, or taking it to his place first. Mason might want to have a lazy morning and have the picnic later in the day. She decided to take the hamper with her.

With a giddying sense of excitement, she knocked on his door. "We're having a picnic!" she cried, but her enthusiasm vanished when she saw his face. At first, she thought he hadn't slept. That he maybe had been out all night with the TV crew, because she had never seen him look so rough before.

"Mason, where is the sugar?"

The sound of the female voice chilled her to the bone. And then a woman walked past in the distance behind Mason's shoulder, wearing a nightshirt.

Roxy blinked. She dropped the hamper. It hit the floor with a SPLAT! Her mind ran riot, calculating the possibilities of what this was. What it meant. Who it was. She glanced at Mason.

"I..." He seemed stunned into silence, no words came out of his mouth, which seemed to have dried up, just like her throat which had suddenly become parched.

"Mason, where is the sugar?" It was French. That accent. And the woman was now more recognizable as she walked towards the door, coming slowly into view, the women whom Roxy had seen in online photos.

Mason's ex-wife.

Roxy didn't know whether to pick up the hamper and flee. Her eyes settled on the woman who was now standing beside the speechless Mason. A flash of anger shot through her. Her eyes couldn't unsee the woman's long legs, or that she wore a sexy nightshirt. No ordinary cotton, or flannel striped nightshirt, of the type Roxy was used to wearing, but something made from silk, or satin, in a sexy deep red color, with half sleeves and tiny butterflies.

Something that only a 'Monique' would wear.

"This is the woman who is on your show?" the woman asked Mason. Mason's face hardened, but Roxy couldn't help but notice the familiarity between him and Monique, or the way she leaned against him, and the way in which he didn't flinch. If she didn't know any better, she would never have known they were divorced.

Something tight gripped her vocal cords, her chest, her lungs —she couldn't breathe, she couldn't speak.

She turned and fled as fast as she could.

~

He picked up the hamper from the doorstep, his knuckles tight, his gut churning. The sight of Roxy rushing to get away filled him with fury. His steely, hard-to-contain patience had vanished. He wanted to call her back, tell her to wait, while he sent Monique on her way.

But he couldn't. He had frozen. Faced with Roxy, with Monique in his kitchen, he hadn't known what to do. Rage coursed through his body, threatening to burst his veins and arteries.

"Found it!"

Monique held the jar up for him to see.

He had to keep it together, otherwise the anger would drive him to destruction. He fought the urge to hurl the picnic hamper against the wall, to slam his fists onto the table. Who did his ex-wife think she was, pirouetting into his home, sucking up his newfound happiness, and leaving a trail of debris the likes of which he might never recover from?

Because he had seen the sheer distrust and disbelief in Roxy's eyes just before she had turned and run.

"Get dressed and leave," he said quietly, walking towards his ex. His fisted hands with the skin stretched so tightly across his knuckles were the only indication of the riot of emotions in his head.

Monique started pouring hot water into a cup, ignoring him.

"Did you hear me? GO!" He set the hamper on the island, struggling to stay calm. Roxy had surprised him. She'd planned a picnic.

What a beautiful day it could have been.

"Who was that?"

Monique walked over, with her cup in her hand, her inquisitive gaze going to the hamper. "You ordered this?"

Eyes widening, he tried to fathom what she was talking about.

"Oh, Mason!" Setting down her cup, she opened the hamper, her squeals of delight piercing his ears as she nosed inside it.

Did she honestly think he had ordered a hamper for them to have a picnic? Her claws hooked inside and she started looking through it.

He wanted to yell at her. He wanted to tell her to stop, to take her hands off everything, but it would be easier for her to believe *this*, than for him to tell her the truth—and she didn't deserve the truth.

Roxy did. Roxy. The hurt in her eyes had twisted his heart, wringing it like a dirty dishrag.

This could be so easily explained but he had to find her and talk to her. Alone.

"This is so sweet of you, Mason." Monique took out the tiny parcels that Roxy had so lovingly and carefully put together.

He suddenly realized that she was wearing a flimsy nightshirt, the first glimpse he'd had of her in it. Roxy would have seen her and thought of a different scenario altogether.

He needed to tell her, he needed to go after her and quickly.

"These are delicious." Monique was eating what looked like a sea bass blini. It took a heroic shift of restraint for him to not yank the hamper away. She was rummaging through it like a feral fox.

He was torn. If she had been a man, he could have thrown her out. How could he get this woman to leave without laying a hand on her?

He looked at the woman who had once been his wife and wondered how he had ever loved her.

Love was blind.

Even though he'd told her to leave first thing, she obviously had no intention of listening to him. He stared out the window, thinking of the time he had wasted, of falling in love and becoming swept up with Monique, in the wrong country with the wrong woman, doing the wrong things for his life.

"Where did you want to have this?" she asked him, as if this was a normal day and they were normal people. Ignoring her, he opened the veranda doors, needing to breathe fresh air, needing freedom and an escape from Monique's clutches.

She was like a leech, stuck to him, and all he could think of was how to fix things with Roxy, because she was the one who mattered.

"This is as good as you make it." Monique's hand slipped around his waist, and in her other she held a half-eaten tart. Roxy must have had leftovers from the event last night. Any pleasure he felt that Roxy had served the types of canapés he'd introduced her to vanished as Monique's fingers squeezed his side.

Overcome with rage, paralyzed by the dilemma of what to do and feeling trapped in his own condo, he grabbed her hand and flung it away.

"What ... why are you—" Her voice wavered a little bit. He didn't answer, didn't look at her. He grabbed the iron railing hard, trying to remain calm and not lose it.

"It's not a hamper for us, is it?" she countered. "These are your creations."

She wasn't stupid. She had figured it out.

"That woman who came, she's the owner. She's on your show."

"And what if she is?" he growled, making the type of noise a cornered dog might make.

"This picnic was for you both." The inflection in her words indicated her surprise as she unraveled the final piece of the puzzle. "She did this for you."

He chose not to respond, not wanting to give her any bait.

"What's happened to you, Mason?" Displeasure mixed with jealousy and stuck in her throat. "Your standards are slipping."

He raised himself to his full six foot two inches, his muscles tightening as he fought to remain calm. "On the contrary, I found something precious."

"She's so ..." Her mouth twisted as she tried to find the words to lacerate him with. "She's so *plain.* "

"Beauty is in the eye of the beholder. Roxy has something you never had, or ever will have."

"And what's that?" The sneer made the corners of her ugly mouth lift.

"A heart."

She would have slapped him had his quick reflexes not stopped her.

ith tears streaming down her eyes, she raced off, rudderless, directionless, broken. Her heavy heart cracked under the weight of Mason's deception.

Everything she had come to learn about the man she was starting to fall in love with now slapped her in the face.

Hailey had been right.

Mason was still hung up on his ex-wife. How this woman had suddenly shown up, she had no idea, but that didn't matter.

What mattered were the facts.

She had come, and she had stayed the night. There was no disputing the fact; Monique, dressed like that, had obviously just crawled out of his bed.

And Mason. Roxy's poor aching heart fractured into a thousand pieces. How could he do that do her? She wiped the tears from her eyes. She had been a fool. A fool falling in love. She had forgotten who she was, and she had forgotten who *he* was.

Seeing his ex-wife had reminded her, had winded her like a punch to her gut. Monique was so incredibly beautiful, her movements, her mannerisms so polished and graceful. Who was she but Miss Plain and Average? There was nothing notable about her. How could she ever have thought that a man like Mason would ever see anything in her?

He had been lonely, and in need of company. And she had been the rebound. Maybe not even the rebound. He wasn't over his wife, despite the lies he'd fed her. He was still in love with her.

She had been something he had used to try to forget her. She was sobbing so hard that when she pulled up at the lights, people gave her concerned looks. She quickly rolled up her windows and blew her nose, trying to make herself see that it was a good thing she had found out now, like this, and had caught Mason red-handed.

All of her guards, her iron-clad defenses, her singular focus on her diner, her refusal to waste her time chasing romantic pipe dreams, her way of living had served her well because what was she now but a wasted shell of the woman she used to be?

This man had taken her heart and pulverized it, leaving her broken.

She drove, far, far away, her mind racing, her spirits in tatters. She would put this behind her. She would learn this lesson, she would claw her way back to the light.

But for now, darkness surrounded her. She couldn't go home, didn't want to go to the beach, didn't want to run into people she knew. She couldn't go to the diner, couldn't let her staff see her in pieces. So, she continued to drive, her mind playing over and over and over again the scene she had just lived through.

He had never been more relieved to see a cab leaving.

Gone was Monique and her Louis Vuitton bag.

Seeing her had only reminded him of the colossal mistake he had made in being with her in the first place.

He had to move fast now that the headache of his ex-wife had disappeared.

He needed to find Roxy. She had turned her phone off and he couldn't get through to her. He had no idea if she'd seen the many frantic messages he'd left her.

He drove to her place, his heart in his mouth as he knocked on her door, ready with an explanation.

This would be easy. He hadn't done anything wrong. She would see that.

But when Roxy didn't answer the door, his fears grew.

He drove to the diner, tried to sound as casual and unworried as he could when he asked her employees if they had seen her.

They shook their heads.

"She might be at the beach," one of them said. He scoured the beach and the shops around it, rushed around the town center, looking for her in every nook and cranny and corner.

There was no sign of her anywhere.

Where else would she have gone? She wouldn't have dared to go to the lake or the woods for fear of being too close to him.

Finally, after a frantic few hours of looking for her and not finding her, he called Hailey, and tried to sound as relaxed as he could.

"Have you seen Roxy?"

"No. Not this weekend."

"Has Jax?"

"He's here with me, so, no, he hasn't seen her either. Why?"

"I wanted to know how her catering went last night." How could he tell her why he was so worried? Hailey and Jax didn't know that there was anything going on between them. They had wanted to keep things that way, with their romance being so new and so fragile. But the stunt his ex-wife had pulled would be enough to derail it, especially if he didn't find Roxy soon.

"She's probably in the shower, and didn't hear your call," suggested Hailey. "Try again in a while. It's Roxy. Where's she going to go?"

Where would she go?

He hung up, his hopes crashing to the ground as the day wore on. He decided to go back home and wait a while. Maybe Hailey was right, maybe Roxy had done chores.

He'd noticed that she went extra wild cleaning the kitchen at the diner when she was all worked up.

Maybe she'd cleaned her house from top to bottom and was in the shower.

He'd try again later.

It was about an hour into the drive, an hour in which she had sobbed her tears dry, that she noticed signs for Whisper Falls on the highway.

She'd driven so far out of Starling Bay that it made sense to keep going. After all, what did she have back at home?

She would only end up staring at her four walls, sitting on her couch with a tub of ice cream and crying some more. And also run the risk of Mason finding her.

What if he wasn't trying to find her?

What if he was happy that Monique was back?

She didn't want to know the answer to that, so she had turned her phone off a long time ago.

When she arrived at the farmers' market, she didn't go for a stroll around the stalls. Instead, she headed straight for the park, to the gazebo with the fairy lights, and sat down. It was hard to imagine not so long ago this had been the place which had been the start of their story.

There were no more tears to squeeze out. Even though her brittle heart was in pieces, she tried to harden herself to the fact that Mason had ever had feelings for her. Maybe he had liked her, and maybe she had taken the edge off his loneliness, but what if Monique had returned? What if he hadn't stopped loving her?

She recalled all the interactions she'd had with him, from the shows and outside them, and now she was plagued with fresh doubts.

Had it all been for the ratings? Had he played with her feelings in order to get a reaction out of her? Twisting and bending her emotions to his will. So many times he had talked about their 'chemistry' and how his producer had often commented on it.

Had this 'chemistry' been something that he had manufactured? People like Mason didn't rise to such high heights doing the things that normal people did.

People like that did whatever it took.

Could it be possible that he had manufactured everything between them, to manipulate her feelings and reactions so that they could get the viewing figures higher?

She didn't want to think that was possible. Didn't want to believe that Mason could be capable of such a thing, but he had changed so much before her eyes. Where he'd been a cold, hard monster at the start, he'd just as quickly turned into someone different.

People didn't change that quickly.

Unless there was something to be gained for their advantage. What if he had used her to his advantage, and kneaded, sliced, and manipulated her feelings for his gain?

Confused and aware of her irrationality, she turned her phone on and all at once a flurry of texts and voicemails flooded into her screen. Many were from Mason, some from Hailey and some from the staff at the diner. She read the texts and messages from everyone at the diner first in case there was something urgent she needed to tend to.

There wasn't.

They just wanted her to know that Mason was looking for her. She didn't read or listen to the other messages, but instead, she made a foolish move and looked at the photos that Mason had taken of them in this gazebo. The fairy lights in the background had symbolized a fairytale romance; it had fooled her into thinking that Mason saw something in her that was worthy.

She tried to still her shoulders, tried to hold back, but the flood gates had opened, and she started sobbing all over again.

CHAPTER 37

She had gone extra heavy on her undereye concealer today, which, given that she didn't usually wear any makeup, made her eyes look even more noticeably tired.

"You don't look well." Ella hovered around her looking worried. "And you changed your shift yesterday. Is something wrong?"

"No."

"Did you come down with something?" Lewis peered at her, a frown on his face.

Brokenheartitus. That's what she had come down with. And paralysis from being jolted with four thousand megawatts of shock.

"I didn't sleep much. I was too overtired from the party, and then last night I couldn't get to sleep."

"Are you sad that it's the last show?" Ella asked.

The last show. She had forgotten. But somehow it felt right that this was. It was the end of her risky venture into letting someone in, into trusting someone who was not worthy of her trust, or of her, no matter who he was.

"No. It's about time we got back to being by ourselves."

"Won't you miss this?" Lewis asked, his tone indicating that he would. There was a fire in his eyes, a new ambitious streak that she hadn't seen in such abundance before. He hung onto every word that Mason said, and Roxy could see Lewis going off and running his own place not so many years from now.

"I won't miss having the camera in my face, or having makeup plastered on my face." She straightened up, determined to get through this final episode in one piece.

Inside, her nerves jangled and jostled. Her stomach turned to concrete and she tried to breathe slowly three times.

In, out, in, out, in, out.

She wished for this day to be over, and although she had tried to block Mason from her mind, every fiber in her body was on high alert, knowing that anytime soon he would appear, and she would have to face him.

It was traumatic, having to pretend to be normal, to get along, to now have to manufacture the chemistry that everyone had noticed. Today was going to be like walking on a bed of nails, just being near him and having to look at him without wanting to claw his eyes out.

She was also nervous that Monique might show up. There was nothing to hide, now that she had seen him with his ex-wife. Would he flaunt her on the set? The old Mason would. And maybe the old Mason was back. The newer, softer man had just been for her benefit, while he made her believe that she was something special.

She walked outside, and headed to the makeup station in the tent, but just as she was about to take another step, Mason appeared and blocked her path. His tight expression suddenly softened as his eyes examined her face. "Roxy. I've been so worried about you."

She clamped her mouth shut tight, felt the muscles along her jaw tighten. She should have dealt with him when it had been just the two of them, even if Monique had been hovering around in the background like a mosquito. She could have had it out with him. Now, here, in front of not just the cameras, but the crew and her staff, she couldn't say anything. She couldn't tell Mason Brandt exactly what she thought of him and how he made her feel.

She looked up at him with an unsmiling face. Those green eyes and those lips were now features that made her recoil. "I'm fine, Mason. Could you excuse me?"

He lowered his head, dropped his lips to her ear and whispered, "I can explain everything. I *need* to explain everything."

She stepped back, not wanting to be reminded of his warm breath against her skin or the smell of his aftershave. "You don't have to explain a thing. I saw what I needed to with my own eyes. You can't explain it away."

He opened his mouth, but someone grabbed him, diverting his attention. She stole away to the makeup station.

Today wasn't going to be easy, but all she had to do was get through it and she would be free of Mason forever.

She wasn't giving him a chance. She didn't want anything to do with him, and he didn't blame her. If he was in her shoes, he would have acted the same way.

But she was wrong. Everything she had seen wasn't what she thought it was, and he needed to tell her that.

Soon enough, the cameras started rolling. He had been meaning to discuss with her how they would handle the last show. It was supposed to be a closing up, a conclusion of all that had gone wrong and how they had addressed various issues that she had encountered along the way. They were supposed to talk about how Roxy had benefited from having him around.

He had intended to discuss this with her on Sunday, except that on Sunday all hell broke loose.

Before he could orchestrate anything, they were in the kitchen, and Roxy was furiously mixing pancake batter.

"This is our final show, Roxy." He attempted a smile he didn't feel because the hurt in her eyes, and the dark circles which he could see despite the makeup, told him how much she was hurting, how much he had hurt her. "What do you say?" he prompted when she continued to stir the contents of the bowl and didn't even look up to meet his gaze.

"She's extra busy today, lots of concentration," this to the camera.

She lifted her head. "I say the end couldn't come fast enough." Her words slapped him like a wet towel. He glanced at the camera and smiled, giving the viewers a reassurance that he didn't feel, that all was okay. Clearly, all was not okay.

"You're not going to miss me then?" he asked a little too cheekily, given the deathly mood.

She glared at him as if she wanted to throw a knife in his direction.

"That's confidence for you. I like it, Roxy. I like it." He tried to sound unfazed by her comment, even though he knew it had nothing to do with the show. She was talking about them.

"It's been a journey and a half, hasn't it?"

"It's a journey that should have come to an end weeks ago," she snapped.

He spoke directly to the camera. "Roxy doesn't need me around. She's learned everything she needed to, and now she has no use for me."

"I did learn a lot." She put the bowl down, wiped her hands

and was about to walk over to the fridge when he grabbed her. As if he'd touched her with a hot iron, she jerked her arm aside.

"We're old friends now. Can you share some highlights and low points of the show?"

This was hard work, trying to cover each sniping comment she made, because she clearly didn't care what was being broadcast. Gerard would have a heart attack when he saw the raw footage from today.

She moved away from the counter, over to a corner of the kitchen, and folded her arms. "What do you want to hear?"

"The truth, of course." And yet he was terrified of what she was going to say.

"This experience hasn't been like anything I imagined. It really hasn't."

"Is that good or bad?" He was still trying to steer her conversation towards some semblance of normality, but an unhinged Roxy was hard to steer in any direction.

"It depends on who's asking." Cold eyes, eyes that once looked at him with softness, now stared back at him, hard as flint.

He frowned, knowing that this conversation wasn't advancing anything on the show, wasn't providing an insight to the viewers. "What negative thing do you take away from the show? Roxy?"

Her eyes bore into his, and the disappointment in them, the distrust leveled at him, made his stomach knot up like a ball of wool. "There have been days when I've wondered why I did this."

"But it worked out in the end, surely? Look at you now, full of confidence, you've redone your pricing structure, you've changed up your catering branch of the business, you've introduced new things, what else, Roxy? What else have you done?"

He was trying to give her a chance to sell herself, to share the things she had learned and which had benefitted her, but her mind didn't seem to be on those topics.

"What positive thing do you take away from your experience?"

Her mask slipped for a few brief seconds, affording him a glimpse into her fragility, the very thing she managed to hide so spectacularly, but which he had been able to see beyond.

"There have been some memorable occasions."

His hope soared. "Such as?"

"There have been so many, I can't pick just one."

The sarcasm, twinned with the hard set of her mouth, told him he wasn't going to get much from her.

"Try," he suggested, needing to get something from her before the show fell flat on its face. He needed a strong ending, otherwise viewers would stop watching and not even consider the next show.

"One thing I have learned is that I'm mostly right about things, despite what some great chefs might have me believe." It was hard to miss the cutting sarcasm in her tone.

"And what's that?"

"That I should know my limits."

"What limits?" he cried. "You have no limits, Roxy. You can do anything you put your mind to."

"We all have limits. Limits of what we will accept."

He had a sense this was personal, directed at him, and that this conversation would be lost on viewers. He had to steer it back before Gerard edited out most of the show.

"Accept? Like what? What are we talking about exactly?"

"Say you convinced a customer to have lobster risotto, but maybe your customer didn't want the lobster risotto. Maybe the lobster risotto wasn't all it was dressed up to be. Maybe a nice mushroom risotto would have tasted better, but somehow you convinced your customer to have the lobster just because it's supposed to be classy. Let's face it, there's a certain perception about lobster risotto compared to the mushroom one. And then your customer tells you he's changed his mind and wants the mushroom risotto after all."

She had lost him.

"And?" He blinked, and tried not to look as concerned as he felt.

"Then he tries the mushroom risotto but realizes that it's plain and boring, and he should have stuck with the lobster one in the first place, because even if it was bland, the price and the perception of it would have made him feel that he was better off with the lobster risotto after all."

He huffed out an irritated breath. Gerard was going to explode when he saw this. Trying to understand what she meant, while reading beneath the lines, and at the same time praying that Roxy wasn't completely baffling the viewers was like performing a trapeze act, and at every second, he was terrified of falling flat on his face. The best option he had was to talk to the other staff members.

"That's, uh … that's … interesting." He smiled at the camera. "Shall we go and see what the rest of the team think?"

CHAPTER 38

She heaved a sigh of relief when Mason left her, and the camera crew followed him.

This could very well be the last time she'd have screen time on the show, and she'd let her emotions take over, rambling away about lobster and mushrooms.

She'd made a fool of herself.

Tears welled up in her eyes and she tried to suppress them. The drama of the weekend, and the rollercoaster ride had left her reserves depleted. She hadn't slept well, and the tension along her shoulders made her muscles feel like lead.

Mason was talking to Lewis and she heard him answering the questions that Mason had directed to her, but which he was answering with greater ease and making complete sense.

She disappeared into her office, glad to see that the attention was off her. In the safety of her room, she tried to get herself together.

A notification ping on her cellphone alerted her, and she fished it out of her apron to check.

Hailey had texted her again asking her if she was okay. She had texted her back a quick, 'All okay here' last night when she'd arrived home after a long, solo day at Whisper Falls.

Roxy: Good, thanks. Busy. Last show.

Hailey: Oh, good luck! Speak soon.

Roxy: XX

A tab on her phone was open at one of the photos of her and Mason at the gazebo. Their happy, smiling faces stared back at her. She couldn't help it when the tears started up again.

Desperate to get control of herself, she deleted the photos, then reached for a tissue to wipe away the fat tears which flowed down her cheeks.

She was so caught up in her emotions and trying to make herself look as if everything was okay, that she was too slow to respond when there was a knock at the door. It opened and Mason's head appeared. Concern was etched all over his face as he walked in and rushed to her.

But the cameraman was behind him, and the camera was still rolling. Mason stepped away, as if he had suddenly remembered they were being filmed.

It was an eerie moment, her wiping her tears, the cameras rolling, and Mason silent.

Somebody whispered, "Aren't you going to say something, Mason?"

But he didn't.

The camera was in her face.

"Get that thing out of her face," Mason barked.

More silence. The camera still rolled, and there was nothing from Mason. "We don't need this. There's nothing to see."

But the camera kept rolling.

"Don't mind me," she said, clearing her throat, feeling the need to say something because this silent movie effect made things seem odder.

"Are you sad because this is ending?" someone asked as Mason walked out.

"Yes." She forced a smile, gesturing towards the camera and crew, lying through her teeth. "It being the last show and all that."

More silence followed, and eventually, the cameraman turned the camera off.

hat should have been a memorable last show had turned into a mess and he regretted every second of filming.

He could see that Roxy wasn't herself, and it was all his fault. Her lobster and mushroom scenario wasn't lost on him, and neither were her tears.

Someone told him that Roxy had slipped out when the cameras had stopped rolling. He had been busy saying goodbye to everyone in the diner, not just the staff but the customers too, signing autographs and taking pictures with them.

He liked to think that this was just temporary, that he would be back here, like he was on most days when he came to the diner, to see Roxy for a while before he went about making the most of his day.

But now he wasn't sure if this would be the last time he would be here. It depended on whether Roxy gave him the time of day to explain himself.

When Roxy still didn't return, when he'd finished signing autographs, Ella mentioned that she had gone to see a supplier. He didn't believe it. On this, of all days a visit to a supplier wasn't the most important thing she needed to do.

She was ignoring him, avoiding him, staying out of his way because she couldn't stand the sight of him.

That evening, alone at home, staring at the lake from the vantage point of his veranda, he called Hailey and asked her if she'd heard from Roxy.

"What's going on?" Hailey asked. "It's like the two of you are playing hide and seek."

If only it were a game.

"Can you talk?" he asked.

"Yes."

"In person? Can I come over?" He couldn't get a hold of Roxy, and he knew from yesterday that she could disappear and he'd only be wasting his time looking for her. Even if he found her, he doubted that she would be willing to listen to him. It would be better to get through to her from someone she trusted.

"Come on over."

When he reached Hailey's place, he got straight to the matter. He told her everything, about the picnic, about him going to Roxy's for dinner and accidentally kissing her, about going to the farmers' market. She was silent, but her blue eyes widened as he revealed what had been going on.

At the end of it, a huge smile spread across her face. "You and Roxy. Wow. I did not see that coming."

"There's more." He told her about Monique showing up.

"Monique was here?" A rare frown crinkled Hailey's brow. He recounted the entire episode from the moment his ex-wife had arrived and shocked the living daylights out of him, to the filming of the final show this morning. But he left out how Roxy had been.

"So, you see, I need to get in touch with her and explain

everything. It can be explained, but she's not giving me a chance." His voice vibrated with indignation. He pinched the bridge of his nose. "Monique stayed the night, in the spare room, and she was there when Roxy showed up. She had planned to spend the day with me, but she saw Monique and thought the worst."

"I spoke to her this morning," Hailey said.

"She was on the show, in the diner, but she left and I can't get in touch with her."

"Let me try. Do you want me to try now?" Hailey's fingers were poised on the button. What would Hailey calling Roxy now achieve? It was him that she didn't want to see. And he was the one who needed to see her to set this right.

"No. Give her some time. She needs time."

Hailey sat back in her chair and tilted her head up at the stars. "You and Roxy," she repeated, the revelation clearly a surprise to her.

"Don't tell Jax yet," he pleaded. At the rate things were going, there might never be a reason to tell Jax. It could be that after this week, he and Roxy would go their separate ways and what they'd shared would be nothing more than history.

Hailey whistled softly. "I can't believe it."

"Well, believe it." He drew in a sharp breath, bracing himself for what Hailey might say next. He didn't want to hear that he and Roxy were so different that they might as well have been chalk and cheese.

Or lobster and mushroom.

"In all the time I've known her, she's never had a boyfriend. She's had a few, Jackson said, but not for a long time. You must have found a way to her heart. You must have charmed her, Mason."

"I didn't charm her, I *understood* her. I saw the real Roxy, not the side she displays to everyone, the cocky, spirited side."

A small smile curved up at the corners of Hailey's mouth. "You care about her."

"I more than care about her. I'm crazy about her."

She lifted her head and sat forward, her eyes studying his face as if she were looking for something. "My goodness, Mason."

"What?"

"You're crazy about her. I was so wrong."

"What?"

"I thought you were sad about you and Monique splitting up."

"Sad?"

"On the later shows you were more introspective, less sarcastic, less *you*. I assumed, wrongly, that you were missing her. I thought you were upset now that the divorce was final."

"No. Never."

"I see that now."

CHAPTER 40

"When will it be fixed?" her mom asked.

Roxy scratched her neck. She hated lying to her parents, but pretending that her water heater was broken was the only way she could end up staying at her parents' house for a few days without them asking too many questions.

She would stay here until Mason left Starling Bay. She didn't want to face him. Didn't want to get sucked into more lies. He had made her believe that he cared about her. Because of him, she had started to think that she could be with someone like that. A man she had once abhorred, a man she had found repugnant.

She'd ended up in his arms. Spending romantic days together, falling for his words, believing him when he told her that she could do anything she set her mind to, that they weren't so dissimilar after all.

He'd made her feel special. Taken care of her, made her slow down and enjoy the world, instead of just concentrating on her business. She'd felt all the better for it.

But he had also broken her heart, even if she hadn't given all of it to him yet.

"Last week's show was a bit odd," her father grumbled as they sat around the table, having dinner.

"It was odd," her mother agreed.

"Was it?" Roxy stuffed food down her mouth at breakneck speed, hoping to be excused on the pretense of another white lie, that she had work matters to take care of, and no, she couldn't work downstairs in the same room as her parents who were going to watch TV.

Her mom nodded. "That said, he's very dreamy looking. If I didn't already know, I would think he was a chef."

Roxy chewed quickly, took a gulp of water to wash it down.

"He's being really good to you," her mom persisted. "You're both joking around more."

"Flirting, it looks like," her father growled.

This was getting to be too much for her. Roxy jumped up. "I need to go. I've got something urgent to deal with."

"At least wait until your father and I have finished eating, honey. This is a treat for us, having you stay with us for a few days. It'll be like the good old days."

"I'll come back later, Mom. I really have to take care of something."

She couldn't get out of there fast enough. When the doorbell rang, she was caught between going to the kitchen with her empty plate or answering the door. When it rang again, she rushed to the door, plate in hand.

"I had a feeling I'd find you here." Hailey walked in.

Clever girl. "What made you think I'd be here?"

"Because it's the last place Mason would go looking for you."

Clever girl indeed.

Roxy set her plate in the sink, while Hailey briefly disappeared to say hello to her parents.

"What did you want to see me about?" she asked when Hailey reappeared. But she knew. She'd received several messages on her phone from Mason, messages which she hadn't read or listened to, and these were followed by several messages from Hailey.

"You know what it's about." Hailey's eyes gleamed with amusement.

"Let's go outside." As far away from her mother's ears as they could.

The back of her parents' house led onto a field. With the sun starting to set, the sky turned a shade of russet splashed with indigo. Roxy stopped for a moment, taking it in. She had never before taken the time to admire so many of the things which she realized she had taken for granted. Rushing around had been the order of her day, but lately she had learned to appreciate the world around her, she had learned to slow down.

Mason might have had a little something to do with that.

"Mason's been trying to get a hold of you," Hailey announced.

"I know." They walked a short distance to the fence which separated her parents' yard from the field. Roxy tilted her head, looking up at the sky.

"He told me about you two."

Roxy lifted a shoulder signaling a so-what? She examined Hailey's expression, bracing herself, listening for a nuance or intonation which might indicate her shock at this news.

Hailey blinked and laughed, a breathy little laugh. "The more I think about the two of you getting together, the more I can't believe I didn't try to get you together sooner."

For a few frozen moments, Roxy forgot to breathe. She waited for her friend to burst out laughing, waiting for the jokey punchline. But her friend was serious, as if she believed that Roxy and Mason being together was normal.

"We're not together anymore."

"I heard." Hailey sighed. "He said Monique showed up

unexpectedly. The first he knew was when he opened his door. He said she told him that she had made a mistake and she wanted to get back together with him."

"It looked to me as if they did get back together." Roxy's skin bristled as she remembered Monique's tall, slim body and how tempting it would have looked to Mason.

"They didn't."

"But she was wearing a nightshirt. You should have seen it," Roxy insisted. "She stayed over. Spent the night with him."

"He couldn't throw her out. He told her to leave but she refused. What was he supposed to do?"

Roxy pressed a finger against her chin, trying to see if this could be plausible. Monique was wearing a sexy red nightshirt. *With tiny butterflies.* She couldn't get the image out of her head. How could Mason not have been tempted? "You didn't see what I saw."

"Then tell me what you saw."

Hailey let her speak, without interruption, and she recounted what she had seen. "You should have seen what she was wearing. I don't have lingerie that sexy."

"He said she slept in the spare room."

Monique made her feel inadequate. She rested her arms on the fence, intertwined her fingers as she reasoned with this new line of events.

"He said nothing happened. He said he told her he wasn't interested, that he had moved on and that their marriage had been a mistake."

Roxy's heart started to dance. "He said that to her?"

"That's what he told me and I believe him." Hailey hooked a thumb in the belt loop of her jeans, adamant.

"But that one time you said he was pining for his ex. You were worried that he might be depressed."

Hailey's cautioning had worried her and it had made her start to question whether what she and Mason had started was real. To make things worse, Monique's appearance had made those doubts as sharp as daggers. The belief in herself and of what she could achieve extended only to her business. So, in that respect, she owed Mason a debt of gratitude because he had helped her. But in her personal life, the earlier scars were still ingrained and more stubborn to shift.

"I was wrong. He's in love with you, Roxy," Hailey said softly.

"In love? Did he say that?" Her insides quivered with emotion.

"He didn't say that—"

"Then don't … don't …lie." She worried that Hailey was trying to put a bandage over her wounds.

"He said he was crazy about you."

"He told you that?" The disbelief echoed in her words.

"Yes. You should have heard the way he spoke about you. When he told me the things the two of you had done, simple things, like having a picnic, your visit to the farmers' market, the gazebo? Where's the gazebo? I haven't seen one around here. He said it was one of the best days of his life. What did you do? Because Mason has led a pretty incredible life, Roxy, and for him to make that claim, it must have been something."

He'd told her everything. Roxy's lower lip trembled, her eyes welled up. "He told you about all those things?" Her calm voice belied the thumping of her hopeful heart.

She hadn't given him a chance to explain, hadn't given him the time of day. Rather, she had sought solace in her parents' home of all places.

"He forwarded me this photo of the two of you." Hailey held out her phone and showed a photo of her and Mason in the gazebo. The photo had caught a precious moment. They'd both smiled but had looked at one another and not the camera. It was her favorite one of them all.

"You two look so good together. It's like you were made for one another."

Roxy stared at the photo until Hailey put her phone away. "Can you send that to me?"

She pulled out her phone and pressed some buttons. "Done. He's leaving soon, for the next show."

Roxy's hopes plunged and fell to their death. "How soon?"

"This weekend. You shouldn't let him go without giving him a chance to tell you his side of things."

Roxy gnawed at her bottom lip. "I guess I owe him that."

CHAPTER 41

"It wasn't the ending we wanted even though there's a lot of emotion, it's still a mess," Gerard told him. "But we're keeping it all in. We'll edit it to make it better, but I'm confident it has enough drama and emotion to grip viewers."

"To grip viewers?" Mason glowered.

"I liked the tears, though I'll be damned if any of her rambling made any sense to me. She's a funny one, that one. I can't say I'll be sorry to get the heck out of this place."

The muscles in Mason's jaw bunched like a fist. "*Roxy* is talented," he bit out slowly, putting the emphasis on her name in case Gerard had already forgotten it. "And if you had any sense, you'd see it instead and recognize it for what it is. You wouldn't depict her as a wreck in the final show."

"The lobster and mushroom speech was a good one." Gerard chuckled. Mason's eyebrows lifted.

"She had a lot to contend with that day," he said carefully. "I want you to kill that scene—"

"What?" Laughter rippled on the other side of the phone and Mason held it away from his ear, until the noise subsided. Gerard seemed to think this was some sort of joke.

Mason wasn't done. "And the scene at the end, when Roxy is upset and crying. That needs to go, too."

"What in the world are you talking about?"

"Exactly what I just said."

"You're insane."

"People have told me that, yes."

"But they're two of the best scenes."

"They don't accurately reflect what Roxy is like."

"I don't care what she's like. The viewers will want to see her in that state."

Mason lowered his head and huffed out a long, irritated breath. "You will cut those scenes, otherwise I won't do the next show."

A gasp of disbelief echoed across the airwaves. "You're not serious."

"I'm completely serious."

The one thing that Roxy had asked him to do was to not make her look like a fool. He was going to honor that request. She didn't look like a fool to him in those scenes, but *she* would feel that she did. She would find her portrayal humiliating. Those scenes didn't show the real Roxy, and especially when she had blossomed as the series progressed, it wouldn't be fitting justice to show her in that light especially when he was the only one who knew why she had broken down.

"I mean it, Gerard. If that episode airs, and those scenes are in it, I will walk." He hung up before Gerard said anything else to darken his mood.

He was heading back to LA next weekend, before flying to New York to start filming the next series of episodes. It had been confirmed that they were good to go with Buffalo Bill.

He had started to pack, even though he wasn't leaving for a few days.

Better to be ready than not.

With no filming to do, and no Roxy to visit, his days had lost purpose. There was no reason to get up and get dressed.

No reason to go to town and visit the diner.

And there was only so much of gazing at the scenery from his veranda that he could do.

He had no interest in going for a walk by himself.

He'd been by himself for a long time. Even during that separation, when he'd tried to make things work. Being lonely wasn't good for him. Getting on with work, filming the next show, meeting Buffalo Bill again would keep him busy and help keep his mind off things. Delving into the man's financials, and seeing his business plan and strategy, would provide plenty of material for arguments and disagreements.

But he had been serious when he'd told Gerard. He would walk if the man didn't cut the scenes he'd asked him too.

He had left Roxy a few messages over the days but she hadn't replied. Hailey had told him to give her time, but time was the very thing he was running out of.

Hailey told her that Mason was leaving.

He had sent her so many texts and messages, telling her he needed to talk. But the final text, the photo of them at the gazebo, made her get up and drive over right away. He'd sent her the photo that Hailey had sent her, the one that was her favorite and also seemed to be Mason's favorite, too.

She knocked on his door, her heart galloping like wild horses.

He opened the door. "Roxy." It was a statement, a soft, sexy statement the way he said her name.

"I wanted to see you before you left," she said, sounding very formal.

"I've been wanting to see you for a few days."

"When are you leaving?"

"Later today."

Today? She gulped, the shock of his sudden departure hitting her like a blast of Arctic frost.

"Come in. I still have your picnic hamper."

The picnic that never was. She looked around anxiously, remembering that last time when Monique had been here, and everything she had seen had torn her hopes to pieces.

Even now, despite what Hailey told her, the ghost of Monique still hung in the air. Roxy had come in order to let Mason say his piece. She hadn't handled things well, but she had also never been hit so hard, falling for a man who was so far out of her league, he might as well have come from space. Seeing him with his glamorous ex-wife had been a further twist of the knife.

She would never forget that feeling of being small. The hurt had been too big. A confirmation that she was nothing special, but ordinary, and therefore would never be able to reach for her dreams.

And that included men like Mason.

"I'm sorry my ex ruined the day."

She felt some comfort from the fact that he couldn't even refer to her by name.

"Sit down, Roxy." He motioned for her to take the couch, while sitting down on a different couch, giving her space.

They had reverted to being strangers again, a fall from the heady heights of closeness they had reached not so long ago.

"Did you go on a picnic?"

He scoffed, consternation furrowing his brow. "The only person I would have wanted to go with fled."

"What did you expect me to do? Your wife was here. I had no idea she was even in the country, much less that she was here."

"She's my *ex*-wife, and she slept in the spare bedroom. Her appearance was completely out of the blue. I'm not in touch with her because there is no 'us' anymore."

"But she was here, and she stayed the night." Try as she would, she couldn't get the image of Monique in that sexy nightshirt--and all that it spelled-- out of her head.

Mason tsked and took in a long breath. The air turned cold and spiky, the easygoing familiarity and delight of their previous encounters belonging to two different people.

"I don't love Monique. I fell out of love with her a long time ago. I hung onto what I thought was love even when we separated because I don't like to lose, and splitting up is, to someone like me, a sign of losing. I like to make things work, I like to fix things, and I thought when our marriage failed that I could fix it. But Monique didn't seem to want to try. She realized long before I did that we were two different people." He looked away, pain turning his face somber. "I told her she needed to leave because I didn't love her anymore."

"But why did she come?"

"Because she wanted to try to make it work. She said her father could help me, we could try again in Paris, and I could turn the new restaurant into my dream Michelin-starred restaurant, while she would get busy with ..."

His voice trailed off.

"Why didn't you take her up on her offer?" Because something that was broken could be fixed. And Monique was everything a man like him would ever want. With her father wanting to help them get set up, why would he not agree?

"Because we are done. It took being apart for me to see that we should never have gotten together in the first place."

He stood up, walked over to the table and leaned against it, his hands sliding into his pockets. "Never lock eyes with a beautiful woman across a crowded restaurant and make a move which you will regret."

She swallowed. "That's not a problem I'm ever likely to have." She would never end up in a situation like that. Men tended not to notice her. She was the proverbial wallflower. Snappy and mouthy in the diner, her domain, but outside of it, she was filled with self-doubt.

She was Jax's sister.

Or Hailey Ross's friend.

At the SBWEB meetings, she was usually the silent one, needing to be prompted to say something.

"But I noticed you, maybe it wasn't a crowded Michelin two-starred restaurant, but it was a pretty good diner."

"Hailey got us together," she clarified. Otherwise, how on earth would she ever have gotten Mason to talk to her, much less notice her? He had been forced to notice her, more than that, he'd been coerced and persuaded into taking her on.

A hook dug into her chest and needled into her heart. It hurt. Everything she had thought about them being together, she was now unsure of.

"And I have to thank her for that," he replied.

"But we got together for the show," she said. No other reason.

"Thank goodness for the show." They fell quiet for a few moments until he spoke up again. "I told Monique to leave because she had no right to be here. She's not a part of my life. I've moved on. You have to believe that nothing happened, Roxy."

"I do believe it." Coming here had dispelled her doubts. Monique had left, he sounded genuine, he looked unhappy. His story panned out. When she looked at him, she saw a man who looked sad and deflated.

"Then ... why are we doing this?" He shrugged, nodding his head at the distance between them. "Why are you sitting there, and I'm all the way here? Why are we wasting time like this?"

He wouldn't understand that she still questioned his feelings for her, even though she longed to go up to him and put her arms around his neck, to sink against his chest so that he could lock her in an embrace.

"Because ... because you'll be gone soon." It was a cop-out, and he would know it.

Feeling hot and bothered, she got up and walked out onto the veranda, needing space and air, and the breeze.

He joined her. "But I'm here now and I want to see you. I want to get back to where we were."

She placed her hands on the railings. "What's the point?" she cried defensively. The barriers around her heart were being fortified. Future-proofed.

"Whatever those teachers told you, Roxy, whatever lies and untruths and short-sighted opinions they might have told you, they're simply not true."

Her grip loosened, the fortified fencing she had started to erect around herself, POOF! Mason's words had hit, like bullets.

"Don't you see?" she cried, schooling herself to breathe, "I will always see a 'Monique', even if we're going for a walk, or sitting in a restaurant, and I will always worry that she will catch your eye."

There. She'd said it. He crossed over to her and wrapped his arms around her before she had a chance to step back and avoid him.

"I see you. I see all that you are, and all that you want to be. It's *you* I want, Roxy. *You.* You are special, and it's time you started to believe that."

She sniffled, burying her face in his chest, needing the heat and comfort, needing to hide her face so he couldn't see that he was breaking her down.

"I'm in love with you, Roxy. I'm trying to slow it down, even though we're going at a snail's pace. I'm trying to put my brakes on because with you, I find myself careening at breakneck speed and I can't stop it. You're the type of woman I might not have noticed, but I see you, for the woman you are, and the businesswoman you want to be. I love so many things about you. I love your spark and your sarcasm. I love your softness and fragility. It makes me want to protect you even more, if you'll only give me the chance."

She wasn't going to cry. She wasn't. She wasn't going to fall apart just because this man understood her so clearly. He understood her in a way that no one, not even her parents or Jax, did.

And that was priceless.

~

She looked up at him, tears glistening in her eyes.

"I look like a mess."

He leaned down and kissed her. "You look like a beautiful mess." He wiped away her tears with his thumbs.

Some women took. He'd met and dated women like that for most of his life. Roxy was a one in a million. She didn't take. She *gave*. She made him see, she made him appreciate things he hadn't appreciated before.

With her, he didn't feel the need to be the best, to be on top of the world and kill himself to stay there. With her, those things didn't matter as much as the smaller things did. Things like watching sunsets, enjoying a walk in a park. Kissing in a gazebo.

"You're leaving when?"

"My flight is at seven."

"I don't want you to go."

The tears threatened to spill over her lashes again. This time she wiped them with the back of her hand. "I don't know why I'm all over the place. It's not like me."

"I know." She wasn't like the person he had first met, and neither was he.

Her eyes searched his face. "I don't want you to go," she whispered. "I've wasted so much time we could have had together."

"You were working things out." He understood that she had needed the space. Knowing the way she thought, and understanding the fire alarms that seeing Monique at his place would have set off, he knew she'd started to question her self-worth again. She had believed the future that people in her youth, people in power, had convinced her was the one for her. But he had shown her that she could be so much more.

He'd seen the upward effect in her business, now he had to convince her of what she was worth.

A sigh heaved from his chest. He didn't want to go. He didn't want to leave her and he hated that this last week of theirs had been ruined. But there were always other options.

"I can take the last flight out tomorrow."

"You'll change your flight?" She sounded surprised that he would want to do such a thing for her.

"It's just a flight." He leaned down and kissed her forehead. "I don't want to leave you, and we have so much time to make up for."

This time she tiptoed up and kissed him. It was warm, and soft, the type of kiss which told him more than words could, that they were back together.

Business was starting to boom in the diner, and she was busy interviewing for more staff.

It had been two weeks since Mason had started filming on the next series of his show in New York. He flew back on Friday evenings and left on Monday mornings.

For both of them, much had changed in a short span of time and this was a period of adjustment. They were both adjusting to being together for two days a week and apart for five.

The cameras had gone, and her life was no longer on view, and Mason had stayed, enriching her life for the better.

She liked to think that she was also getting better at achieving a sense of balance--that elusive thing which she had never tried to find before because she'd never thought she had needed such a thing.

Life was no longer about working hard all the time. These days, she looked forward to her weekends, to seeing Mason and taking time away from the diner.

This evening, she had decided to attend the SBWEB meetings, having missed the last one. Francine had begged her to come because everyone in the town had seen the show and the businesswomen were eager to hear from her. When Francine asked who would like to go first and share what each of them had been up to, she raised her hand. "I'll go first."

Francine sat forward eagerly, her warm eyes encouraging. "I was hoping you would say that. We're all dying to hear from you."

She addressed the table of women, a burst of confidence sweeping over her, boosted by a new interest in clothes, only for occasions such as this. It had required a shift of mindset and a change in how she saw herself, for her to feel at ease among these women. It also helped being dressed in a smart skirt suit, instead of just taking off her apron and rushing over in the comfy clothes she'd worn at the diner.

She was still Roxy, but she no longer felt the need to sit on the sidelines or hide, and while she loved her comfy clothes, she felt empowered by dressing in smart clothes for these events.

The women at the SBWEB meeting gazed at her with smiling faces.

"I suppose you want to hear about what it was like to be on the show, rather than the strategic changes I had to make to the business?" Laughter rippled around the table.

"I can tell you that it was a great experience. Stepping out of my comfort zone and going on that show changed my life." She went on to recount her experience, noting how in the beginning she hadn't wanted to be on the show at all, but Hailey had forced her to. "It was the best thing I ever did."

"I'll say," someone shouted out.

"You got Mason Brandt out of it!" said another.

She gave a shy smile, but that was all they were going to get. She wasn't going to go into her personal life, even though it was public knowledge that she and Mason were together. That was all that anyone needed to know.

A chorus of questions spread around the table as the women

started asking her questions. She answered them all. Having spoken for longer than was usual at these events, she discovered that she felt so much more at ease now.

The meeting ended, having run longer than it was supposed to, and just as she was leaving, Francine approached her and asked her if she would consider doing a talk. In her segment of the meeting, Francine had mentioned that the Institute of Business Management in Massachusetts was looking for successful women in business to talk about their experiences. Francine had passed a sheet of paper around the table for anyone who was interested to put down their names. They would also need to submit a two-page document about their business and how they ran it. The chance to speak was by invitation only and at the institute's discretion.

"I notice you didn't put your name down," said Francine. "I'm going to apply. I think you should too."

"Me?" Successful women? A business talk? How could she? She was about to say that she would think about it, but instead, she took a deep breath, and then took the jump. "Where's the list? I'll add my name."

Mason waited outside in the hotel lobby. Roxy's SBWEB meeting had taken place in one of the conference rooms at The Grand Hotel this time.

He glanced at his watch again. She should have come out by now. As women started to file through the lobby, he looked out for her. Mackenzie noticed him and immediately came over. They exchanged welcome greetings.

"Good meeting?" he asked.

"It was great! Listening to Roxy was the highlight of tonight."

His eyes widened with interest. "Yeah?"

"Roxy was so inspirational. She sounded invincible."

He was proud of her. "She is."

"She said you were commuting from New York. How's that working out?"

"Not as bad as you would think."

"That's great."

"Wouldn't have it any other way," he told her. "It's working, but it's tough having to leave after a few days."

It was hell, actually. But Monday soon turned to Friday, and time flew by. He couldn't complain too much.

"The things worth having don't come easy, and the things that come easy aren't worth having."

He blinked at this slice of wisdom she had just imparted, but before he could say anything, she told him, "My grandma used to say that."

"Your grandma is very wise."

Mackenzie glanced over her shoulder. "Roxy should be coming out soon. I saw her talking to someone."

Just then he caught sight of Roxy. Their eyes met across the lobby floor, and she raced as fast as she could in her stilettoes; she was still getting used to them.

As soon as they met, she fell into his arms, her hands sliding around his waist tightly, gripping his back as if she would never let go. He would have scooped her up in his arms, were it not for where they were. Instead, he dipped his head and kissed her, short and sweet, not the usual Friday kisses which were filled with need and longing. Missed-you-like-crazy kisses. Couldn't-wait-to-see-you kisses.

In the hotel lobby, they had to show restraint.

"Bye, have a good weekend," they heard Mackenzie say. By the time they looked up, she had vanished.

"Sorry. We ran late." Roxy's soft hand squeezed his as they walked out. She told him about the meeting, and that someone had mentioned about doing a talk at a business convention and she had put her name down.

This pleased him. "You're going to be awesome."

"It's by invitation only. I probably won't get asked to speak."

"How do you know?" He entwined his fingers in hers and kissed her hand. He remembered the time she hadn't wanted to go to the front in the tent at Reed's engagement party, with everyone watching. He'd heard the pleading in her voice as she begged him to let go of her hand.

Most people didn't like addressing a crowd, but for Roxy, the fear of being nothing, of amounting to nothing, of failing, had burrowed itself deep.

She hadn't been able to see in herself what he had. She had never looked deep enough to discover that she had more courage than she thought, but she was becoming more daring as time went on and it pleased him to see the change already.

"Fellini's?" he asked. He'd left his luggage at the condo and come straight over. Eating out would be easier.

"I made risotto."

"Risotto? What type of risotto?"

Amusement swirled in her eyes. "What type did you want? Mushroom or lobster?"

He cocked his head. "Is that a trick question?"

"Is that too hard?" Mason asked, his fingers gently hooking into her flesh.

"No, it's perfect."

They had set up near the lake at what was now affectionately referred to as 'their spot.' The day was unusually warm for early fall, prompting them both to have their last picnic. The summer had quietly slipped away; a summer Roxy would always look back on as being the one that changed her life for the better.

"You don't have so many knots these days," Mason remarked.

"Hmmm. I wonder why." She bit back a sigh as his fingers massaged her. But then he pressed his thumb into one spot and she felt it. "Owwww!"

"Found one, sorry. I'll try to ease it out gently." He worked on her, slowly and gently, and with a tenderness that made her love him even more.

The stiffness in her neck and shoulders had melted away, just like the worries and the sleepless nights. Reaching back, she placed her hands on his, wanting to freeze the moment so that she could savor it.

"What?" he asked, squeezing her shoulders.

"I wish I could have you for longer."

"I know it's not ideal, Roxy, but two days out of seven is a win. It could be worse."

She didn't want to think about that. He had been filming with his third candidate in Pennsylvania and the flight time was slightly longer than before.

He coughed. "The next candidate is in Alaska."

"Alaska?!" She spun around in her chair. "When were you going to tell me?" She raised her eyebrow, then stared at his hands.

"This is how." He bent down and kissed the top of her head, before pulling her to standing. "It will only be for eight weeks."

She opened her mouth to protest when they heard a shout.

"Spart!"

It was Chloe, the teenage daughter of the owners of the gift store nearby. She was struggling to restrain the biggest dog Roxy had ever seen. Spart, a Great Dane, was making a beeline for their picnic table.

She and Mason sprang apart at the same time and stood in front, trying to shield the food from Spart's ravenous eyes.

"Is he hungry?" Roxy asked, wondering if they should give him something as recompense.

"Hey," Dylan rushed towards them, and took the leash from the teenager. "Sorry about that, *again*." The poor guy really did look apologetic. This wasn't the first time Spart had sniffed out their picnic.

Behind Dylan, his wife, Merry, waddled along. She was huge, and expecting a baby in a few months' time, apparently sometime around Christmas.

"We're going to have to find another forest," Merry said, sounding out of breath as she cradled her baby bump. "This isn't fair on you guys and your picnics."

"It's not a problem," Mason reassured her. "The picnics will be stopping soon enough anyway."

"Would you like to join us?" Roxy asked. They had come to know this couple well, as they often ran into them on their walks and picnics. Chloe took the leash back from Dylan and raced towards the field, enticing Spart away from them. Dylan took Merry's hand. "Thank you, but no. You guys carry on and enjoy what's left of the summer."

"You only get to spend the weekends together," Merry pointed out.

"See you around." They waved as they left.

"She looks as if she's going to have that baby soon," Mason commented. His arm went around her shoulder, and he hugged her to him. The scent of his aftershave was familiar as home and she leaned against him, resting her head against his chest.

"She's still got a few months to go." Though she had to agree, Merry's top was pulled so tight that the bump was hard not to notice, and it did look rather big.

Speaking about clothes, she needed to go shopping. The Institute of Business anagement had selected her to come and speak at their event next week.

"Can we go to Whisper Falls tomorrow?" she asked.

"To the farmers' market?"

"I need to find something to wear to the business talk."

"The business talk." Admiration echoed in Mason's voice. He had been so happy when she'd told him. "We can do that. You could do that talk in your jeans and sweatshirt and you would still blow everyone away."

She tilted her head up, her heart overflowing with all she felt for him. "Thank you, but I happen to like dressing up for these events because it makes me feel more confident."

"I get that." He kissed her nose. "But you have more

confidence in your finger than most people have in their entire body."

She tip-toed up and pressed her lips against his. Mason loved her just the way she was, but this was something she was doing for herself. For too long she'd been taking care of the business instead of taking care of herself. Now she was making up for lost time and putting herself first.

The only problem with going to Whisper Falls tomorrow was that it would take up most of Sunday and Mason would leave first thing on Monday morning. She wanted time to stop when they were together, and fast forward when they were apart.

"Alaska is far, Mason."

"It's not forever." He lifted her chin up, his eyes soft as he wrapped his hands around her face. "So what if the flying time is longer? I'll still come home every weekend."

Home.

He'd said home.

It might have been a figure of speech. She searched his face for confirmation, but instead he kissed her again deeply, with longing. His kiss was a reassurance, a claiming of her lips and her heart. She curled her fingers around his neck and moaned against his mouth.

"I love you," he whispered, his voice so low, his words reverberated inside her chest. He'd told her this many times, but each time he said it, it was like hearing it for the first time. Her insides danced for joy.

"I love you," she answered back.

Their paths would not have crossed were it not for his TV show. This man had walked into her life in the strangest way and rendered these last few months unforgettable.

That life could be like this was a revelation. He'd opened her eyes, and her heart. He had shown her the possibilities of who she could be, what she could do, and what she could have.

She loved him with a passion that sometimes scared her, because she had never loved so deeply before.

"Alaska is for eight weeks, Roxy. You and me? We're forever."

"Forever," she whispered, their lips so close together, they shared the same breath.

His gaze locked onto her, full of promise and reassurance, and goosebumps shivered across her skin in anticipation of the good times they had yet to share.

Thank you for reading ***Table for Two.*** I hope you enjoyed Roxy and Mason's story!

You can hear from them, as well as other characters from earlier Starling Bay books, in ***A Bouquet of Charm***, which is Mackenzie's story.

If this is the first Starling Bay book you've read, you might want to start with the first book in the series, ***Winter's Kiss.***

And if you'd like to be notified of new book releases and more, please subscribe to my newsletter here:

http://www.siennacarr.com/newsletter

Thank you so much,
Sienna

ACKNOWLEDGMENTS

I would like to thank my amazing group of proofreaders who check my manuscript for errors, typos and inconsistencies.

I am eternally grateful for their help and support:

Marcia Chamberlain
Nancy Dormanski
April Lowe
Dena Pugh
Carole Tunstall

I would also like to thank Tatiana Vila of Vila Design for creating this awesome cover.

ABOUT THE AUTHOR

Sienna Carr is the sweet romance pen name for an author who has been writing romance since 2013. She lives in the UK with her husband, three children, and a parrot.

Connect with Me

I love hearing from you – so please don't be shy!
You can email me at: sienna@siennacarr.com